IF ONLY YOU KNEW

By

LOUISE MERCER

IF ONLY YOU KNEW

By

LOUISE MERCER

Cover design by Carly McCracken

Published By
Crimson Cloak Publishing

ISBN: 978-1-68160-721-4

ISBN: 1-68160-721-2

Edited by Denna Holm

Publisher's Publication in Data

Mercer, Louise

If Only You Knew

1. Fiction 2. Romance 3. Women's Fiction

To David, Thomas, and my guardian angels
watching from above.

Kind regards,

Louise

CHAPTER 1

Laura breathed a sigh of relief as she turned off the busy dual carriageway, joining the country lanes down to the Yorkshire Coast. Her nerves jingled at the thought of what future lay ahead for her. Only two months had passed since Lazy Leon (as her mother called him), suddenly announced he was leaving her, commitment being too much for a thirty-five-year-old. She could hear him now, 'so many women to get to know and so little time'. Not that he was much of a catch, to be honest. Buying residential and commercial properties and renovating them to sell on didn't bring in much money. They'd relied more on her wage than his. Looking back, she wondered what had attracted her to him, not his recently acquired podgy stomach or increasing bald patch, for sure.

She wound down her car window and allowed the warm July breeze to filter through her blonde hair. She hoped this venture would be a success. After being made redundant from the estate agents she had worked in for years, she desperately needed some good luck.

If there was an opportunity to chat with Jemima one last time, she wondered what her godmother would say to her. The conversation would most likely start with 'you're braver and stronger than you think, my darling,' and end with 'You've got this'. Laura gave herself a mental shake. Of course, she could do this. She could run her own B&B.

Admittedly, she was still shocked at discovering her inheritance. Not everyone gained a seaside B&B upon the death of their beloved godmother. She still missed Jemima dreadfully. Although they hadn't often had the chance to meet, they'd messaged and skyped each other frequently. Her eyes prickled at the thought of no more handmade birthday cards or thoughtful gifts sent to celebrate even the smallest of successes. The effects of a stroke were so cruel.

She turned at a stone hump-backed bridge over a wide peaceful river that shimmered under the warm sun. Laura smiled as she passed a beautiful thatched country pub called 'The Fat Goose'. The succulent hanging baskets covering its red brick frontage and riverside seating area looked so inviting. She planned to visit that establishment regularly!

A sharp turn led her into the village of Lambsdale. On the steep, cobbled streets, white cottages lining the harbour glinted in the sun. The well-stocked gardens brimmed over with a kaleidoscope of pinks, blues and whites all competing for space. Tiny shops selling traditional buckets and spades were sheltered under blue and white canopies, while the boats in the harbour bobbed around in the faint breeze, their bells tinkling. The beach, as usual, was full this time of year with couples and young families sitting on picnic mats or deck chairs, some paddling in the sea while others snoozed with an open book on their lap.

Her possessions banged and wobbled around as she manoeuvred the uneven roads, watchful of the many tourists milling around. As she neared the bottom of a steep, narrow street, her sat nav informed her only three more minutes to destination. She shivered with both excitement and nerves as she started to climb another steep hill to the left of the harbour.

Laura pulled up outside a large, double-fronted whitewashed cottage with roses and wisteria climbing lazily around the light-blue front door that overlooked the sea. The well-maintained little garden at the front, defined by a white picket fence, boasted brightly coloured shrubs and flowers. In the garden, a pale blue B&B sign swayed gently in the summer breeze, proudly stating 'Harbour Cottage B&B'. Underneath, on a white chain, 'No Vacancies'.

She sat for a few moments, taking it all in. "This is stunning," she whispered. Of course, she'd seen photographs on the web and in the details from the solicitor, but they really didn't do it justice. The butterflies in her stomach fluttered around even more as reality started to hit home. Could she do this? Such a responsibility. She texted her mum quickly to say she'd arrived safely, then took a deep breath to calm herself.

As she got out of the car, she stretched out her arms, put back her head and took a deep breath of the tangy, salted air. From the front of the cottage she had a full view of the village and harbour to her right, and the blue sea to her left that stretched all the way up to the equally blue sky. She could see why Jemima had stayed and made her business here. Why would anyone want to live anywhere else?

Her thoughts were interrupted by Aunty Maria rushing out of the front door and down the little garden path, swinging open the white picket gate and enveloping Laura in her arms. Aunty Maria had always loved the simple pleasures in life, and her sense of dress style reflected that. Rarely had she been seen without a comfy pair of shoes, jeans and a fleecy top. Two years older than her sister, Laura's mother, appearance-wise they were similar, petite, blonde hair and pale blue eyes, but their characters were quite different. While her own mother was strong, quiet and thoughtful, content with retirement, her books and occasional baking, Maria was outgoing, and not satisfied unless she was involved in the hub of everything.

"I've been pacing at the window for the last hour. I knew you'd be driving, so I didn't want to ring you. Have you had anything to eat yet?" A flood of other questions fired at her as they walked to the car for Laura's luggage.

"Just a sandwich and a coffee," Laura replied, "but I must admit I'm a bit peckish again. Must be the relief that I'm finally here."

"Cup of tea and dinner first then." Aunty Maria helped Laura unload the bags from her car. Together they carried them through the colourful front garden, into a pleasant white and light grey entrance hallway. "We'll do a tour of the B&B in a bit, after you've had something to eat. Come on, let's go straight to your annex so you can rest for a short while."

"Annex?" Laura puffed as she struggled with her many bags. "I thought I'd be sleeping in the B&B."

"Oh no, my love, you'll not be sleeping here," her aunt replied as she dragged a particularly heavy bag down the hallway. "Every room is a huge money maker, especially at this time of year. The plus of this B&B is the views. Each bedroom has a wonderful view of either the harbour or the sea. They are highly sought after."

They struggled down the hallway, straight through to the back of the cottage B&B, into a sunny yellow boot room with original stone flooring. The many windows let in the brightness from the large garden. Raincoats of different sizes and colours hung off coat hooks, and Wellington boots resided happily underneath. "For the guests," Aunty Maria explained as she wiped away a smear on one of the windows with the arm of her fleece. "Not everyone comes equipped for the Great British weather. Either that or they don't want to pile their cars up with what they hope they won't need, unlike you, of course." She smiled, looking into Laura's bags full of waterproofs, fleece jumpers, walking boots and wellies.

Aunt Maria opened the boot room doors, leading them into a large flower and scent-filled garden overlooking the sea.

"Wow! This is amazing." Laura took in the mature flowering shrubs, rose gardens and apple trees. Seagulls cawed above them, their cries mingling with the sound of waves from the sea just below. Near the end of the garden, facing the ocean, stood a small barn conversion with a pitched beamed roof, accessed by large glass patio doors and a little wooden decking area.

"Your annex," Aunty Maria said as they approached the barn conversion, curtseying as she waved Laura inside.

"I didn't expect this." Excited, Laura walked inside. "It's so homely. Oh, and a real log burner." She stood in the middle of the room, savouring the cosy feel of the barn with its chintz-covered furniture, bookcases and deep pile rugs. Laura could see herself curled up in here on a cold night in front of the fire. At the end of the room was a small but perfectly equipped clean kitchen.

Aunty Maria bustled around, plumping up the many cushions. "There's a hut around the back, which is great for storage. You can look at it later if you wish."

Laura nodded her thanks and continued to explore the annex. A wooden door led through to a small sunny bedroom with windows looking out over the sea, while the last door led to the back of the building into an equally clean and smart little bathroom. Feeling overcome with emotion, she stood in the middle of the annex, thinking all this now belonged to her. It was so much to take in.

"She wanted you to have this, child," her aunt said quietly. "She wrote her will around two years ago. She never hesitated or changed her mind about you inheriting. I don't know if she ever regretted not settling down and having a family of her own, but she lived life to the full, working abroad, teaching languages, and all her charity work before she retired and bought this."

"It's such a responsibility."

"The annex is only five years old," her aunt replied. "Jemima looked after the B&B too, so I don't expect it to suddenly start falling apart. This isn't beyond you. Oh, it's hard work. I grant you that, but you'll have help."

"You're already busy with your own B&B in the next village," Laura said, panicking slightly.

"I meant Amy from the Post Office. She's willing to continue to work here once you re-open. If you want her, of course, and John next door is a dab hand with a hammer and a plunger. If all else fails, sell it to me and I'll turn it into a brothel. That'll raise your mother's eyebrows!"

Together they brought most of Laura's luggage into the annex and unpacked the essentials. "There is central heating," Aunty Maria shouted from the bathroom as she placed freshly laundered towels on the radiator. "Jemima preferred the log burner. It warmed the whole annex. Most of the summer you'll be in the B&B, but this is a great retreat during the slower months. Now, I've prepared a bit of lunch, so go and sit down and I'll bring it through."

*

Her aunt brought a tray of sandwiches into the room. "Take a plate, then tell me everything that's gone on with Leon. No need to pretend with me, I'm neutral, so spill the beans."

"There's not much to tell," Laura said, sighing. "He said he wanted his freedom, to relive his youth. He started spending more and more time out with his mates, and less time with me. I must admit I did suspect he was having an affair. He packed while I was at work. It seemed so cold and calculated, no kiss goodbye."

Her aunt shook her head. "You're worth a thousand of him, my girl. It sounds like you've had a lucky escape to me. You're young, beautiful, clever, and you deserve much better than the Leon's of this world. Coming here will give you a chance to get over him. You wanted a distraction. Well, believe me, there's nothing like good, honest hard work to provide that. Now go and freshen up and I'll show you around the B&B."

Laura walked back through the garden with her aunt, armed with a folder containing details on the B&B, from room tariffs to laundry bills. "It seems so real now," Laura said, as they headed into the dining room. "When do I need to re-open?"

"Soon, to bring in the finances. I had to put a message on the answering machine explaining that due to a bereavement, the B&B was closed until further notice. Don't forget to place adverts in shops too, letting them know you're open, not forgetting the website. It's all in my notes."

"That's something I am good at, websites." Now on familiar territory, she started to feel more positive.

The sunny dining room, to the left of the hallway, looked out over the sea, while the sitting room, with its warm red sofas and open fire, had a clear view of the harbour and the village. Exposed brick walls held white shaker style cupboards in the homely kitchen, while pots of fresh herbs sat on the windowsill, giving off their woody and citrus scent.

"All the bedrooms are named after roses," her aunt explained as they climbed the spindled oak staircase to the first floor.

Laura noticed the name plates on the three doors, "Charlotte, Alnwick and Olivia," she read. "Jemima's favourite English Roses. I remember their names."

Laura unlocked the door to the first room, finding herself in a bright, sunlit double room with views of the sea. Voile curtains, with their tiny sprigs of pink flowers, floated in the open sash windows. She looked out over the sparkling ocean. As tea-time approached, trails of families were leaving via the sand dunes, while a small yacht could be seen in the distance, it's white sail prominent against the blue cloudless sky. She breathed a little sigh at the serenity of the scene.

They headed onto the second floor, to the rooms named 'Emily' and 'Bronte'.

"These are your best sellers." Her aunt unlocked one of the doors. A four-poster bed covered in white voile dominated the room. Instead of sash windows, this room had full length patio doors that looked out over the sea. "Make sure you mention these on your website. 'Emily' is a replica but overlooks the harbour."

It was so much to take in. "When can I open?" Laura asked.

"I knew you'd get the bug once you saw the place! We have an appointment with the solicitor Mr Pickwick tomorrow afternoon, then you're good to go. Right, I'm going to leave you to it and let you settle in. I'll meet you tomorrow, outside the Post Office on the harbour front."

Her aunt opened the front door to leave, just as a small curly-haired dog flew out from the kitchen and started to scramble for attention at their feet.

"Bronte!" shouted a male voice from the kitchen. In followed a man that Laura guessed to be in his early sixties. His twinkling green eyes smiled in greeting. "Laura, I presume," he said, reaching to shake her hand. "I see you've met Bronte already. He's a handful. I hope you're ready for him!"

"Ready for him?" Laura asked. "What do you mean?"

"Ah." The man directed his eyes at her aunt. "You've not got around to Bronte yet then?"

"I knew there was something else," her aunt replied, looking sheepish.

"I'm still waiting," Laura said, bending down to stroke Bronte, while simultaneously stopping him from jumping into her arms.

"Bronte is a two-year-old cockapoo. Jemima's much-loved companion. I took him in after Jemima died, temporarily, until you arrived, unless..." The man looked embarrassed. "...unless you don't want him."

"I've never had a dog before," Laura replied. "I've no idea how to look after one, and isn't it against health and safety to have one in an establishment like this?"

"Bronte lived in the annex with Jemima. He had the run of the garden, but didn't enter the B&B, other than the boot room. I'm John by the way, from next door." He extended his hand in greeting.

"You're American?" she asked, while still struggling to calm the little dog and his wagging tail.

"Yes, from San Francisco. So, are you able to take Bronte?"

"I'll have a go." Laura smiled at her aunt. "Were you planning on springing this little surprise on me tomorrow?"

"You looked quite overwhelmed earlier. I thought it best to leave this until tomorrow. Let you settle in first and so on…"

"And I spoiled the plot." John looked relieved that Laura had agreed to take on his little charge. "He seems to have taken to you quite well."

"He will be company for me, I guess. Is he a good guard dog?" she asked hopefully.

"Oh yes, he'll lick any intruder to death." John laughed. "I've left some instructions in the kitchen around his feeds, and walks. There's also an emergency vet number, not that I think you'll need it. Don't forget, I'm only next door. I've left my mobile number on the kitchen worktop. I'm an ex-army man, good with DIY. Just shout if you need any help, okay?"

Laura sighed as she locked the B&B front door behind them. Tiredness had suddenly overcome her, and she looked forward to going back to her little annex, lighting a few scented candles, and opening a bottle of wine. She would read the instructions to the B&B tomorrow.

After reassuring herself that the building was secure, she headed down the garden to the annex. Bronte's little wet nose bumped into the back of her knees as she walked, most likely feeling confused about his change of ownership. The sun had started to set, turning the sea a golden yellow. The gentle hush of the sea waves and evening bird song had replaced the seagulls' caws.

Laura turned on the central heating to take the chill out of the air, making a note to buy wood and kindling tomorrow for the log burner. She heated the lamb stew—kindly left by her aunt—as she washed up and changed into her pyjamas.

Bronte barked hopefully as she opened a cupboard door. Instead of crockery, she found a dog bowl helpfully labelled

'Bronte', four large tins of dog food, and a dog lead. Laura felt sure they hadn't been there this afternoon. Maybe her aunt was craftier than she thought. At least she could cross those off her massive list of things to buy.

Laura opened a tin of the dog food, smiling as Bronte dived into his meal, snuffling the bowl around the kitchen floor, his little tail wagging furiously. She carried her hot bowl of lamb stew into the living room and curled up to watch the small TV, while appreciating the sunset over the sea from her window. Bronte soon joined her, licking his lips as he jumped onto the sofa and curled up at her side.

"Bedtime soon," she said to Bronte, as she started to feel sleepy. "Once I've phoned home."

"Hello, sweetheart," her mum answered on the fourth ring. "I've been worrying about you all day. How are you finding everything?"

Laura described the B&B and annex. "You'll have to come and stay with dad. I think I'm going to be very happy here."

"Still, I'll worry about you, but I know you'll make a success of it. I saw Leon in the supermarket today, by the way. He looked a bit rough, if I'm being honest. He asked after you. I said you'd gone to work in Yorkshire, but I didn't tell him anything else."

"Thanks, I appreciate that. Each day I think about him less."

"He didn't deserve you, darling. Your dad still wants to kick his skinny little bottom into next week. Speak of the devil. Your dad wants to talk to you."

Laura listened patiently to his fatherly advice on home security and staying safe. They finally said their goodbyes, and Laura promised to ring them in the next few days.

The bedding was soft and welcoming as Laura sank against the plump pillows, shifting her feet to accommodate the little dog at the end of her bed. The sounds of the sea calmed her as she read a few pages of her book. Finally, after hearing Bronte's rhythmic breathing, she turned off her little bedside light and fell into a deep and peaceful sleep.

CHAPTER 2

"Good morning, Bronte." The little dog pattered into the kitchen, following his morning snuffle around the garden. "Today is opening day." Laura rubbed Bronte's ears excitedly as he jumped onto her knee and licked her face. "Thank you." She laughed, wiping her cheeks with the sleeve of her t-shirt.

Heading onto the decking in the morning sunshine with her cup of tea, she watched the fishing boats come back into the harbour. The beach, already busy with dog walkers, inspired Laura to walk Bronte along the sands, at least once a day.

She had dressed casually this morning, planning to give the rooms in the B&B a quick clean after making up the beds. Grabbing her list of things to do, they headed over to the cottage, Bronte lolloping around the shrubs, then settling on a comfy spot on the boot room doormat.

The rooms didn't take much cleaning, but making up the beds turned out to be harder work than she realised. "I need to get in touch with the girl from the Post Office to make sure she can still help," she muttered, while wiping loose strands of hair off her now red face. The rooms sparkled in the warm sun streaming through the windows. Looking down at her grubby clothing, she smiled with satisfaction and headed for a shower, keen to make a good impression on her first visit into the village.

Bronte whined impatiently at the annex door as Laura struggled to clip his lead onto the collar. Unsure of the dress code for a trip to the solicitors, she had finally decided on a white cotton dress with blue flowers and a pair of strappy white sandals. She felt fresh and summery with a shimmer of bronzer on her cheeks that highlighted her blue eyes and a slight lick of lip gloss.

"Come on, Bronte," she said excitedly as she headed down the steep street into the village. Seagulls flew high in the sky, cawing to each other, and tourists strolled past with ice creams, buckets and spades. Tables outside the restaurants overlooking the sea were already preparing for a busy day ahead. From this height, she spotted the tantalising view of The Fat Goose, the beer garden already full of people relaxing at the side of the snaking river.

"Laura!" Her aunt waved. "How was your first night then?"

Laura briefly explained her relaxed evening, then her busy morning cleaning.

"Oh, making up new beds each day, you'll soon have muscles the size of Popeye's," her aunt said, laughing. "Come on, we'll take Bronte into the Post Office. Amy will keep an eye on him. We shouldn't be too long."

Sweetly scented hanging baskets and stands of postcards almost obscured the bright red door leading into the stone-built Post Office. Behind the desk stood a girl in her mid-twenties, a tumble of dark curls falling over her big brown eyes. Her low-cut, bright yellow top and tight blue denim skirt did little to cover her voluptuous figure.

"Hi!" said the bubbly girl as she came from behind the counter, bending down to stroke Bronte. "I'm Amy. Are you Laura?"

"Yes, it's lovely to meet you. Aunty Maria has been telling me about you and how you've helped Jemima in the past at the B&B."

"I'm so sorry about Jemima," Amy said. "I always liked her. I worked for her for nearly five years at the B&B. She didn't nag like my mum did, although she did insist I suck a mint in the morning if I smelled of alcohol from the night before! She talked about you a lot, showed me photos. That's how I knew you when you walked through the door."

Laura was pleased to meet someone so friendly. "I plan to do her proud and hopefully make a success of the B&B. We're just off to the solicitors now to finalise everything. Once I'm up and running, would you be willing to come back and help in the B&B? Same terms and conditions, of course. My aunt recommended you."

"Of course I will." Amy smiled. "To be honest, I've missed the money. This might be a nice place to visit, but I was born here, and I can tell you, it's not cheap getting a glass of wine and a packet of crisp around here! Just give me the nod and we can sort out the arrangements. Why don't you leave Bronte with me while you go into the solicitor's next door? Hopefully, I can close this place up for an hour during dinner, then we can head to The Goose for a vino to celebrate your good news."

"That was my plan exactly." Laura laughed. "Yes and yes, and thank you!"

Thankfully, the appointment at the solicitors was brief and simple. Mr Pickwick was surprisingly young, in his early thirties, she guessed. His dark-brown hair, worn short and gelled tightly to one side, contradicted his wide friendly smile, half covered by thick, framed glasses.

"I wish you all the best, Miss Thompson," he said, standing up and shaking her hand, surprising her with his height. "You're in a unique position inheriting such a good business at your age, but I'm sure you'll be a success."

"I think you've made quite an impression on our Mr Pickwick," whispered Aunty Maria. She gave Laura a wink as they walked next door to pick up Bronte.

"What are you smiling at?" Amy asked, bangles jiggling on her arms as she locked the Post Office door.

"I think Laura has taken the eye of Mr Pickwick." Aunty Maria giggled.

"Oh please!" Laura said, poking her aunt. "I don't need any matchmaking. Do I make myself clear? I'm done with men for the time being. I'm going to concentrate on my business and myself for a while."

"Good job really." Amy bounced along on her high red wedges. "There're no men in this village, I can tell you. I've been searching for years. They're either married or due to get married, or just not worth bothering with."

"What about Mr Pickwick," Laura asked. "Is he married?"

"Good God, no. Sam Pickwick!" Amy snorted. "He's so square he's unreal. Do you know, all he ever wanted to do was be a solicitor? I went to school with his sister. He was the most boring kid EVER. Top of the class for math, English, history; you name it, he studied it."

Laura laughed at Amy's description of Sam. They walked past the harbour shops on the way to The Fat Goose. Laura marvelled at their well-kept exteriors, all painted a different pastel colour, their pale blue and white striped canopies sheltering their wares outside. Laura paused at a little toy shop, its baskets full of brightly coloured buckets and spades, windmills, and kites. She called inside and treated Bronte to a red ball.

"I'm going to get some blackcurrant and liquorice." Amy skipped into a traditional sweet shop called 'Rupert's'. Shelves upon shelves of jars of sweets lined the inside walls of the sugar-pink fronted shop. A pale blue counter boasted large round lollipops, sticks of rock and bags of fudge. An old-fashioned bicycle leaned ornamentally against a wall, its basket full of fudge and toffee.

"I lurrrve this shop." Amy stood, looking up at the shelves. "If I won the lottery, I'd buy this place, no hesitation. Although I'd probably eat half the profits. Janet Henderson runs it now, but I know she's getting too old. If it was ever up for sale, I'd sell my soul to buy it."

They paid for their sweets and walked the small distance to The Fat Goose, sitting at a table close to the riverside. Bronte remained on his lead and headed under the table in the shade. Laura tucked the end of his lead under her chair.

"To the Harbour B&B!" they toasted and clinked their wine glasses.

Laura sighed happily. She'd made a good friend in Amy already, and her business was about to open its doors. As the sun shone warmly on her bare shoulders, she watched the ducks climb out of the river and waddle their way around the beer garden, pecking at crisps on the grass. Out of the corner of her eye, she caught sight of a red estate car pulling into the car park. Its owner, a tall dark-haired man, strode into the pub.

"Penny for them," her aunt asked, busy stripping off layers of fleece.

"I'm thinking how lucky I am," Laura replied. "I hope this feeling continues."

"Cheers to that!" Amy giggled while applying more red lipstick.

Laura stretched out her legs and took a sip of her cold wine, her attention momentarily distracted by the owner of the red estate car appearing in the beer garden. She squinted to make out a tiny kitten in his arms. His dark hair was cut short, and slight stubble suited his olive complexion. Laura guessed him to be in his mid-thirties. Despite a few ladies in the beer garden waving at him, he kept his head down and studiously ignored them.

Amy caught her looking at him. "Don't bother," she said, yawning widely. "He's the rudest man ever, the local vet, Lucas Chamberlain."

"He does have a reputation for being good with animals, but not very talkative," added her aunt, finishing off her drink. "He's been here a few years now. The ladies like him, obviously." She winked at Amy.

"Thinks he is someone," Amy huffed. "He reminds me of Arsey Darcy, only I can't see him offering to sieve my blue soup." She laughed, mimicking one of her favourite rom-com movie scenes.

"Aww, don't be mean," her aunt chastised. "I've never heard a bad word about his practice. He just prefers to keep himself to himself, that's all. Not easy in a village like this. I think he gets a bit fed up with the ladies making excuses to visit his practice. I call them the lipstick brigade. That's them waving at him now. There's nothing wrong with their pets. They just want to attract his attention. I like him. He's always been polite to me. Aiden Stokes, the other vet in the practice, has a lot of time for Lucas. He's always said he's good to work with."

"Well I don't like him," Amy said with a pout. "Although, if you do like him, Laura, I know he goes biking on his days off with the lads from The Goose. He looks good in Lycra." She winked.

"I need to get back to your Uncle Peter before he blows the place up." Her aunt stood up. "Enjoy your drinks, ladies, but don't get too drunk."

"I need to go as well," Laura said. "I've lots to do, and I can't do it with a muzzy head."

As she stood up to leave, a duck waddled under their table. The next few minutes whizzed by in a blur as Bronte shot at the duck, tipping over Laura's chair and freeing his lead. In his excitement, he charged at the ducks, sending them scattering into the river. Never one to be outdone, he continued to chase one brave duck around the garden, upsetting chairs with his long lead. As the duck spread its wings and gained flight, Bronte lunged at it, knocking over the vet holding the kitten.

"Bronte, come back here now!" Laura shouted, as she chased the dog around the garden. "Bad dog! Back here now!" But Bronte had other ideas and carried on his chase of the ducks.

Laura's cheeks burned with embarrassment as Bronte barked wildly and continued to ignore her shouts and commands. One kind woman eventually managed to grab his lead before he jumped into the river.

"Thank you so much," Laura puffed as she ran over and grabbed the lead. "I'm so sorry for all the mess."

The woman laughed. "I think you should be apologising to Mr sour pants over there. He seems to have come off worse."

Laura turned around and saw the vet on his knees, looking under the summer house. As she neared him, she realised he was trying to coax something out from underneath.

"I'm so sorry," she mumbled. "Can I help?"

He turned his head around to face her, then stood up. His face was red with anger and he seemed to be wearing most of his lemonade down his shirt and trousers. "I think you've done enough," he whispered to her. "Get that dog away from here. You obviously have no control of it."

"Excuse me!" she replied indignantly. "My dog was on a lead. It was the ducks that excited him. That could have happened to any dog or any owner."

"But it happened to your dog, in this garden, and now I can't get the kitten out from under this damned summerhouse," he hissed. "Please take that dog away. You're not helping."

Amy came rushing over, her bosom jiggling with her curls as she ran. "Are you okay?" she asked Laura.

"Is she okay?" asked the vet, his voice rising. "I'm covered in sticky lemonade, I've got a thousand wasps buzzing around me, the bloody kitten is still stuck under here, and you ask is she okay!"

"Fine, fine," Laura backed away. "I offered to help, but you're obviously too angry to listen. Come on, Amy, let's go." She turned around again to see the vet back on his knees, looking under the summerhouse. "I really am sorry."

The vet turned again and looked at her, then sat back on the grass. He pinched the bridge of his nose and sighed deeply. "Look, can you get your hands under here? The kitten can't go any further under, but I can't quite get to it."

Laura bent down and looked at the small gap underneath the summerhouse. "I think so," she said as she lay down on her stomach and put her arm through the gap. She felt around underneath, at first feeling only dirt, then eventually a little quivering ball of fluff. "I've got him, I think." She shuffled around on the grass to get a better grip.

"Careful," said the vet, "don't drag him. You'll hurt him."

"I won't drag him," Laura replied angrily. "I'm not an idiot!"

"Could have fooled me," the vet said under his breath. Unfortunately, Laura heard him. She stood up and brushed angrily at her knees. "I don't need comments like that. I've said I'm sorry. You're on your own."

"Just get the kitten out for me, please! It belongs to the pub. I was checking it over." Laura stared at him, and he stared back. She was determined not to apologise again for the situation they'd found themselves in, given his rudeness.

"I'll get the flipping kitten." Amy bent down, giving the vet a good view of her cleavage, but her arms were too wide for the gap.

"Alright, I'll do it!" Laura pointed at the vet. "But one more smart word from you and you're definitely on your own."

The vet put up his hands in surrender, then pretended to draw a zip across his lips. Laura lay down on the grass again and managed to grip the kitten, aware of her undignified position. Her dress had worked its way almost to the top of her thighs, and her knees were splattered with grass stains and dry mud, but at least she had the kitten in her hands. She handed it straight to the vet, who checked it over thoroughly.

"Thank you," he said begrudgingly.

"A pleasure," she replied as she pulled down her dress, wiped her knees and pushed away her hair from around her face.

"You need to keep that dog on a lead," he said, pointing to Bronte.

"He was on a lead!" Laura shouted. "I told you that."

"Come on, Laura." Amy pulled at her arm. "Let's go before we start a slanging match."

Laura picked up her handbag and the ball she'd recently bought Bronte.

"That ball is far too small for that dog," said the vet, looking at it.

"None of your business," Laura replied as she turned and left the beer garden with as much dignity as she could muster.

Back at the annex, Laura was still fuming after her altercation with the vet. Bronte, completely oblivious, snuffled around the garden as if nothing had happened. "You're in big trouble, little dog," she shouted as he lolloped around with his tongue dangling from the side of his mouth, chasing his new ball.

She made herself a cup of tea, opened the box of chocolates from the fridge, and sat outside in the sun on the decking. As she munched away at the delicious chocolates, she realised the 'No Vacancies' sign was still up.

"My moment of glory," she said to herself as she stood in the garden, removing the sign. "And I'm not going to let anyone spoil it for me, including that vet."

As she headed back inside the B&B, a couple in their sixties stopped her.

"Excuse me," said the woman. "Do you have any vacancies for tonight and tomorrow, a double if there's one available?"

Butterflies flew excitedly into Laura's stomach as she replied, "Yes, of course, come on inside. I'll show you the rooms."

The couple were delighted with the room they chose. "I've only just opened," Laura admitted. "You're my first guests."

"Well, what a privilege. My name is Christine, and this is my husband, Robert. I hope you remember us for the right reasons." They laughed.

Laura explained where they could park their car, and they walked back down the garden path to collect their luggage.

"Oh my God!" Laura shrieked as she jumped around in the hallway. "My first guests." She turned around in circles, not sure what to do first.

Christine and Robert were back within fifteen minutes with their luggage and soon settled into their room. Laura immediately texted her aunt and her mum to let them know the good news. Her aunt replied with a smiley emoji face, while her mum replied with 'Well done, darling. Good luck! Xx.'

"I must read those notes my aunt left me," she said to herself as she went back to her annex and pulled out the folder. She sat on the decking with a fresh cup of tea and went through the papers. Bronte sat nearby, his tongue lolling out of his mouth, panting over her. "You're not forgiven yet," she said to him, stroking his ears. He simply licked her face. "Daft dog, you're too cute to be angry with. Come on, let's sort the dining room out and get the tables set for breakfast."

She walked back into the B&B as her mobile rang with an unknown number. "Is this the Harbour B&B?" asked a woman. "We've just seen your advert in the newsagents and wondered if you had a twin room for one week starting tomorrow? We're staying on the other side of the village, Marjorie and myself. We only booked for four nights, but we're having such a wonderful time that we want to stay on. Our hotel is full and they can't accommodate us."

"Well, thankfully I have a twin room free." Laura happily took down their details. She really needed to get the electronic system up and running. "But could I ask, did you say you saw an advert in the newsagents?"

"Yes, lovey, it's in the window there. Why, is there a problem?"

"No, no, of course not." Laura smiled. Her aunt had obviously been busy after their visit to The Goose. At this rate, she would have all her rooms occupied in a few days.

As evening approached, Laura grabbed Bronte's lead from the back of the patio door, along with her fleece. "Come on," she called to Bronte, as he came flying to her at the sight of his lead and new red ball. "You don't deserve a walk after this afternoon's disaster, but I'm ready for some beach therapy."

Instead of walking along the path outside her B&B to get to the beach, she walked down to the end of her garden and scrambled down the series of steps carved into the cliffs. The beach and sea were vast; nothing could be seen for miles. She kept Bronte on his lead until they came to a more deserted part of the beach. He ran straight off at top speed after his red ball, his ears flying behind him. Into the incoming tide he went, time after time, getting wetter and wetter. Laura settled herself on a large rock, watching him roam around while listening to the incoming tide against the sand. Rock pools filled and then emptied noisily as the water glugged away, mesmerising her. A few other couples passed by, saying hello, some with dogs, others out for a walk after their evening dinner.

Despite her fleece, the cool breeze soon started to make her shiver. Together they made their way back towards her

B&B. In the distance, she noticed a man walking a golden retriever down the beach, heading in her direction. As he got closer, she recognised with dismay the vet from The Goose. Putting up the hood of her fleece and tilting her head down, she hoped to walk by unnoticed, but their four-legged friends had other ideas.

"Hello," the vet said to Laura's fleece-topped head.

Laura decided not to reply. Instead, she whistled to Bronte to come to her. Of course, Bronte took no notice and carried on playing with his new friend. Laura, desperate to get away before being noticed, once again whistled. Bronte didn't just ignore her, but also ran the other way. The golden retriever naturally gave chase.

"Oh bugger," Laura groaned, "not again. Bronte! Heel, now!"

The vet, also shouting after his own dog, turned and looked at her more closely. "You again!" he said incredulously. "Have you not learned yet to keep a pup on a lead? Bella!" he hollered to his own dog. Naturally, Bella came running to her master straight away, while Bronte frolicked in the sea with his red ball.

Sighing with frustration, she took off her converse, rolled up her jeans, and waded into the incoming tide to grab Bronte's collar. "Why do you always play up in front of him?" she growled between gritted teeth as she hauled him back onto the dry sand. She tried to hold on to his lead while hopping around putting on her shoes and waited for another torrent of insults from the vet. She walked back to where he stood to pick up her discarded fleece, not to be disappointed.

"Is that dog even yours?" he asked rudely. "Why do you insist on letting it off the lead when it obviously doesn't listen to you? Don't you realise it's not safe for the dog if you can't control it?"

"The dog is mine, and I'll have you know that when he's not around you, he's well behaved, which says a lot about you, doesn't it? In fact, I happen to know that dogs are good judges of character. If my dog plays up around you and no one else, then you're obviously the one with the problem, not me."

"I'm the one with the problem? Are you serious? I'm not the irresponsible dog owner here, and I see you're still letting it play with that ball. It's far too small for a dog of that size. I really don't understand why you're being so rude to me when you're the one who's caused yet another issue."

Without his sunglasses, Laura could see his dark brown eyes firing missiles of anger.

"Well, wouldn't we all like to be as perfect as you?" she snapped. "Can you tell me if you get vertigo sitting in your ivory tower, or if your halo glows in the evening while you're asleep?"

Laura knew she was being petty, but she couldn't help it. This man's rudeness frustrated her beyond belief.

"You're being extremely childish," he replied as he clipped a lead onto his own dog. "Are you always so determined not to accept when you're in the wrong?"

"If I wanted to be patronised, I'd become one of your customers, and accept it alongside your huge vet bills!" she shouted, flouncing off towards the steps, up the cliff face, leaving him stunned and speechless.

Her hands still shook with anger as she reached her annex, muttering to herself, "How dare he speak to me like that. He's arrogant, abusing his professional role to boss people around and make them feel insignificant."

The remainder of her evening passed by without any event, although her latest encounter with Mr sour pants, as she had nick-named him, did bother her more than she liked to admit. Never one for confrontation, she'd surprised herself as to how readily she had retaliated. Maybe living with Lazy Leon had taught her a few things. Whatever the reason, she replayed the confrontation repeatedly in her mind.

Unsurprisingly that night, she dreamt of swimming with golden retrievers and fiery brown eyes.

CHAPTER 3

Bacon and sausages sizzled away under the grill, while her two guests munched away at their cereals. Laura hummed gently to the relaxing songs on the radio whilst cracking eggs into the frying pan.

Christine and Robert had arrived downstairs at eight o'clock prompt, both ordering a full English breakfast, much to Laura's gratitude. She'd cooked many of those on a Sunday morning for Leon.

This is easy. She sighed happily while collecting their empty plates. Seconds later, she dropped the tableware as eight pieces of charred bread shot out of the toaster, setting off the smoke alarm. "Typical," she muttered to herself.

Despite her smoky start, breakfast proved to be a success. She finished wiping down the kitchen surfaces, then sat with her laptop to survey the B&Bs website. Her computer skills enabled her to make the slight alterations that it needed, and for good measure, she added a photograph of herself above her name and new job title. A further two bookings confirmed four of her five rooms would be full tomorrow. She felt the time had come to seek the help of her friend, Amy.

"Come on, little dog." Bronte skipped excitedly around her ankles at her command. "You're staying on this lead today. No chasing ducks, dogs, anything. When I say 'heel,' you come straight to my side. Are we understood?"

"Woof!" Bronte replied. He jumped up, scrambling at her knees for love and attention. She couldn't be mad at him for longer than thirty seconds.

The small cobbled roads were teeming with tourists, the good weather attracting plenty of trade. Seagulls swooped around the harbour restaurants, hoping to catch scraps of food, while the bells of the fishing boats in the harbour tinkled in the slight breeze.

"Hello, stranger." Amy stood behind the Post Office counter, wearing a sexy red gypsy top that laced up over her ample bust. "What can I do for you?"

"I'm here to ask a favour. Would you be able to start work at the B&B tomorrow? I know it's short notice, but I've a further two bookings coming in tomorrow and two guests arriving around four o'clock today."

"Not a problem. Will seven in the morning be okay? That's what time I used to arrive for Jemima."

"Perfect. What time are you having lunch, by the way? My treat for helping me out."

"Just give me five." Amy looked at the clock on the wall. "My stomach thinks it's been cut. Shall we get chips and sit outside?"

"My mouth is watering already, and if you're really good, I'll treat you to a latte at the same time."

"You're my new BFF." Amy made a love heart shape with her ring covered fingers.

*

Laura sat on the harbour wall next to Amy, eating the most delicious fish and chips she'd ever tasted.

"Do you fancy a drink at The Goose this evening, Laura?"

"Oh, I don't know. After yesterday's embarrassment, I've sort of gone off that place."

"Old news." Amy scrunched up her chip-papers, wiping the grease from her hands on them. "The Goose is normally full of tourists this time of year. They'll be gone and replaced by new sunburned versions today. Lucas might not be there either."

"I had another run in with him last night on the beach." Laura stood up and took their chip papers to the nearest bin. "He's very obnoxious."

"Told you he was." Amy listened to Laura recount last night's events. "He either doesn't like people or doesn't know how to communicate."

"Well, I plan on staying out of his way," Laura replied.

"Quick, hide. Sam Pickwick is coming." Amy walked briskly away to examine a jewellery stand on the other side of the narrow street.

"Afternoon, Miss Thompson. I hope all is going well with the business." Sam nervously touched his hair, causing Laura to smile.

"Please, call me Laura." She craned her neck to spot Amy hovering discreetly a few metres away. "The business is going well. I've got a few guests booked in over the weekend, and I'm learning lots as I go."

"I'm glad. It's always busy here Fridays and Saturdays, especially in the evenings. The Fat Goose is a good place to visit at the weekends. Have you been there?"

"Yes, I called in yesterday. We are planning to go again this evening, aren't we, Amy?" Her friend pretended not to hear and continued to fiddle with the jewellery stand. Laura realised she'd put herself in an awkward position. "You're quite welcome to join us, Mr Pickwick. Isn't that right, Amy?"

"Oh, well, I'm not sure." Mr Pickwick had noticed Amy rolled her eyes. "If I'm free later, I may pop down to join you. Thank you for the invite, though. Good evening, ladies."

"I'm sorry, Amy." Laura cringed. "I had to invite him. Do you not like him?"

"I don't dislike him." Amy sighed. "He's just so boring. He'll talk about parking fines and house sales. He'll consider himself ever so riveting." She mimicked him flattening his hair.

"Well, we'll just have to get him drunk." Laura linked arms with her friend. "Or, we could talk about women's problems. That will most likely have him running for the hills!"

CHAPTER 4

Laura noticed couples and families mingling together on the decking area of The Goose, while waitresses bustled past with delicious plates of food.

She found Amy sheltered under a parasol near the river. "I got here early for a good table, otherwise we'd be stood up all night, and believe me, even I can't stand in these shoes." Amy lifted her feet from under the table to reveal a pair of high yellow wedges. Her dark curls complemented her brightly printed Bardot top and skinny white jeans.

Laura looked down at her plain pink t-shirt and blue chinos, feeling frumpy and boring. She promised herself a wardrobe overhaul if the B&B business took off. They ordered their food and drinks with a passing waitress before settling down to enjoy themselves.

As the evening went by, young families were replaced by couples and groups. Strings of lights lit up flower-filled pergolas as the music became livelier.

"Hello, ladies, mind if I join you?" Laura looked up. Her eyebrows raised as Mr Pickwick approached them.

His normally flat gelled hair had been fashioned into a messy style. His glasses, she presumed, replaced by contact lenses, which emphasised his deep blue eyes. All in all, she had to admit, with his white cotton shirt, light blue Levi's and casual sports shoes, he looked very attractive.

"I'll get us some drinks, if you don't mind me joining you."

"Of course, we don't mind." Laura looked with amusement at Amy's shocked face. "The more the merrier."

"Oh my God!" Amy leaned over the table towards Laura, watching Mr Pickwick walk to the bar. "Get Clark Kent over there. He's a bit of alright when he's not dressed like a stiff. He's got a cute ass. I've never noticed that before."

"It's a shocker." Laura giggled. "I've got to admit he scrubs up well."

Mr Pickwick returned with their drinks and sat at their side. He looked nervous and out of place.

"So, Mr Pickwick, what kind of work does a solicitor do around here?" Laura asked, desperate to fill the awkward silence.

"Well, all kinds really. House sales mostly during the summer." Sam looked suspiciously at Amy's dilated pupils. "You keep calling me Mr Pickwick. My name is Sam. I prefer Sam."

"I used to be an estate agent, Sam," Laura replied, thankful to have something to talk about. "I understand how pressured it must be. So, how long have you been a solicitor?"

"Erm, around ten years, give or take. I've got quite an analytical mind, a good skill in this profession." He laughed nervously, trying to straighten a pair of non-existent glasses. "I loved that film, the court scene, you know, *A Few Good Men*. It inspired me."

"Oh my God, I love that film." Amy leaned over the table towards Sam, her incredible cleavage on show. "'You can't handle the truth!' I love it when Colonel Jessup shouts that out. Such a classic."

"I'm impressed," Sam replied, his eyebrows raised. "Most people know it was Jack Nicholson, but not his character. Ten points, Miss Sharples."

"You know my surname?" Amy asked, sitting back down with surprise.

"Well, yes, of course I do. You went to school with my little sister, Lucy. You were always at our house, playing with dolls, hair, makeup, screaming lots, whatever little girls do. Do you not remember me?"

"Yes, I do. Of course I remember you. You always came across as a bit, I don't know…"

"Square?" he asked, raising his eyebrows once again.

Amy blushed. "Yes," she replied.

He laughed. "Well, I suppose it comes with the profession, and the glasses, of course."

"Where are your glasses?" Laura asked. "You look very different without them."

"Oh, I invested in contact lenses. A client of mine suggested I should try them. I dropped a pair of glasses last week, and they smashed. My spare pair were at home. I was due in court so…"

"You go into court?" Amy whispered, leaning even further over the table.

"I'm training to be a barrister." Sam looked concerned by Amy's eagerness.

"Like Judge John Deed?"

"Yesss." He tried his best not to stare at her full cleavage. "I guess so. Do you want another drink? You look hot and flustered."

"I'll get them." Amy jumped up, fixing her off-the-shoulder top whilst twining a finger flirtatiously around her curls.

Laura smiled as Sam watched Amy sashaying away in her tight white jeans. "So, do you two only know each other through your sister?"

"Yes, through Lucy. I've not spoken to Amy in years. We work near each other, but our paths don't tend to cross. I don't live in the village. I only work here. I don't know if Amy has already told you, but she and my dear sister took great delight in making my life a misery, as younger sisters do. I did my best to keep out of their way!"

"That's girls for you." Laura smiled. "I've got to say, Sam, you look much different out of work."

"And is that a positive?" he asked nervously.

"Well, this look is definitely more relaxed. It's kind of cool. I know Amy likes it."

"Really, does she?" he asked, looking pleased. "Well, that's good to know."

Amy returned, her hips swinging more than usual, holding three gin glasses and packets of peanuts between her teeth. As she reached their bench, her heel stuck in a patch of grass, and she tumbled slightly.

Sam jumped up and caught her elbow.

"Thank you," Amy said breathlessly.

"Not a problem, Miss Sharples." Sam looked at her with new interest. "Dry-roasted peanuts, my favourite." He juggled the three packets before throwing one at Amy and one at Laura.

"You can juggle?" Amy squeaked.

"I can do a lot of things, Miss Sharples."

*

Feeling much like a fifth wheel, but happy that Amy and Sam seemed to be getting along, Laura left her friends and walked back to her little annex.

Bronte barked and scrambled at her knees as she walked inside the cosy lit room. She rubbed his ears, much to his delight. "Bedtime soon, little dog," she said as he had his night-time sniff around the garden. "Busy day tomorrow. Four to feed at breakfast. Beds to change and laundry to sort."

She changed into her pyjamas and climbed between the cool sheets. Bronte, as per usual, jumped onto the end of the bed and turned around three times before settling himself on Laura's feet. She took out her book and started to read, but her head filled with the evening's events.

She smiled as she thought of Amy and Sam. They were cute together. Chalk and cheese quite obviously, but quite often opposites attract.

She suddenly realised that Lucas hadn't turned up at The Goose after all. The fact that she didn't get to insult him again strangely disappointed her.

CHAPTER 5

Her alarm woke her at the unearthly hour of six thirty. Groggily, she reached out a hand to turn it off. The annex felt cooler today. She shivered as she pushed her feet into her slippers. Bronte, still at the bottom of the bed, simply sighed and moved his head to a more comfortable position. "Oh, what I'd do to change places with you right now."

The Gin and Tonics had left a staleness in her mouth. Leaving The Goose early had been the right decision. She showered and dressed in her customary jeans, t-shirt and converse, while wondering how Amy and Sam had got on after she'd left.

For the first time since she'd arrived in Lambsdale, clouds could be seen in the sky. Laura unlocked the patio doors to the boot room and stepped inside, firing up the central heating to take the chill off the air. Amy arrived in time to warm up the large oven. *I really need to re-think my wardrobe,* Laura thought, admiring Amy's exotic palm printed maxi dress, tangerine cardigan and matching pumps.

Amy launched straight into the events of last night without even drawing breath, "Oh my God! Last night was amazing. Sam can do magic tricks too. I can't get over how good looking he is, and he likes the same movies as me." Amy rummaged around in a drawer Laura didn't even know existed and pulled out an apron, tying it around her voluptuous figure.

"So you got on well then?" Laura laughed.

"He's just perfect, and a gentleman too. He offered to walk me home. I was all prepared for a really good kiss, but do you know what he did instead? He walked me to my garden gate, placed a flower in my hair, then kissed my hand. It was so romantic, like something Jack would have done for Rose in the Titanic. I can't wait to see him again."

"When are you meeting up?" Laura asked as she filled the kettle and put it onto boil.

"I don't know." Amy groaned. "That's my only problem. He didn't say he wanted to see me again. Do you think that's a bad sign? Normally, I ask men for another date, but I couldn't with Sam. It seemed wrong. I want him to take the lead. I don't know what I'm trying to say, really."

"You want to be wooed, I think is the phrase. Nothing wrong with that. Quite romantic."

"I know, but so frustrating at the same time. I hope he rings me today." Amy pulled out her mobile and checked the signal before sighing dramatically. "Anyway, guests to serve, see you later."

Laura smiled as Amy disappeared into the dining room with her pad and pen, already proving to be worth her weight in gold. She jumped as her phone beeped with a message from her mum. Reading it quickly, her eyebrows raised.

"Ex-boyfriends are a nuisance," she said when Amy returned to the kitchen. "Mine turned up at my parents' house last night, wanting to know how he can get in touch with me."

"Does he not know where you are?"

"No, he doesn't, thankfully, and I want it to remain that way. I changed my mobile number after we split up. He doesn't know my address here, either. Some people you need to leave in the past. He's definitely one of them."

"Good decision, move onwards and upwards." Amy pointed to the laden plates. "Marjorie doesn't like egg, so I've given her extra bacon. Sylvia doesn't want beans, so I've fried up extra mushrooms. I'm telling you, those two can talk nonstop. I couldn't get a word in edgeways. John and Christine had full English with everything. We're done."

Amy ran around, quickly clearing the dining tables, scraping off the plates and rinsing them, before placing them in the dishwasher.

"Does the Post Office not mind you coming here in the morning?" Laura asked, struggling to keep up with her whirlwind friend.

"Nah, in a small village like this, everyone knows you've got to follow the money and help each other out. Polly Pocket will cover in the Post Office until midday. I'll take over then."

"Is she really called Polly Pocket?" Laura laughed.

"No, she's called Polly Pickett. She married Don Pickett, from the brewery. I call her Polly Pocket though. You have to get the laughs where you can." Amy boiled up the kettle again. "Brew time for us now. There are two bacon sandwiches under the grill. Grab them and we'll have a break."

"You really are a star." Laura smiled. "Heaven sent, as Jemima would have said."

CHAPTER 6

Laura groaned after a morning cleaning rooms and making beds. She stretched her back and aching muscles, sighing as the doorbell interrupted her mid-flex. Cursing Amy for most likely forgetting something, she limped down the two flights of stairs.

"Hello, Laura, have you missed me?"

Laura stared in disbelief at her visitor. "What do you want? How on earth did you find me?" Her heart thumped painfully in her chest.

"I've come to see you," Leon replied, looking hurt and a bit put out. "I set out this morning at stupid o'clock to get here. I'm knackered and ready for a brew." He looked over her shoulder into the hallway. "Any chance I can come in?"

Laura, about to slam the door in his face, noticed a family studying her room rates pinned near the garden gate. "Five minutes, that's all you get."

She walked into the kitchen, her head full of questions, dazed and stunned at Leon's sudden arrival. Leon followed, having a quick nosey in the living room before coming to stand near the kitchen window.

Laura pulled out her bar stool and sat on it to steady her shaking legs. Leon, looking around for another chair, and failing, eventually shuffled his feet and coughed, preparing for his speech.

Laura took this opportunity to take a good look at the man she'd once loved. Her mum's description of him rang true. He did look rough. He'd also put on more weight, resulting in a very tight shirt.

"Laura." He held out his hands, reminding her of the vicar back home. "I've driven all this way to try and put things right. I've been an idiot. What can I say? I know I treated you badly. I didn't know just how good I had it until I lost it."

"You didn't lose it, Leon. You chose to leave." Laura replied calmly.

"Yes, yes, I know." He stuttered, obviously put out that his well-prepared speech had been interrupted so early. He coughed and wiped his nose on the back of his hand, a habit that had always driven her mad. "I know now I made the wrong decision. You were the best thing I ever had. I had my head turned by the single lifestyle. Spending too much time with the young ones from the office, I suppose."

"So, did you not enjoy the bachelor lifestyle then? The one-night stands, gigs, weekends away with the boys, poker nights."

Leon had the grace to cringe. "I had a mid-life crisis. I had to get it out of my system. We all make mistakes. Look at how you pranged the car last year. That cost me two hundred quid, but I forgave you."

"That was a car, Leon, you idiot. You can fix a car. And incidentally, you didn't forgive me straight away. You ignored me for three days until I paid for the repairs."

Laura gripped the side of the barstool tightly. How could he stand there and use a dent in a car as a comparison to what he'd done to her? His lack of compassion astounded her.

"Leon, don't you get it? You caused me hurt, pain and embarrassment. How can you be so blasé about what we had built together?"

"Hey, you can't blame all this on me." Leon had one hand on his hip, the other out at the side, reminding her of a teapot. "You weren't exactly easy to live with!" Beads of sweat formed on his upper lip as they normally did when he got angry or agitated. "You were always working late, demanding takeaways because you couldn't be bothered to cook. I've driven all the way here to try and get this relationship back on track. Give me a break, at least!"

"I worked late four times, Leon, and take-aways are what normal couples do on a Friday night. Do you even know what a normal relationship is? You've been here less than five minutes and already you're turning the tables on me." Laura's eyes filled with tears at the injustice of his words. How did she manage to spend so many years with this man? "You humiliated me. I lost my beautiful home because of your selfish behaviour. I cried myself to sleep every night for weeks."

"Oh, Laura," he replied, sensing weakness. She noticed him changing tactic again. God, she knew him so well.

He walked over to her chair, his sneakers squeaking on her freshly mopped floor. "We can work this out. We're not over. Come back home with me. Sell this place and we'll buy a nice, detached four bed with the profits. I've already done the sums. You can even buy yourself a nice car to get to work and back. And well, listen." He coughed, nervously. "I've been doing some thinking, maybe we could get engaged."

Leon got down on one knee and held her hand in his sweaty palm. "I don't have a ring, but we can buy one." He lifted her hand to kiss it, but Laura withdrew it quickly.

"You've done the sums? What do you mean you've done the sums? How did you find me, Leon?"

"Erm, off the Internet. I Googled your name, found your photo attached to this place. Never mind that now. Are you going to say yes?"

As the sun chose an unfortunate moment to come out from behind the clouds and shine upon his spreading bald patch, Laura experienced a mix of emotions. Firstly, sadness that their relationship had come to this. They'd been so happy at the start. Leon had been attentive and caring, generous and amusing. She'd moved in with him without any doubts. Anger filled her the most now. Leon had come here to cajole her into selling the Harbour B&B so he could reap the profits.

Her disappointment and humiliation came up from her toes, spreading through her entire body. "I'm going to say something now that you'll thank me for in years to come," she replied, looking down into his sweaty face. "I'm going to tell you to piss off back to Manchester. Sleep with half the population while you're there if you must, and never, ever come near me AGAIN!" Laura took in a deep breath to steady her racing heart. She felt brilliant, exhilarated. Adrenaline pumped through her body as she stood up to leave the room.

"You can't mean that? Laura, Laura." Leon steadied himself against the barstool in his haste to stand up. He followed her into the garden, his head on a swivel, taking in his surroundings.

"Heel, Bronte!" Laura stood at the door to her annex. Her little charge obeyed her, baring his teeth whilst growling loudly.

Leon backed away, eyeing the dog warily. "I fear we've got off to a bad start," he mumbled, holding out his hands in his vicar pose again. "I'm sorry for my grumpiness. I'm tired from the journey down and I'm hungry. Maybe if we had a bite to eat, things will look much better." He looked over her shoulder into the annex.

Laura sighed. He did look tired. Plus, she didn't want the guilt of him crashing his car driving home because he felt hungry. "Okay, you can have bacon and eggs, then I want you to leave. You've got one hour and nothing more."

"Leave? But I've only just got here," Leon complained. "Can we at least talk after you've made us something to eat?"

"No, Leon. My answer is no to coming home and no to an engagement. I'm not going to play with your feelings and let you think there's hope. I've moved on, and I suggest you do the same."

"What do you mean you've moved on?" he snapped. "Are you seeing someone?" Laura watched him look around the annex for evidence of a male.

"Not that it's any of your business, but no, I'm not."

Leon sighed with relief. "That would have been a bloody slap in the face after five hours of driving. Okay, let's eat and take it from there. You put some dinner together and I'll have a little snooze."

Laura shook her head at his audacity. She walked back into the B&B with shaking legs. Bronte followed closely at her heels, his little nose bumping against her ankles every now and then. She bent down and ruffled his ears, his tail wagging in delight. "You are a fabulous dog, my knight in shining armour." He licked her face repeatedly whilst trying to climb onto her knee. "Come on, you softy, get down."

She headed back to the annex, her arms piled up with ingredients to make a bacon and egg muffin. She found Leon sitting on her sofa, one leg swung over the other, the remote control in his hand.

"Thanks, love. You know I like my bacon nice and crispy. The egg not too runny." He absentmindedly swapped TV channels.

Laura slapped the goods on the small worktop. "There you go. Sort yourself out." She walked back to the B&B with a smile; his face was a picture.

*

"You won't change your mind then?" Leon walked into the kitchen with egg on his chin. He picked up his jacket and slung it over his shoulder. "I won't ask you again. Once I walk out of here, we're over. I won't beg."

"Leon, please leave," Laura said softly. "I won't be coming with you. Not today, not ever. Whether I decide to stay or sell up, either way, you won't be in the picture. Do you understand?"

Leon lifted his head in arrogance. "Your loss," he sneered, swaggering down the hallway. He jumped into his car and wound his window down. "You'll regret your decision when you're old and grey. Living on your own, like the geriatric spinster who left you this shithole. I'll make my millions selling property while you slide into the sea with this friggin' dump."

Laura deigned not to reply, but quietly closed the front door and leaned her head against it.

CHAPTER 7

"He said what!" Amy exclaimed, rapidly stuffing chips into her mouth as her legs dangled over the harbour wall. "What an absolute friggin' tool. I'd have chopped his bloody knob off. Well, Laura, absolute respect to you." Amy held up her hand for a high five. "So, where's knob-head now? On the way back to Manchester?"

"I've no idea. I guess he's part way down the A40 by now. I hope so, anyway."

"You've had a lucky escape there, my girl."

"I know. Funnily enough, that's what Aunty Maria said to me the day I arrived here. Which reminds me, I need to phone her and my mum. Let them know what's happened."

"What's your plan for this afternoon then?" Amy asked as they walked to the coffee shop. "Oh, I forgot to tell you, Rupert's sweet shop is up for sale. Mrs Henderson fell down the stairs a few days ago. She's okay. A few cuts to her head, but it could have been so much worse. Anyway, she's decided to move closer to her daughter."

"Where are you going to get your blackcurrant and liquorice from if Rupert's closes for good?" Laura teased.

Amy sighed and looked out to the sea with a wistful expression. "I don't know, but I wish I could buy it. I've always felt at home in there."

"Could you not get a small business loan? You could buy it then."

"What, me!" Amy stopped and pointed to herself. "A bank lend ME money. Pigs might fly."

"Amy, I'm being serious. Why ever not?"

"Because I've never run a business before. I'm twenty-five-years-old. I work in a Post Office part-time and cook breakfasts in a B&B. No offence," she quickly added.

"Non-taken. But, Amy, most people who apply for a business loan are starting from scratch. At least you have retail experience. You know the area and understand the footfall. You're better placed than most to run that shop."

"Oh, I don't know." Amy scuffed one of her heeled wedges against the kerb. "I wouldn't know where to start. I mean, forms and all that legal bollocks. I wouldn't have the first clue."

Laura grinned and nudged her shoulder. "I think you need to speak to someone with a legal background. I wonder if you should make an appointment with a certain solicitor for some much-needed advice."

Amy slowly turned to look at her, "I like you, Miss Thompson. I like you a lot."

*

The heavens opened as they finished off their drinks. Laura ran up the hill to the Harbour B&B, her handbag raised above her head to protect her hair. The sea started to disappear under black clouds as tourists came off the beach in droves. She opened the door to the B&B and ran inside, wiping her sodden shoes on the doormat, shaking raindrops from her hair.

"Oh, Laura, I am sorry, love." Marjorie appeared down the stairs, looking embarrassed. "I don't mean to bother you, but we can't close our bedroom window and it's quite chilly."

"Of course, don't worry." Laura followed them to their room. "These old sash windows do stick. I'll sort it."

They walked up the stairs together, exclaiming at the rain and thunder. Laura found the sash window well and truly stuck. She heaved and pushed using her weight, but to no avail. Marjorie and Sylvia looked frozen. Laura took them down into the warm living room and made them both a cup of tea.

"Just give me five minutes." She grabbed her raincoat. "John, from next door, might be able to help."

Thankfully, John came around straight away. He worked his way around the window sash with a putty knife and a small hammer, gently tapping the chords in the insets. He pushed gently on the sill of the window, smiling as it started to move.

"Here you are, Laura, a candlestick. It's cheap WD40 and less messy. All done!" John moved the sash window open and shut with much more ease. "That should move smoothly for a while now, but if it starts to jam again just run this candle along the chords."

"John, you are an absolute star. I don't know what I would have done without you."

"Not a problem," he replied, running lightly down the stairs. "Just knock. You know I'll always help."

"It works both ways, John. I'm no use at DIY, but I can cook!"

John paused. "Actually, you can do me a favour, if you don't mind. Nothing urgent. I've got myself a laptop, but I'm struggling with it. Technology, not my area of expertise, I'm afraid. Now, ask me to rewire this place. No issue at all."

"So, you were an electrician in the army?"

"Yes, ma'am." He saluted. "Corporal John Thistle at your service. I served in the US Army for twenty years before coming back to England."

"Oh, so you're from England originally?"

"Yes, I was born in a small village near Lancaster called Heppleworth. I lived there for almost twenty years before moving to America." John smiled, as if lost in his thoughts. "Anyway, if you get a chance, could you pop round, see what I'm doing wrong?"

Laura looked at her watch. "I've got an hour before my guests are due to arrive. I can come now if you're free?"

Laura threw on her raincoat again, and they ran around to John's house. His laptop sat on a dining table surrounded by paperwork. "I open the browser and no matter what site I try, BBC, Google, whatever, I get some nonsense about no connection."

Laura looked at the screen. "It says you're connected, but the Internet's not available. I'll just check your router and turn it off and on again."

"Brilliant, you're a genius." John clapped his hands as the Internet service returned.

Laura shrugged. "The on-off switch is the oldest trick in the book."

"Well, I'm kind of relieved. I've been having lessons at the library. I just assumed I'd done something wrong. I've only had this laptop a few weeks. Would you like a brew, by the way? You look cold."

"Oh, yes please, that would be perfect." Laura noticed the paperwork around her related to births, marriages and deaths. "It's pretty powerful, the web. You can find the answer to almost anything these days."

John sighed, "Not all answers, though. I'm afraid I'm coming to a dead end with my research."

"I hope you don't mind me asking, but are you trying to do your family tree? I've noticed your papers, and I may be able to help. I did mine a few years ago."

"No, not quite," John replied, looking thoughtful. "I'm trying to find a certain person, but I don't have a lot to go on. The Internet was my last hope."

"An old friend?"

"Kind of. Well, a bit more than that, really. It's a long story."

"I'm sorry," Laura said. "I didn't mean to pry."

"No, you're not. I've never talked about this before. It's not a secret, as such, more a buried past that bothers me the closer I get to the pearly gates. When I lived in Heppleworth, I met a young lady whilst working at Woolworths. Lizzie Flanagan. We were both eighteen at the time. She stole my heart. I was smitten the minute I laid eyes on her. She was the best-looking girl in the whole of Lancaster by far, and the nicest too. A bit shy, but that just added to her charm.

"Every day I all but ran into work so I could see her. It cost me a fortune in hair gel and aftershave. She had hair the colour of chocolate, eyes that matched the sky, and talk about a figure. Oh my, she turned plenty of heads. Anyway, we'd known each other about four weeks when I finally plucked up the courage to ask her out to the cinema. We agreed to watch 'The Three Musketeers'. I can't say as I remember much about the film. I was in seventh heaven just sitting at her side. I walked her home after. I didn't expect a kiss, and I didn't get one either."

"You strike me as a gentleman." Laura smiled. "Did you see her again?"

"Yes, a few dates later and she agreed to become my girlfriend. From then on, we spent nearly every waking hour together. Her parents didn't approve, though. They wanted better for their daughter than a shop worker. They never invited me round, so most of the time we were at my house. I shared it with my brother Stan, stealing moments together when he was out. Anyway, one afternoon she asked to meet me at the back of the shop. I just presumed she'd had enough and wanted to end the relationship. She was too good for me, you see. Anyway, she told me she was pregnant."

Laura's eyes widened. "What did you say?"

"I was over the bloody moon. I knew from that moment on we'd be together for the rest of our lives. I couldn't think of anyone more beautiful to make a baby with. I got down on one knee and proposed to her there and then. I didn't have a ring, of course. I went into the store and bought her a costume jewellery ring instead, just as a stand in, until we could get the real thing." John laughed lightly at the memory.

Laura thought about the proposal she'd received earlier from Leon. They were poles apart.

"What did her mum and dad say?"

"We agreed to tell her parents together. I thought we could move in with Stan after we'd got married. Just until we could afford a place of our own. Anyway, I turned up at her house as we'd agreed, but Lizzie wasn't there. Her dad answered the door, and I knew the minute I saw him that he already knew our news. He threatened to knock my lights out if I so much as even walked within a mile of their garden gate. He also said Lizzie had gone. He didn't say where. He didn't say when, only that I'd never set eyes on her, or hear from her ever again. He was right. I never did."

Laura gasped. "That's awful. What about the baby? Do you even know what she had?"

"Six months after Lizzie left, I received a letter in the post from Surrey, England. Well, not so much a letter as a photograph of a newborn wrapped in a pink blanket. On the back it says, *'Baby Flanagan - 25/12/1974'*. This was the last thing I ever received. No letter, no note, just this. All I know is I have a daughter born on Christmas Day 1974."

"So, this is your research? Do you not even have a first name?"

"Possibly. I caught the train to Surrey not long after I received the photo. I asked around for their local maternity hospital. I found one called Queen Victoria. Unfortunately, they'd suffered a large fire a few months previous, and not all birth records survived. I did find out four babies had been born on that date, three girls and one boy. The girls were named Alice Rosendale, Deborah Spencer and Catherine Myers. None of them had a surname of Flanagan, but I do wonder if she gave a false name to protect her identity."

"She could have put the child up for adoption, John. Have you considered that?"

"Oh, I've thought about every scenario. Even the fact that the date of birth could have been a ruse to put me off the scent. If she did put the child up for adoption, then maybe I'll never find her."

"Oh John, I don't know what to say. Have you tried finding Lizzie instead?"

"Yes, I tried for a long time. Her mum and dad moved not long after Lizzie went away. I did wonder if they moved to be closer to her and the child. I've tried finding her on Tree Roots. You know, that ancestry website, but I've had no luck. Anyway, Stan, my brother, he died in 1975. A motorbike accident. He was riding my bike at the time. Our parents died young, so we just had each other. Well, after a year, there was nothing keeping me here anymore. The memories of Lizzie were too painful. I left England, and well, you pretty much know the rest."

"I do hope you find her one day, John, I really do. I'll help you with your research if you wish. Two heads are better than one."

CHAPTER 8

John's research filled her thoughts as she settled down in the annex later that evening. The ferocious winds whipped around the small building. Rain lashed against her windows, and she could hear the crashing of the sea from the cliffs at the end of the garden. Laura lit a fire in her log burner, closed her curtains, and settled down on her comfy sofa. Bronte curled up in front of the fire on the fluffy rug, quite content.

The weather worsened as the evening wore on. She could barely hear the sound from the television over the falling rain. She hoped no fishermen were out tonight. They'd be in for a treacherous time if they were. She put more logs on the fire and pulled a throw around her even tighter. Bronte gave little grunts every now and again, his ears occasionally twitching. Laura watched him with fondness. She'd grown close to him so quickly.

An hour later, the storm showed no sign of slackening off. Lightning had now joined the torrent of rain and whipping winds. As she watched the effects of the storm from her window, she heard a faint banging noise in the distance. *I hope it's not my beautiful white picket gate,* she thought, listening to the repeated noise.

She groaned as she realised she would have to go outside and check. One of her guests must have left the gate open. She cursed the life of running a B&B as she shrugged herself into a knee length raincoat over the top of her white cotton nightie. Her Wellington boots were still by the door and she pulled these on over her stripy bed socks. Aware she was naked under her nightie, she hoped she wouldn't be seen wearing such dubious outdoor gear.

The wind whipped around her, and within seconds her raincoat had torrents of water flooding off its hood. She stepped inside the B&B and closed the door behind her.

"Damn it!" she whispered, watching her gate open and bang shut repeatedly. She grabbed a powerful torch from the kitchen, and string to fasten the gate shut.

The storm pounded around her as she struggled against the wind walking to the gate. As she formed the final knot, she heard shouts from the cliffs. Shining her torch in the direction of the sea, she spotted figures in the distance.

"Help us, please!" Two fishermen approached carrying a lifeless form between them. "He's badly hurt."

Laura rushed over and shone her torch on the man they were carrying. Blood oozed from a huge gaping cut in his head. "In here!" she shouted above the sounds of the wind, and directed them into the B&B.

"We need to lie him down," panted one of the men. Laura recognised him as Bill, a fisherman from the village. His clothing dripped all over the floor. "I'm pretty sure he's broken his leg. Do you have a bed on this floor?"

"No, but there is one in my annex if you can carry him another minute. There's running water in there too. I think we're going to need it."

"Phone Dr Fishwick, young lass," shouted Bill. "We're going to need him."

The men followed Laura through to the annex and into her bedroom, where they gently lay the injured man down. Now they were in full light, Laura could see the extent of his injuries. She worried if he would survive. The wound in his head spurted blood at an alarming rate, while his face, all swollen and bloody, looked like it had been battered with a hammer. Laura noticed his leg angled in an awkward position. Through his trouser leg more blood seeped. She grabbed as many tea towels as she could find to try to stem the flow before running into the boot room to call Dr Fishwick.

The phone call filled her with dread. Laura rushed back to the annex, panicking. "The doctor can't come. He's already been called out. I've asked for an ambulance, but the area is flooded. They're doing their best, but it could be a few hours. And they might not get through at all!"

"He won't last another hour!" shouted Bill. "Phone Lucas. He's the only one can help us now." Bill ran his large, blood-stained hands through his hair.

"Lucas? The vet? Are you sure?"

"If he can stitch the backside of a cow, he can work on Olly. Ring him now, lass, before it's too late."

Laura didn't need any further encouragement. She ran back into the boot room, looking for the emergency vet number John had left her. Her fingers shook as she punched the numbers into the keypad. She had to try twice before she hit the right buttons.

"Lucas Chamberlain," he answered almost straight away.

"Oh, thank God," Laura replied breathlessly. "Lucas, we need you quickly. There's been an accident. One of the fishermen, he's badly hurt. His head and his leg. They're bleeding, and we can't stop it!"

"I'm a vet!" Lucas replied with frustration. "Have you tried Dr Fishwick?"

"He can't come! This fisherman, he's bleeding to death. Bill doesn't think he'll last another hour."

"Bill Mather from the village?" Lucas asked, now sounding more alert.

"Yes, Bill is here with him. Please, can you come?"

"I'm on my way," he replied, firmly. "I need your address. Listen, put as much pressure as you can on those wounds. Every drop of blood will matter if he's as bad as Bill makes out."

Laura ran back to the annex and gave the fishermen her update. The deterioration in the unconscious man shocked her. The bed sheets around him were now saturated with blood. She found more tea towels in the main kitchen along with bath towels from the laundry room. She instructed the men to put pressure on the wounds while she waited outside for Lucas.

Her legs shook as she stood at the garden gate. She strained her ears for the sound of an approaching car up the steep hill, but so far could hear nothing. "Please, please be quick," she pleaded as she waited in the lashing rain.

"Laura! Are you Laura?" In the distance she could see Lucas running up the hill, a large medical bag in his hands. "Quicker to run. The roads are flooded." He panted for breath as they both ran through the B&B and into the annex.

"Thank God!" Bill shouted. "We're losing him."

Lucas listened to Olly's heartbeat while the fishermen pressed on Olly's wounds. He worked quietly, observing the patient's breathing and heart rate. "You've done well," he said calmly to the fishermen. "If we work fast, we can save him. Laura, I need hot water."

Laura removed the hood of her raincoat as she carried a bucket of hot water into her bedroom. Lucas looked at her briefly before rolling his eyes, "We meet again. Okay, there's too many in this bedroom. I only need one person for the time being. Laura, you know where everything is, I need you to stay. I'll keep you updated, Bill. I promise."

The men obeyed him without hesitation. Bill patted Lucas' shoulder as he passed, "His name's Olly. He's a good man, Lucas. Look after him."

Lucas worked quickly, instructing Laura calmly and firmly. "Cut his pants up to the top with those scissors. I need to see where the wound begins and ends."

Laura cut the heavy material, exposing more of the wide, deep wound. She retched as she saw a jagged piece of bone protruding from the cut.

"Are you okay?" Lucas asked with concern as he held towels against Olly's head wound. "Do you need to swap with Bill?"

She wiped her mouth as her hands shook. "I'll be okay. It's just the shock. I've never seen anything like this before."

Lucas didn't reply. He moved her out of the way and examined the wound. "He's suffered a severed artery. We'll need to clamp it quickly." Lucas concentrated on the wound, trying to stem the blood flow. "This isn't working." He checked Olly's pulse again and grimaced. "His pulse is too slow. We need to stop this bleeding fast or we're going to lose him."

"What can I do?" Laura asked.

"Bring my bag closer." He went through it with speed and efficiency, finding the tools he needed. "It's bleeding so fast, I'm struggling. Damn!" he exclaimed as a fresh outpouring of blood spurted out. "I can't clamp it. The blood flow is too strong."

He acted without hesitation. "Right, I'll need to cauterise it. Laura, hold this towel firmly against his leg."

Lucas dove into his bag. His swift movements amazed her. Laura's heart banged painfully against her chest.

"Right, here goes. I'm going to try and cauterise this artery. Laura, this may smell. Can you cope?"

"Yes." She nodded, preparing herself for the stench of burning flesh. She watched him placing the cauterising tool on the artery for two to three seconds at a time, his forehead creased with concentration.

"Check his pulse for me," he ordered. "If you don't know how, place your finger on the inside of his wrist, above the thumb. Feel for a pulse. Can you feel it?"

"Yes, I can. Now what?"

"If you're wearing a watch, count the number of pulses over fifteen seconds. If you're not wearing a watch, I'll tell you when to start and when to stop. Okay?"

"I have a watch." Laura started to count the number of pulses in her head. She told Lucas the result, he nodded. "Better. Still not good, but better."

Lucas listened to Olly's heart again. "I've managed to cauterise the artery in his leg. It should stop some of the bleeding."

Lucas switched places with her and started to look at Olly's head wound. "Wash his head well, but don't disturb the open wound. I need the area around it clean. This guy is out of it. I've given him morphine. He can't feel anything now. No need to be gentle."

Laura started to dab at the wound, her hands and body shaking. Lucas roughly took the cloth off her. "No time to be gentle. I said wash it well." He roughly scrubbed the skin around the wound.

"It's fine. I can do it!" Laura snapped, grabbing the cloth from him.

He watched her for a few moments before returning to concentrate on his patient. "Remove that raincoat. You're dropping rainwater all over the wound."

Laura hesitated for a few seconds, aware that underneath her raincoat she was naked, except for a white cotton nightdress. But now was not the time to be shy. This man could still die if they didn't work quickly. She removed her raincoat and threw it on the dressing table, cursing herself for not dressing more appropriately earlier. "This wound is clean, Lucas. What now?"

Lucas looked up at her. He made no comment and showed no surprise at her lack of clothing.

He surveyed the wound. "Good. Now the same with the leg. He won't feel anything. Just clean it well."

Laura rubbed around the wound, trying not to look at the protruding bone. Once or twice she retched.

Lucas looked up at her. "Are you sure you're okay?"

"Yep," she replied. They worked together calmly over the next few hours, Laura obeying Lucas' clear directions.

"Pass me those scissors." He cut the thread that he'd used to stitch the head wound and exhaled. "Laura, do you have anything that we can use as a splint on his lower leg?"

Laura went through the kitchen cupboards and found a large spirit level. "Will this do?" She noticed that Olly had some colour returning to his face and lips, and she breathed a sigh of relief.

"That's perfect. Wash it well and bring it straight back. I can't do anything about the open fracture, but I can make him more comfortable. Right, stand over there and hold the splint tightly against his leg. Don't let it move."

Laura bent over, aware that her nightie was gaping at the front. She looked at Lucas, engrossed in his work. He frowned with concentration as he fastened the splint tightly to Olly's leg, stopping frequently to check his heart rate and pulse. Eventually he finished and used his sleeve to wipe the beads of sweat off his face.

He looked up at Laura and puffed out his cheeks. She noticed he kept his eyes directly on hers. "He's stable now. His pulse is stronger. That's all we can do for him tonight. Take off your gloves, wash your hands, then come straight back. We need to make him comfortable before the painkiller starts to wear off."

Laura scrubbed at her hands in the small kitchen. She shook with a mix of cold and shock as she returned to the bedroom. Lucas pulled the stained sheets from under Olly as gently as he could. "You'll need a new mattress."

Laura simply rolled her eyes. "That's the least of my worries tonight."

For the first time, Lucas gave her a small smile. Laura felt herself return it. It was short lived though, as he started to order her around again. "Hold his head and put a pillow underneath it. Now grip his arm and roll him towards you. It's called the recovery position. I'm worried about him vomiting."

Laura grabbed Olly's arm and pulled it towards her. "I can't. He's too heavy."

Lucas moved quickly to the other side. "You pull his arm. I've got my weight behind him here. I'll push, on three."

Laura bent over Olly and pulled hard. With the pressure from Lucas, he rolled easily. She placed the pillow more comfortably behind his head. "Is that okay?"

Lucas raised his eyebrows, then turned away, a slight blush entering his cheeks. Laura smiled to herself as she fixed the front of her nightie. Could he be human after all?

CHAPTER 9

They were shattered, emotionally and physically. Laura crossed her arms self-consciously across her chest, looking for her fleece. She found it on the living room floor covered in blood.

Lucas sensed her discomfort. He took off his jumper and handed it to her with no comment. Laura pulled it over her head, grateful for its warmth. "I'll make us a hot drink."

It seemed strange to be doing such mundane things after the last few traumatic hours. She glanced at her watch, shocked to see the sun already coming up over the hills. She would have to start making breakfasts for all her guests in a few hours, then try to clean this place up.

"Tea or coffee?" she asked wearily.

Lucas sat on the sofa, rubbing his drained and pale face with his hands. He didn't reply. Laura hadn't taken into consideration that this wasn't normal work for him either. He was a vet, not a doctor. The pressure on him tonight must have been vast and his knowledge of medicine tested to its limit. She brought his cup of tea over. He took it gratefully, then grimaced when he tasted the sweetness.

"I'm not in shock. Just shattered, but thanks anyway."

Laura jumped violently when Dr Fishwick rang on her mobile rang. She handed it straight to Lucas, who took the call outside.

"Dr Fishwick has only just got back home." Lucas walked back into the annex, looking relieved. "I've talked him through what we did. He agrees with all the decisions and medications. Apparently, the ambulance tried to get through, but the roads were flooded. They were forced to turn around."

"Are the roads still flooded, or do you not know?"

"Still flooded, but the levels are going down. The river burst its banks too. Dr Fishwick has called for another ambulance, but we may need to wait a few hours. Olly still needs to get to the hospital."

"But he's out of danger, isn't he?"

"Yes, he's not in any immediate danger now, but I'll stay here with him until the paramedics arrive. If that's okay with you? I'll let Bill know how things are. The men are still in the main house. They must have stayed there all night."

"I'll come with you," Laura replied. "Just let me change. I'll be with you in a few minutes."

The effects of the storm were evident in her garden. Rose petals scattered across the lawn alongside debris from broken tree branches. Many of the garden tables and chairs were upside down at the side of the hut, obviously forced there by the vicious winds.

In the boot room, Bronte scrambled delightedly around her as she rubbed his ears.

Bill stood up and clapped Lucas on the back. He didn't say anything; he didn't need to. His eyes were full of tears as he sat back down with his head in his hands, trying to compose himself.

"You alright, skipper?" Rob, the other fisherman, asked gently. "You need a stiff drink, mate."

"Aye, I need a stiff drink alright." Bill replied, wiping his eyes. "I thought he was a bloody goner."

"What happened?" Lucas asked, still nursing his cup of tea. "It was more than a thrashing in the waves. His face has taken a battering against something."

"Aye, the fishing boat," Rob replied. "We went down to the harbour about ten o'clock last night to make sure the boat was secure. We'd been in The Goose having a beer when the storm really took hold. That boat, it's our livelihoods. Anyway, it was adrift in the harbour. The blasted cleats and pilings had come away in the storm. It wasn't the lines that had come loose. We secured it proper last night. The waves beached the boat near the cliffs. We ran down to the shore, planning to tie it up somehow. We all had hold of the lines when a bloody big wave hit us. Bill shouted to us to let go and run, but it was too late for Olly. He went out on a massive wave, the boat too."

"I went in after him," Bill continued. "We both went in. It's what we do, look after each other. It seemed like bloody hours before I found him, his leg trapped around the fender. The waves had smashed him against the side of the boat over and over."

"Thank God it was the fender he was stuck to," Rob said. "He wouldn't have stood a chance otherwise."

Laura looked at her watch again. "You've all had a traumatic night. I've plenty of food in the freezer to make bacon and sausage muffins. We all need to eat. Who wants one?"

The fishermen raised their hands in agreement. Lucas simply nodded, then headed back to the annex to check on Olly.

Laura felt bone weary, but these men deserved something substantial to eat. They were determined to see

Olly off in the ambulance, despite them being in the wet clothes they'd arrived in last night.

"Sit down. I'll do that." Amy walked into the kitchen, looking solemn.

Laura looked at the clock on the wall in confusion. "What are you doing here, Amy? It's not even six o'clock yet?"

Amy shrugged. "I heard about last night. How's Olly?" She looked at the fishermen, acknowledging each of them.

Bill updated her, and she breathed a sigh of relief. "The whole village is in a mess. There's water everywhere. The Goose is completely flooded out. There's quite a few in there already trying to work through what can be salvaged. They're all talking about Olly, and your boat, Bill."

"I've no idea what happened to the bloody boat." Bill rubbed his tired eyes. "Probably sixty miles out to sea, smashed to smithereens. I'll need to try and find her after. Hope she's salvageable."

"I'll come with you, skipper," Rob offered.

Bill shook his head. "You're shattered, lad."

"There's no need to look for the boat, Bill." Amy served them their breakfast. "The other fishermen were out first thing this morning looking for it. It's back in the harbour, tied up. John from next door is in it now, fixing what he can. The villagers think you're all heroes."

Bill's eyes filled with tears again. He sat down and placed his head in his hands and sobbed.

"You need to rest, mate," Lucas said. "Olly is doing fine. I'll ring you if there's any change. I'm heading back to sit with him again, but you need to go home, Bill."

"Did Lucas really perform open surgery on his leg?" Amy whispered, her quest for a bit of gossip returning. "That's what everyone in the village is saying. Was it like casualty? Did he order you around and make meaningful looks at you while holding a scalpel?"

"No and no," Laura replied. "But he did save Olly's life. I have to admit his work is impeccable."

"Oh, God, it sounds so romantic. Him sweating under the pressure; you handling the instruments while wiping his brow with a swab."

Laura laughed. "You really do live in the film world, Amy. Believe me, it was nothing like that at all. I was terrified and covered in blood, while Lucas stayed calm and methodical."

The sounds of running water and squeaky floorboards alerted Laura to her guests waking for breakfast. She sighed and turned on the oven again. No rest for the wicked.

Her doorbell rang, and Bill went to get it, thinking it could be the ambulance. Instead, her Aunty Maria came through the door. Behind her were two women Laura recognised from the village.

"We've heard the news," her aunt said. "We've come to help. Show us what we can do. We've got bedding, towels, food. The job lot."

Aunty Maria led Laura into the living room of the B&B and ordered her to lie down on one of the sofas, covering her with a thick throw. "I'll let the guests know what happened. They won't disturb you." She handed Laura two paracetamol, and then shut the living room behind her. Despite the drama and her rapidly beating heart, Laura immediately fell into a deep sleep.

*

The sounds of the ambulance crew removing Olly on a stretcher woke her. She checked her watch. She'd been asleep for three hours. She rushed to the door, relieved to see Olly with his eyes open, replying to the paramedic's questions.

"John's going to the hospital with Olly." Lucas picked up his medical bag. "He'll keep us all updated. I need to get some sleep. I have surgery in a few hours."

"Lucas, thank you. You were amazing." Laura bent down and picked up a whining Bronte.

Lucas frowned. "You've not taken that ball off your dog yet. I told you it was too small for him, and you feed him far too many treats."

Laura stared at Lucas in astonishment. After all they'd just been through, he seemed to be trying to pick another fight with her over Bronte. She laughed at the absurdity of the situation.

Lucas frowned at her again. "Why do you never listen? I'm trying to help you."

"Lucas, we've been through enough tonight. I'm happy to listen to you, but not when you're ordering me around. I'm not your Nurse Nightingale now."

"I'm not ordering you around. I'm stating a fact," he replied, acting frustrated by her reaction. "You just seem to reject everything I say to you."

"Because you don't say it nicely." Her voice started to rise as she became more agitated.

"Well, maybe that's where I'm going wrong." Lucas held his hands up to the sky. "An epiphany! I'll say nice things to ignorant people, and their pets will magically get better."

"Are you calling me ignorant?" Laura shouted, aware that she now had an audience in the kitchen.

"Oh, there's no talking to you! Goodbye, Laura. If you need me, you know where I am."

CHAPTER 10

Laura walked down the beach with Bronte, shivering in the autumn breeze. She had finally accepted she needed a wardrobe update and agreed to join Amy for a spot of retail therapy and a much-needed haircut.

They arrived back in Lambsdale many hours later, laden with shopping bags full of clothes that Laura looked forward to wearing. She'd left one of the dresses on and teamed it with a pair of ankle boots. She felt feminine and trendy, especially with her freshly blow-dried hair.

"A coffee!" Amy pleaded, limping down the bus aisle in her high-heeled boots. "I need coffee and cake."

The bus dropped them off outside the Harbour coffee shop in Lambsdale. They carried their shopping bags inside, sitting down gratefully at a table by the window.

"You know," Amy mumbled through a mouth full of buttered scone. "Last night I rang my mum and told her about Rupert's. She said she'd lend me the money if it meant a step in the right direction. So, I think I'm going to make an appointment with Sam and find out what's involved."

"Amy, I think that's brilliant. I'm sure Sam will go out of his way to help you. Speaking of which, are you no nearer to sorting out another evening together?"

"No." Amy scowled. "I know he goes for his dinner at twelve o'clock every day. I make sure I'm outside, fiddling with the postcards, but he just smiles and says hello. I don't know what to do. I want him to ask ME!"

"Okaaaay!" Laura replied thoughtfully. "I get your dilemma. Let me have a think. How to get a man to notice that you're interested in him without coming on too strong. Men are simple creatures. They love to feel in charge..."

"Speaking of feeling in charge," Amy said. "Look who's just walked in."

Laura turned around to see Lucas come through the coffee shop door in his medical scrubs. He walked to the counter with his head down, looking at his phone, unaware of the many admiring glances. He ordered a coffee and a sandwich then sat a few tables away, still engrossed in his phone.

"I'll ask him over," Amy whispered, standing up.

"No!" Laura hissed. "Please don't. We don't get along. I've accepted that we're never going to be friends. We just need to be civil to each other. That's enough for me."

"Pity, though, isn't it? You'd make beautiful babies." Amy lowered her voice further. "He'd tie you to one of your four-poster beds with his stethoscope and then order you to growl while he—"

Lucas chose that unfortunate moment to walk past. The amused expression on his face suggested he'd heard the sordid tale of the stethoscope.

Amy, not in the least embarrassed, grabbed his arm. "Hi," she said, twiddling a finger through one of her curls. "Would you like to join us while you finish your coffee?"

"Not really. I'm due back in surgery in ten minutes, and I have a parcel to post on the way."

"I can do that for you." Amy pulled out a chair for him to sit on, winking discreetly at Laura. "Take a seat and tell me the address it needs to go to."

"Well, okay. If you don't mind."

A waft of his aftershave hit Laura. "Lucas, I still have your jumper. How do I return it to you?"

He looked up, a slight amused look on his face. "Don't worry, there's no rush. How is Olly? I hear John spends a lot of time visiting him at the hospital. They've formed a good friendship, I gather?"

"Yes, they get on well together. Olly's wife and his son live over forty miles away, so he's grateful for the company. I'll let him know you've been asking about him. I'm seeing him soon, taking him some extra clothes."

Amy winked at Laura, "Speaking of clothes, Lucas. We've been shopping today. Laura bought a new dress. Do you like it?"

Lucas stood up and passed Amy the small parcel. "I prefer her nightwear."

Laura looked at him, completely shocked, her cheeks as red as Amy's dress. He simply grinned and walked away.

*

Laura headed back to the B&B with her shopping bags, her arms aching under their weight. She stopped at the B&B gate and looked down into the harbour. The twinkly lights lining the row of restaurants glowed in the dusk light as the occasional sound of clinking glasses and laughter carried on the wind. *I'm so lucky to live here.*

She lit the log burner and a few scented candles as the cold evening drew in, glad she had invested in warm throws, cushions and curtains. She placed a bottle of red wine near the fire to warm for later before taking Bronte for a quick stroll along the beach. Laura looked out to sea, remembering the night Olly had arrived at her door. It was hard to imagine now, looking at the sea, that it could turn so frightening so fast.

Back at the annex, she heated up her soup, put on her pyjamas, then curled up on the sofa with Bronte. She couldn't put down her latest book, a mystery thriller. However, her mind soon began to wander to John's own mystery and the search for his daughter. She logged onto her laptop to see if she could make any progress.

She typed in the search box for 'Deborah Spencer, 25/12/1974, Surrey, England'. As usual, lots of options were returned, but quite often the date of birth and place of birth were missing from the search results.

Unperturbed, she topped up her wine glass, added another log to the fire, then carried on searching websites, breaking off as her mobile rang. "John, are you okay? I don't often hear from you at this time of night."

"Laura, can you log into that Facebook thing?" John asked, his words falling over themselves. "I've found someone on Tree Roots, born under the name of Alice Rosendale, on 25th December 1974. She is currently on the UK electoral registers in Surrey. This could be her. Could you find her on that Facebook thing?"

"Already on it, John. Just hold on while I Google her first. So, I'm looking for an Alice Rosendale in Surrey, England? Okay, I have an Alice Rosendale who is a magazine journalist, based near Dorking, Surrey." Laura went into the web page and viewed the contents quickly.

"Well, she looks around the right age, John, but it's most likely not the same person. It's too much of a coincidence. I'll try and find more about her."

Laura typed a new search, including the name of the magazine that Alice Rosendale worked for. She scanned the contents, reading out loud the occasional update. "Hold on, John, I think we may be onto something here."

"What!" he exclaimed. "Oh, this is daft, I'm on my way round."

Bronte immediately scrambled at John's knees as he rushed into the annex.

"Sit down, John, pour yourself a glass of wine. I'll show you what I've found. This particular Alice is doing research on the best beauty products to buy for people with December birthdays. In her column, she says she has a December birthday herself." Laura clicked on a photograph of Alice Rosendale, studying carefully the strawberry blonde hair and green eyes of the face that appeared before her.

"I have green eyes." John touched the screen in front of him. "I'd say she looks around forty, wouldn't you? Do you think she looks like me?"

"Oh, John, it's so hard to tell. Look, let me find her on Facebook. Her column gives the impression she's got a profile. We should find out more about her on there."

Laura soon found the Facebook profile and logged in. Most of Alice's personal details were private, but Laura searched through her public posts. Sure enough, she found what she was looking for. Her hand shook slightly as she pointed out her findings. "Look, John, all these posts are to Alice, wishing her Happy Birthday. They were all sent on 25th December."

John snatched the laptop from Laura's knees and gazed at the posts, reading through who they were from. "Find one from Lizzie," he whispered, wringing his hands.

Laura clicked through the many birthday and Christmas wishes. "There's nothing from a Lizzie, or an Elizabeth or a Beth. John, this may not be the person you're looking for."

John stood up and started to pace the room. "I need to find this Alice. I need to go back to Surrey, then I'll know if she's mine!"

"But what are you going to say to her, John? You can't just walk up to her and ask her does she know who her father is, or if her mum is called Lizzie. We need a plan, let's sit down and think properly about this."

John reluctantly agreed. He sat down with the laptop on his knees, still open on the photo of Alice. "I know it's her. I just know it is."

Laura didn't reply. She wanted to believe he had found his daughter. Coincidences did happen, after all. She watched John's animated face as he discussed possible reasons to contact her.

Laura chewed the end of her pen as she listened to his rambles. None of them seemed plausible. "We need to be honest with Alice. We should email her and explain why you wish to meet. She may reply and say she knows who her parents are, or she may say she's adopted and doesn't want to find her birth parents. Either way, we need to approach her with the truth."

John sighed before nodding in agreement. "Will you help me?"

"Let's strike while the iron is hot and do it now. I'll private message her via her Facebook site."

They sat down and drafted a message from John to Alice. After many deletions and re-hashing of sentences, they eventually agreed on a final version.

> *Dear Alice, I know this message will come as a surprise. I'm hoping you will be able to assist me in the search of my daughter, born on 25th December 1974 in Queen Victoria hospital, Surrey. Her mother was called Elizabeth Flanagan. Recent searches of Tree Roots have alerted me to your existence, and I'd like to know if you are my daughter. I hope we can at least have a telephone conversation, so we can be better acquainted. I promise not to contact you again if we are not related, and if we are, or possibly could be, then I will take your lead on whether to meet, or simply say goodbye.*

With a nod from John, Laura pressed send, then closed the laptop. They sat silently for a few minutes, with only the sounds of Bronte's snoring and the log fire crackling to break their silence. Laura squeezed John's arm affectionately, filled his wine glass and turned on the TV. They watched most of a late-night horror movie, laughing at the over acting of the virgin bride, forever running from a persistent Christopher Lee. John left a few hours later. Laura promised to ring him the minute she received any news.

CHAPTER 11

"Are you ready?" Laura stood outside the solicitors building with Amy.

Amy's choice of clothing surprised Laura. Her black-and-white striped maxi dress and strappy red sandals were demure in comparison to her usual choices. She oozed serious and sexy at the same time.

Sam welcomed them both into his office, asking them to sit down opposite his tidy desk. Laura noticed he'd ditched his glasses again in favour of contact lenses and kept the same messy hair style he'd sported at The Goose.

She looked at Amy, expecting to see her on the edge of her seat, her eyes fixed hungrily on Sam. Instead, Amy stared indifferently out the window, paying Sam no attention at all. A fact that wasn't missed by Sam, who looked, Laura thought, a bit disappointed.

"Well, Amy." Sam coughed uncomfortably to clear his throat. "Rupert's is currently on sale for the value listed here. Mrs Henderson wants a quick sale and is quite insistent that the offer mustn't be any lower than the asking price. So, the first question is, can you afford it, and can you afford to buy it now?

Amy simply nodded and politely asked Sam to continue.

Laura watched Sam frown with confusion. He looked ill at ease and confused. "Well, in that case, I suggest you meet with your bank or building society to discuss your finances before making an offer. I can help you write a business plan and factor in cash flow forecasts, etcetera. That's if you want my help, of course..."

"Of course she wants your help," Laura quickly added, while kicking Amy under the table. "Don't you, Amy?"

Amy nodded slightly, "Thank you, Sam, that would be most appreciated."

Amy had really taken Laura by surprise with her detached attitude, especially as she'd been so keen to make this appointment. If she didn't know any better, she'd have said Amy was playing hard to get. Then the penny dropped. The tightly pinned up curls and more formal clothing were worn to impress Sam. Amy must think if she dressed more elegantly and acted more refined, Sam would ask her out again. In Laura's eyes, this was madness. They had got along so well that night at The Goose, just being themselves.

At this point, if these two were to have any chance of getting together, Laura knew she would have to intervene. She also knew her next words would have to be chosen carefully. "Can I suggest you both get together over a bottle of wine one evening this week, then you can discuss what you find positive about the business. I really believe being in an informal and relaxed environment lends itself to new ideas and great decision making."

Laura surprised even herself at how persuasive she sounded. Her surprise grew as Amy and Sam both nodded in agreement, then looked at her to continue. *Really? Would she have to arrange the whole thing?* It seemed that way.

"When are you next free, Sam?"

"Erm, I'm free this evening."

Laura glanced at Amy; whose eyes had now gained more of their mischievous brightness. "Amy, are you free this evening too?"

Laura half expected Amy to drag a diary out of her bag and pretend to consult it. Instead, in typical Amy style, she nodded like an eager puppy.

"So, why don't you both get together this evening at The Goose for something to eat? Then you can decide on the content of your business plan. I'll book you a table for, let's say, seven this evening?"

Sam smiled like he'd just won the lottery, and even Amy had a twinkle in her eyes. Laura let out a breath she didn't even know she was holding. The attraction between them felt almost tangible, yet neither of them could see it. This frustrated Laura. Surely, they must both know how much electricity buzzed between them.

*

"Amy, I can't believe you thought that would work!" Laura said as they left Sam's office and walked outside. They put on their coats and fastened them up against the strong breeze. "Sam was really confused by your behaviour today. He no doubt thought you'd gone off him. You normally look at him as if he's a chocolate pudding with cream on top. You were trying to pretend to be all business like, weren't you, in the hope he would fancy you more?"

"Well, nothing else has worked so far. I've tried wearing less clothing, wearing my hair up and down, more makeup, less makeup. I've tried talking about films, television, music, cider. But ... nothing." Amy raised her hands in frustration. "I want him to look at me the same way Lucas looked at you in the café last week when he talked about your nightie. I want lust!"

"What on earth are you talking about." Laura turned to her friend in astonishment. "Lucas most certainly does not lust after me. He can't even look at me without starting an argument, and I feel the same way about him."

Laura realised her voice had risen a few octaves. She took a deep breath. Had Lucas really looked at her that way? She certainly didn't think so. Okay, so his comment about her nightie had been slightly flirtatious, but knowing Lucas, he'd have said it to embarrass her. That's how he worked, after all, rude and not very complimentary. Regardless, she knew she would end up dwelling on Amy's comment until she could put it in the right pigeon-hole in her head. The one that said all men were bastards.

Amy looked at her with raised eyebrows, "See, I can tell you're thinking about it." She held her hands in a heart shape. "Lucas and Laura, up a tree, k-i-s-s-i-n-g."

Laura hit her with her handbag, laughing along as well. "Anyway, this isn't about me and Lucas sour pants. This is about you and Sam. You got on so well that night at The Goose. If you ask me, I think Sam is waiting for you to ask him out. After all, didn't you say you normally ask a guy for another date? If Sam knows this, he must think you don't like him."

"Yeah, I suppose," Amy admitted. "I guess I could ask him out tonight for a proper date. You know, like the cinema or something."

"That's my girl. Just go with the flow. You've got him all to yourself tonight. Make the most of it. Be yourself, let the evening progress and help him out a bit. He's obviously a gentleman, a rare breed. He likes you, but maybe he's unsure how to express it. I think he needs to know that you're still attracted to him. Let him know you are. How you do that? Well ... you're a grown woman. I'm sure you can think of a way."

"Oh, I can think of a few ways." Amy winked. "Anyway, I'm going back to the Post Office now to take over from Polly, but I'll see you around seven tomorrow morning for breakfast. I'll let you know how tonight goes. Are you seeing Olly today?"

"Yes, I'm going with John." Laura took out her phone to check for any messages from Alice. Still nothing. Laura hadn't told Amy about John's search for his daughter. Not because she didn't trust Amy, but because it was John's story. If he wanted Amy to know, he would tell her himself.

John waved from his car window as she walked back up the hill towards the Harbour B&B. He looked at her, hopeful of a message from Alice. Laura simply shrugged. He nodded to say he understood, but the disappointment was evident in his face.

The drive to the local hospital gave them both a chance to catch up on other news.

"Will Katie and Danny be at the hospital?" Laura asked.

"Most likely. They go as often as they can. Sometimes I take Danny out for a few hours, give them a bit of quality time on their own."

"Olly gets discharged next week. Where's he going, back home to Ruddlesford?

"That's a bit of an issue really," John replied, as they came off the motorway and headed down the smaller roads to the hospital. "They live on the fifth floor of a flat in Ruddlesford, which is fine because all rooms are on one level, but not so easy for him getting in and out of the building in a wheelchair. Katie works all week, so he'll be stuck in there on his own."

"What about the house he bought in Lambsdale? The one he's renovating in his spare time. Can he not move into there, temporarily, until he's fit to start work on it again?"

"The house still isn't ready. I've been working on it while he's been laid up. He needs a downstairs toilet too; he can't manage stairs in a full leg cast. He won't entertain the idea of a commode. Can't blame him, to be honest. His flat seems the best option for him. It's a shame, really, I would have liked him closer to me. I could keep my eye on him."

"If only the bathroom in your house was on the ground floor, he could have moved in with you, John."

"That would have been perfect. I could have taken him and little Danny fly-fishing in his wheelchair. I'd have loved that. A proper treat for all of—"

"My annex, John. He could stay in the annex."

John turned to look briefly at her, his eyes lighting up for the first time in a few days. "Well, that would be a perfect solution. But where would you stay, lass?"

"Well, I want to be in the grounds of the B&B, so I'm thinking that hut at the side of the annex. I'm sure Jemima did some work to turn it into a shepherd hut. I could sleep there and shower and cook in the main B&B."

"Or," replied John, excitedly. "Olly can stay in the hut. I'm pretty sure there's a small toilet put in it. If not, I can do that easily. It makes more sense. Olly can't cook or have a shower with his cast on, so he's no need for your annex. But a bed and running water will be perfect until he gets that cast off."

"Brilliant." Laura smiled. "I can't wait to get back now and see the inside of the hut properly. I've only been in it to store a few bits and pieces. It would definitely fit a single bed in there, and maybe a set of drawers. I know it has electricity already because I've seen the switches."

By the time they reached the hospital car park, they were both brimming over with ideas. Laura and John practically ran down the hospital corridors and into the lift in their haste to receive Olly's agreement. They had a frustrating ten-minute wait in the corridor while the Consultant finished his rounds. Once the doors were opened, they rushed into Olly's room.

Olly grinned with delight. "That will be just perfect. I'll have my own space, but help on hand if I need it. I must admit, I'd started to worry about going home. I really didn't want to struggle in a flat on my own all day. I'm being discharged in three days. Do you think the hut will be ready for me?"

"Not a problem," John replied. "I'll get started as soon as we get back. Katie and Danny can stay with me when they visit you at weekends. Did you say your mum might come too?"

"Eventually, yes. She had an operation a few weeks ago, otherwise she'd have been here visiting. I've told her to rest and come when she feels fit. I've spoken to her almost every day, though."

On their way back to Lambsdale, John called at the local DIY Centre and bought paint for the hut, alongside other essentials, like a bed, fridge, sink and cabinet. Laura could already imagine the hut inside her head, complete with a little heater and bedside lamp. She felt quite envious of how cosy it would be. Olly would be able to go into the garden any time he wished as the hut had no steps to try to navigate, although John did plan to build a temporary ramp while he still needed his wheelchair.

CHAPTER 12

Laura picked up her post from behind the front door and placed it on the kitchen worktop before joining John in the little hut. He had his trusty pencil behind his ear, notepad in his back pocket, and tape measure in his hand. He walked around, whistling to himself as he measured up. Laura flicked on the light switch, tutting when the overhead bulb didn't come on. John didn't seem concerned; he simply added it to his list of things he would need to fix.

Confused, Laura looked around the hut. "John, there's no toilet."

John looked up, still whistling. He walked to the back of the hut where an old piece of worktop rested against the wall. "Nice piece of wood, this. Would you mind if I used it? Now look, behind here, another door."

Laura pulled on the slightly stiff door handle and the door opened to reveal a very small but perfectly equipped bathroom with toilet and sink. "Trust Jemima to have a shepherd hut in mind." Laura helped John carry the piece of worktop into the garden for cleaning.

"Oh, she was always up to something, that woman. Never one to stand still. She had the annex built, you know. It wasn't here when she arrived. And those patio windows in your top floor rooms, she had those put in too."

"I bet you miss her," Laura said.

"I sure do, lass. She was good company. That's all, mind you! She made it known from day one that two single oldies wouldn't make one happy married couple. She liked her independence, but she also liked a chat and a bloody good argument over anything at all. She always made sure she won as well." John winked at her.

Laura's spirits lifted to see John looking so much happier. She left him to his measurements while she headed back into the B&B. She picked up her post, smiling as usual, to see her name above the address of the Harbour B&B.

Her smile faded as she read the contents of the letter.

Dear Miss Laura Thompson,

We are writing to inform you that the land on which your property stands (Harbour Bed and Breakfast, 12 Harbour Lane, Lambsdale, West Widdington) has recently changed hands and is now owned by Tepping & Co. Oldham, Manchester.

We enclose drawings of the boundary and land concerned.

The new owners of the land have requested a full investigation as to the legality of some of the recent additions to the property. These include a one storey, stone-built annex and the main cottage itself. It appears these were built without prior consent.

Failure to have consent is a criminal offence. This is being investigated as a priority. As such, we will need to assess any alterations to the property.

If consent cannot be proved, you may be ordered to destroy any recent additions, or the landowner can claim the property as his own.

On a separate note, we have received a complaint regarding your food safety legislation. The complaint relates to you preparing food for guests outside of an assessed area. If this is proved to be correct, we need to warn you that you have broken food safety rules. This may lead to your rights to serve and prepare food within the property revoked.

We enclose further detail regarding building consent. Also, a contact number so you can arrange for an Environmental Health Officer to reassess your food preparation areas.

Kind regards,

Jack Simms

Historic Buildings Inspector/Conservation Officer

Heritage Department

West Widdington Council

Laura sank down onto the bar stool in the kitchen, her shaking legs unable to hold her up any longer. She re-read the letter two or three times, unsure whether to be more shocked at the possibility of her annex and B&B being destroyed, or at the complaint about the food preparation.

She thought back over the months she had been open. She had never prepared food outside of the kitchen for any of her guests.

Suddenly, she raised her head and spat out the words. "You bastard, Leon. You bloody bastard."

She now realised why Tepping and Co. sounded familiar. It was one of the companies Leon dealt with. A nasty group of low life, from what she could remember.

She stood up and started to pace around the kitchen. She had cooked Leon a bacon and egg muffin in her annex and now he aimed to accuse her of breaking food safety laws to shut her down.

She picked up her phone and quickly dialled her aunt. Was she really in trouble for cooking for Leon within her annex even though he wasn't a guest? Could they really take away her rights to prepare food? What about her reputation in the village? The B&B would have to close. Everything she'd worked for in the last few months, the friendships she'd made, and worst of all, letting down Jemima. Tears of anger and frustration started to flow. She desperately needed words of comfort and support. Aunt Maria's mobile went straight to the answering machine. Laura left a message asking her to ring as soon as possible.

She splashed her face with cold water and tried to dry her eyes, but each time she wiped away the tears, more followed. She really didn't want to alert John to the contents of the letter. He had enough on his plate and this news could jeopardise their plans for Olly.

How she hated Leon at this moment. She knew he had the ability to sink low. She'd seen it first-hand with some of his clients. This was him all over. If he couldn't share what Laura had, then he would make damn sure she wouldn't have it either.

Well, he wouldn't take it from her. She would fight him every step of the way. She needed to find Amy.

Her legs shook all the way to the village. Tears brimmed in her eyes as she envisaged the worst. Her B&B being ordered to close. A sign on her front door saying, *Not fit to serve food on this property*. She could lose everything.

"What on earth?" Amy ran straight to her side. "Look, give me five minutes. Let me serve these customers. Go straight to the Harbour Café. I'll meet you in there. Whatever's happened, we'll fix it. Okay?"

Laura sat at the back of the café, facing the wall, aware her eyes were red and swollen. Her hands shook as she picked up her phone to check if her aunt had returned her call. A kind waitress brought her over a cup of tea and put it down on the table in front of her, placing a hand on her shoulder as she left to serve other customers. This simple act of kindness brought on another flood of tears. They slipped steadily down her nose and into her tea.

Someone pulled out a chair at her table and sat down. Laura turned her face away, determined not to be drawn into any conversation. Her cup of tea slid towards her and she recognised the watch on the wrist that rested on the table.

"Hey, what's wrong?" Lucas asked softly.

Laura didn't reply. Her chin shook from the effort of trying not to cry in front of him.

"Laura, I don't like seeing you like this. Are you on your own?"

Laura nodded, the question of her being on her own broke her again. Fresh tears fell down her face.

Lucas took a tissue from his pocket and tenderly wiped away her tears. "Talk to me," he said gently.

"I've messed it all up," Laura sobbed.

Lucas placed his arm around her shoulders. "Let's go somewhere quieter. We can talk properly."

"I can't. I'm meeting Amy. He's made an idiot out of me. I thought I could do this, but I can't."

Amy's loud voice interrupted them. "Move on, Lucas. She doesn't need your insults today. Come on, shift!"

Lucas didn't move, not taking his eyes off Laura. "What can't you do. Let me help."

"Shift, Lucas," Amy snarled.

He reluctantly stood up, still looking at Laura in concern. "Amy, don't leave her on her own."

"I know how to look after my mates, Lucas. Thank you, but you can leave now."

Lucas hesitated before picking up his drink and slowly walking away. He turned around one last time before closing the café door behind him.

"Drink your tea, Laura, and tell me what's wrong," Amy whispered.

"It's Leon, the absolute bastard." Laura pulled the council letter from her pocket and handed it to Amy to read.

"Right!" Amy shouted, pushing back her chair with such force that it tipped over. "Get your coat on. We're going to see Sam now."

She cupped Laura's elbow and guided her outside the café and down the short street, marching them both up the staircase to Sam's offices.

His secretary jumped up in shock. A nice lady in her fifties, normally welcoming and polite, she now bore the stance of a bodyguard.

"You can't just walk in there, young lady."

Amy simply ignored her and grabbed hold of the doorknob to Sam's office and flung it open.

Laura gave Sam his due. He didn't react in any sudden way. He simply ended his phone call and stood up slowly. Without saying a word, he pointed to the two chairs opposite his desk. Instead of taking his own seat, he sat on his desk, directly in front of them. Stern faced, his broad shoulders held back, and his chin raised, he addressed Amy. "Talk, now."

Laura and Amy had never seen this side of Sam before. The Sam that could make you feel nervous just by looking at you. Laura could sense how annoyed he felt at this sudden and unexpected intrusion. He towered over them from his position on his desk. His status of authority in the room quite clear.

Amy pushed the council letter into his hands. They both watched him for facial expressions as he read it. His face gave nothing away. A good trait in his profession. He lifted his eyes, looking at Laura's tear-stained face.

"Should she be worried?" Amy asked.

"Quite frankly, without looking into this in more detail, I can't answer that yet, and—" He raised his hand to silence Amy as she started to demand a more detailed reply. "I will not undermine my position by providing a reply now that may not be accurate."

He picked up a pad and pen and started to fire questions at Laura. She answered as honestly as she could, noticing that Sam's eyes never left her face. Any lies would not go undetected by him. His intensity made Laura feel quite intimidated.

"Do you know who complained?" he asked.

"I'm pretty sure it was my ex-boyfriend, Leon Finch. He works with the company Tepping and Co. Leon came to see me a few weeks ago. He tried to convince me to sell the B&B. I refused, but I did make him a meal in my annex before he left. Have I broken the law?"

"No, Laura, you've not broken any law. He needs evidence that you cooked a meal for him as a paying guest.

If he didn't book a room with you, then he can't prove that. You can trust me on this. Regardless, I'd advise you to go ahead with an inspection from Environmental Health. This will prove you've nothing to hide. If you wish me to be in attendance when this occurs, I'm happy to do so."

Laura nodded gratefully. "What about the building permissions? What happens now? How did I not know that I didn't own the land?"

"I'm afraid I can't answer your question right away. Our firm of solicitors did not deal with the inheritance or transfer of the property to your name. I wish we had, because these are basic checks. I'll need to go through all the details with a fine-tooth comb."

Sam jumped off his desk and opened his office door to speak with his secretary. He came back within a few seconds. "I've arranged for tomorrow morning to be set aside so I can do some research on this. That's all I can say for now. If I have your permission, I will represent you in fighting this."

"Thank you." Laura shook his hand. This was a version of Sam she wouldn't like to cross.

He walked over to the door, indicating their impromptu meeting was over. "Amy. Seven o'clock tonight at The Goose. I take it you've not forgotten?"

Amy stood up, almost bowing to him as she left his office. "I'll be there, most definitely."

They left the solicitor's building and walked outside into the pouring rain. Amy placed her arm around Laura's shoulders and guided her back to the B&B.

"Laura, isn't that your aunt running up the hill?

Laura turned to see her aunt, all red faced and flushed. "Whatever was that phone message about? I only listened to it about thirty minutes ago. I've been out of my mind with worry."

They all headed down to the annex where it was more comfortable. Amy made three cups of strong tea, one with extra sugar for Laura, while they explained to Aunty Maria about the letter from the council.

"Leon, the little sneaky sod," said her aunt. "Just wait till I get my hands on that pathetic excuse for a man. It's plain jealousy that's made him do that. If he can't have something, then neither can you."

"I said the exact same thing earlier," Laura replied. "The thing is, he must have planned this right after I sent him packing. He's obviously done a lot of research. Leon knows his stuff about property, planning permissions and the like. He would have been thorough before contacting the council. I honestly think the complaint about the food being cooked off the premises was just an added extra to kick me in the teeth because he couldn't find anything else to go on."

Amy and Aunt Maria both nodded in agreement.

"Well, he won't win. I've worked bloody hard over these past few months. He's not taking it from me. Sam has agreed to represent me in fighting this, so I'll have some legal backing, thankfully."

"Wasn't Sam just amazing?" Amy giggled. "He made my knees tremble just listening to him demanding answers from you. God, he was good, wasn't he?"

"He certainly made me feel better," Laura replied, amazed that Amy had gone a full hour before even mentioning the powerful Sam they'd just experienced. "I can't say he made my knees tremble, but I'm pleased to have him on my side and not against me."

"I wonder if he'll be like that in bed?" Amy sighed dreamily.

Laura stuck her fingers in her ears and squealed. "Amy, please. I don't want to think about you two in bed, and don't forget my aunt is in the room!"

"Oh, don't mind me." Her Aunt smiled, making herself comfortable amongst the throws and cushions on the chair. "I'm enjoying watching this love story develop."

"Anyway, Laura, you're only jealous. I get to date Clark Kent, who it seems can turn into Superman anytime I want him too, while you get sour-pants covered in dog hair. Although, I have to say, he seemed pretty worried about you earlier."

"Who was worried about you earlier?" asked her aunt.

"Lucas. I must admit he came across as being kind. Well, at least I thought he was being kind. He didn't insult me or call me an idiot today."

Laura opened a bottle of brandy, a gift from her first guests, Christine and Robert. She sighed as she poured three small glasses. "After the excitement of the plans for Olly's home-coming, to this. How can a day turn from sunny yellow to gloomy black in just a few hours?"

"Have you told your mother about Leon?" asked her aunt.

"No, I don't want her to know. She would worry herself sick over this. Plus, my dad would try and kick Leon's backside into next week. My dad's too old to be kicking anything other than leaves in the garden. I won't be telling them unless I have to."

"Do you want me to stay with you tonight, Laura?" Amy asked, pouring them all another brandy.

Laura looked at her watch. "Amy, have you seen the time? No, I don't want you to stay with me tonight. You've got a date with Mr Hotshot Lawyer in less than an hour."

Amy shrugged. "My girl comes first."

"Oh, Amy." Laura gave her a massive hug. "You are such a wonderful person inside and out. What would I have done without you today, or for the past few months, in fact? Now, get that cute little ass down to The Goose and go and give Sam the evening of his life. Tomorrow, I want to see a business plan. I also want to hear about some snogging at your garden gate. Do I make myself clear?"

Amy giggled like a schoolgirl. "If you say so. But seriously, are you okay?"

"I'm staying here for a few hours," replied her aunt. "Go and have some fun."

Amy disappeared into the small bathroom to refresh her hair and makeup before diving out the annex at top speed.

"You'll not go far wrong with her in your life," said her aunt, pointing to the door where Amy had just left.

"I know," Laura replied. "She's amazing. I just hope Sam's ready for her."

CHAPTER 13

As the evening drew in, Laura put more logs on the fire, opened her book and settled down on her snuggly sofa. Bronte snored gently, curled up as close to the fire as he could get without singeing his fur.

It did occur to Laura to get out her laptop and do some research on the planning permission the council letter had referred to, but she knew that would only increase her anxiety.

Instead, she thought about Amy and Sam. She could just imagine Amy twiddling with her curls and licking her lips, going all out to show Sam she found him attractive. It was an unusual coupling, but no one could deny they were perfect for each other.

Her phone beeped to announce the arrival of a text. She smiled when she saw the message from Amy, *Really hope this man is made of steel :) xx*

Laura remembered how it felt to be in the first few months of love. How you couldn't wait to see each other, share those first kisses, and slowly undress each other. Laura envied the journey Amy and Sam were just beginning.

As for herself, she planned to take a year off men. Especially after Lazy Leon and all his recent bastardly moves.

She could no longer imagine her life back in Manchester. Living in their cramped townhouse and working at the estate agents. Stuck behind a desk all day and then climbing into bed at the side of a sweaty and snoring Leon. Now she had her own business in this beautiful part of the world, her own bank balance, good friends, and no one to answer to. Leon wouldn't win.

Despite that, she felt something was missing. Laura sighed; brandy always made her feel maudlin. She made herself a cup of tea and decided to concentrate on her book instead. She read the blurb on the back:

'So, can they ignore their differences and allow their love to blossom?'

A bit like me and Lucas, really, she thought. They didn't get along. They fired off each other at every occasion. The only time they'd managed to be civil to each other was the night of Olly's accident. Not a promising start to a love story.

Okay, she found him attractive, but so did most of the females in the village. His intelligence couldn't be denied either.

But no... Laura shook her head violently. It would never work. Lucas struggled to be civil to her. He'd called her an idiot and ignorant. Mr High and Mighty obviously had his sights set on better things. Well, good luck to him. She pitied the woman who had to try to break those barriers down.

Laura sighed and opened her book again. She would accept her state of spinsterhood and eventually be eaten by Alsatians.

God, she was turning into Amy!

CHAPTER 14

Laura stacked the cereal bowls in the dishwasher and prepared to serve the hot breakfasts. She jumped as Amy rushed in via the boot room door.

"Sorry, sorry, sorry. I know I'm late." She grabbed her apron and tied it quickly around her waist before rushing into the dining room. She returned a few minutes later carrying a toast rack that needed refreshing. Laura couldn't help noticing her flushed cheeks and sparkling eyes.

"How did it go?" Laura whispered, placing bacon and sausage on each of the hot plates.

Amy gave her a quick thumbs up. "I'll be back in a minute, let me serve this toast while it's still warm."

"So?" Laura leaned back against the worktop and smiled at Amy. "I want to hear about last night. Did Sam kiss you at the garden gate before heading off home?"

"Nope, he didn't." Amy grinned.

"What, still no kiss? How did you let him get away with that?"

"I didn't say he didn't kiss me." Amy fiddled with her curls. "He just may not have headed home after."

Laura gasped. "He didn't. You little minx. Did Sam spend the night at your place?"

Amy nodded, while jumping around on the spot. "He did, he did, he did! It was bloody marvellous! Oh God,

Laura, I'm in love. Completely and utterly in love. I can't believe I've spent all these years working opposite this absolute Romeo and I didn't realise how gorgeous he really is."

Laura giggled. "I don't think I want to hear anymore."

Amy swooned around the kitchen. "He ordered us a bottle of wine when we arrived. He sat so close to me. God, he smelled so good. He kept staring at my mouth. It was like the sexiest, most sensual thing I've ever experienced. Then he leaned over and kissed me gently. It was soooo romantic. Well, we didn't finish our meals. We left."

"Oh, Amy, you look so happy. I'm really pleased for you both. So, did you come up with any ideas for a business plan?"

"Nah, no business plan, but I've had plenty of sex."

Laura shook her head in mock disgust. At least Amy was getting her fair share of romance. Maybe she needed to step up her own game and join a dating website before her ovaries shrivelled up.

"Come on, Foxy Lady. Can you put Sam out of your head for ten minutes while we get these beds stripped? Olly's discharged today. We'll head into the village together when we've finished. I need to stock up on bits for Olly's fridge."

*

Laura stood in the long queue at the Grocers, her basket full. She placed it on the ground and pushed it forward with her feet when she recognised the back of the person in front of her.

Damn! She didn't fancy another run in with Lucas today. She had enough on her plate. Pushing her basket forward, she prayed he wouldn't turn around.

"Morning, Laura." Bill, the fisherman, gave her a thumbs up as he headed outside with a newspaper tucked under his arm.

Oh crap. Laura cringed as Lucas turned and gave her a brief nod. He picked up his shopping after paying and left the building. She breathed a sigh of relief. Another bullet dodged.

She struggled outside with her shopping bags, keen to get home before the downpour started.

"Laura! Wait. How are you?"

Laura groaned. She really didn't need this. "I'm fine, thank you, Lucas." She started to walk away, keen to keep her distance from the irritating man.

But Lucas had other plans. He gently took hold of her shopping bags and placed them at her feet. "You really did seem at your wit's end yesterday in the café. I was worried."

"No need to be. I can look after myself."

"I'm sure you can. I know it's none of my business but—"

"You've hit the nail on the head, Lucas. It's none of your business."

Laura's cheeks started to colour as he stared at her intently. He really did rattle her.

"Hey, are you sure you're okay?"

"I've said I'm fine. I appreciate your concern, but it's nothing to do with you. Bronte is healthy. That's enough for you to know. I've not managed to kill him yet with the trash that I feed him."

Lucas raised his hands in defeat. "Okay, I can tell I'm annoying you. It wasn't my intention. I apologise. I'll leave you to get along with your day."

Laura felt awful. He walked away, obviously hurt by her shortness with him. Now that she thought about it, he had looked quite down himself. Laura sighed heavily. Why did life have to be so bloody hard? If she didn't have enough problems to deal with, now she had to add guilt to her ever-growing list of negative feelings.

She considered following him into his surgery to apologise, but something stopped her. Lucas struck her as a private man. Would he feel grateful to have his surgery interrupted? What if he compared her to the lipstick brigade her aunt had talked about? Just another female coming in with a lame excuse to talk to him.

She decided it was only right to apologise, but it could wait until the next time she bumped into him. In a village this small, the chances were good she'd see him again soon enough.

CHAPTER 15

The hut did look homely. John had made the bed up the day before and hung curtains at the little window to give Olly some privacy. Laura turned the little heater on to take the chill off the mid-September air. She glanced at her watch. Only one hour until John would return with Olly.

Laura opened her laptop to search for details around land ownership. She couldn't carry on burying her head in the sand. The more she knew, the more prepared she could be. After a while she had to admit that each search returned much the same information. It seemed Leon had the upper hand. She sighed and closed her laptop. The thought of her home being under threat filled her with dread.

The sound of laughter disturbed her gloomy thoughts. She gave herself a little shake. Olly had arrived.

"Hey, Laura, good to see you." Olly wheeled himself over and pulled her into a hug. "John is just parking up the car. He'll be here in a minute."

"Glad to be home?" Laura helped to steer him towards the hut.

"You know, this place really does feel like home. Guess it's because I left a large part of me here on my last visit!"

"You certainly left your mark, Olly. All over my mattress."

Olly covered his face in embarrassment and groaned. "I can't even imagine the amount of cleaning up after. Lucas did tell me you spent hours trying to stop the bleeding. I'll be honest, I have no recollection of any of it."

"Good job, really. You were in a right mess. So, when did you speak with Lucas?"

"Oh, he came while I was in hospital with Bill. Do you know Bill? He's my skipper."

"Yes, I know Bill. He shed a few tears here that night."

"You're having a laugh? Bill wouldn't shed a tear if a bloody shark took his leg off. Hard as nails, that man."

"Well, don't let on that I told you. If you break my trust, I'll tell Bill about that tattoo on your thigh."

"I don't have a tattoo on my thigh! Oh, I get it. Blackmail. I'll have to keep my eye on you. Does Lucas know you can be a bit tricky?"

"Actually, I don't know Lucas that well. Our paths don't tend to cross."

"Oh, right. My mistake. Well, he's a good bloke. He did say he almost shit himself when my pulse went down. He said your calmness stopped him panicking."

"Really? I'd have said the other way around. He seemed as cool as a cucumber."

"Well, either way, I'm still here, and that's down to you both, so thank you. I know I've said thank you a million times already, but I really do mean it." He took Laura's hand and squeezed it.

"Now, no getting emotional." John grinned, joining them on the lawn. "You have to save your gratitude for me when you see your new home."

"Bloody hell, John. It's like Buckingham Palace in here." Olly pushed himself up the ramp into the cosy hut. "Do I need to take my one shoe off before we go in?"

John grinned from ear to ear. "There's an alarm in here that's wired to my house. If you need anything, day or night, just push it and I'll come down. There's a small worktop area where you can make a brew or a sandwich. You can come to mine for your main meals. In here's your toilet and sink. You'll have to use your crutches in here. It's too small for a wheelchair, but there's a rail for support and another alarm there."

"Blimey, John, I'm blown away. I was expecting a hut, not a show home. Thanks so much, mate."

"Right, I'm going back to my annex," Laura said, keen to leave the men to settle in. "Olly, I've put some beers in your fridge. Keep the noise down and no getting drunk and falling over. I'm afraid my stitching skills are not as good as Lucas'."

Laura could hear the men laughing. She smiled as she thought how much happier John had seemed this week. Life seemed to be coming together for many in this village. John and Olly. Amy and Sam. What would her happy ending be, she wondered?

CHAPTER 16

Laura pulled her coat tightly around her as she walked into the village. Sam had asked to see her this morning. She prayed he would give her some good news. Her head spun with different scenarios. *It's all a big mistake,* was her favourite. *You'll have to close today for the foreseeable future,* was her least favourite.

Laura climbed the stairs to Sam's office, feeling surprised to see Amy already sitting in the waiting room.

"Hi, Amy. What are you doing here?"

"Sam rang me this morning. He said he wanted to see us both together. I don't know why."

The door opened, and Sam ushered them both inside. "My news affects you both," he said by way of explanation as he noticed their confused faces.

"Is this about my B&B, Sam?"

"Yes, Laura. I'm afraid the claims are correct. Leon now owns the land your B&B is built on. The land was originally owned by the Henderson's who ran the sweet shop. I've spoken to Mrs Henderson who confirmed her grandfather Rupert gave planning permission for your B&B. Unfortunately, there is no formal documentation to state this. To be honest, I'm shocked this wasn't picked up by the solicitors when you purchased the property."

"So, what happens now?" Laura asked, her heart thudding against her chest.

"I need proof that the B&B was built with permission. Without that, Leon can claim the building is encroaching on his land. Now, I have found an informal copy of an agreement between Rupert's family and the builders back in 1912. Or should I say, Mrs Henderson's daughter pointed me in the direction of a copy."

Laura's eyes lit up. "Will that do?" she asked.

"Unfortunately, it was never witnessed." Sam shrugged. "Therefore, it's not a legally binding document."

"What's the worst-case scenario?" Laura gripped the arms of her chair.

"Your worst-case scenario is that Leon will claim encroachment and demand the B&B be demolished."

Laura gasped as Sam raised his hand to reassure her. "I will fight this every step of the way."

"Sam, why am I here too? Is it to offer Laura support?" Amy asked.

Sam shook his head, "I'm sorry, Amy. I asked you here for a different reason, but still connected to this same situation. Leon bought Rupert's sweet shop this morning. The sale went through two hours ago. The land and shop were sold as a package."

"What!" Amy shouted, tears brimming in her eyes. "He can't! That shop is mine!" Amy's chin crumpled as she tried hard not to cry.

Laura looked up, feeling stunned, "How?" she asked. "How did he manage to do that without us knowing?"

Sam sighed softly, "He's done his homework. He contacted the Henderson's directly, offering them a deal for the shop and the land. It all went through his own firm of solicitors. I only found out this morning. Amy, Laura, I'm so sorry."

Laura sat in a complete daze. She now understood Leon's game completely. He was determined to ruin her life here in Lambsdale and have a front-row seat while it happened. He didn't care about the shop. She'd seen him do things like this before. Buy a business, sell it on, make more money.

Laura swallowed back her tears. "Amy, I don't know what to say. This is all my fault. If I hadn't come here, Leon wouldn't have followed me. You'd still be buying Rupert's and this whole mess would never have happened."

Amy wiped her tear-stained face. "This isn't your fault. I'll get over it. It's only a shop, after all. The important thing is we fight Leon together. He's a bastard treating you like this."

"It seems Leon is a very unpleasant character," Sam replied. "I'm a great believer in what goes around comes around. However, my job is not to quote how the law of cause-and-effect works, but to find a loophole in all this. Something we can hang him with."

"What an absolute mess." Laura groaned. "I'm so stunned that I can't actually feel anything now; no emotion at all."

Amy took her hand. "Oh, Laura, we'll get over this. We've got to trust in Sam."

Laura nodded. "But your lovely shop, Amy. All your hopes and dreams."

"Oh, I'll get over it." Amy shrugged, obviously used to disappointment. This hurt Laura most of all. People like Amy had to work hard for everything they had, yet they always put others before them.

Laura slammed down her coffee cup, making Amy and Sam jump. "Right, we're going to The Goose tonight to get drunk, okay? It's Friday and I've no guests booked in tomorrow. I want us all in our glad rags. We're going to show that bastard Leon that we are not people to be messed with!"

"I like the sounds of that one," Amy replied. "You're on. Seven-thirty. I'll meet you in there."

*

True to her word, Amy turned up at seven-thirty on the dot, dressed to kill in a tight, black leather mini skirt and a gold halter top, her curls flowing freely down her back.

Sam approached Laura with a large glass of red wine and a sympathetic smile. "Hey, drink this. Our usual group is over there at that table."

Laura looked around. Dressing up had been the right decision. The clientele tonight was younger and trendier than the Sunday afternoon revellers. Her new wrap around red dress showed off her small, rounded breasts and tiny waist. She had left her hair down after curling it lightly with her curling wand, while her minimal makeup made her skin glow. If her world were falling apart, she'd do it with style. That had been her motto this evening.

She spotted the boys from the cycling club, laughing and being raucous. Laura twisted her head around to see if Lucas had joined them. He hadn't.

Her fifth glass of wine went down with ease and she started to enjoy the relaxed feeling. So what if she drank more than normal? There was no harm in letting your hair down now and again. People were chatting and mingling around her, all in good humour now that the weekend had arrived. Laura had pushed through the crowds to buy the next round of drinks when she spotted Lucas walk inside the pub.

With his white shirt and fitted jeans, he attracted a lot of attention from the lipstick brigade, who giggled into their gin glasses, trying to catch his eye. He simply ignored them, ordered his drink, and walked over to the group he'd come to join.

Laura spied her chance to apologise for the way she'd snapped at him earlier that week. She ordered herself a fresh drink, then eased her way between the packed tables. The glasses of wine she'd already drank, combined with the heat from the pub, created a muzzy alcohol feeling that helped to calm her anxiety. She watched as Lucas leaned casually against a wall whilst chatting with his friends. Her eyes took in how good he looked tonight. His shirt clung to his taut frame, her mind wondering how frequently he worked out to gain such a toned figure. She shook her head. The alcohol had obviously started to play with her hormones too.

Her legs felt like jelly as she got closer to him. *Will he reject my apology? Only one way to find out,* she thought. Laura waved to catch his attention. Lucas, still leaning against the wall, gave her a hesitant wave back.

As she approached, his expression turned to slight amusement. He lifted an eyebrow as she steadied herself against a table. "Been drinking, I see?"

"Maybe I have." She twiddled with her hair, stopping abruptly as it reminded her of Amy in full flirt mode. She hadn't come to flirt with Lucas. She'd come to apologise. That's all. She looked around for somewhere to place her wine glass while she spoke. Failing, she held the glass out for him to hold. Lucas took it without saying a word, his lips raised in a slight smile.

"I've come to apologise." She stared at him, fixated by his beautiful, dark brown eyes that were trained fully on her.

"What?" he shouted back. "I can't hear you!"

"I've come to say I'm…" *Argh, this is no good*, she thought. She couldn't hear herself think in this place. She grabbed his arm and pulled him outside into the beer garden. Her ears rang from the noise inside the pub and the fresh air hit her like a bullet causing her to sway.

"Whoa, Laura." Lucas laughed, grabbing her elbow. "How much have you had to drink?"

She looked into his eyes again, distracted by their deepness. "I've come to say I'm sorry. I'm really sorry. Cos I was rude to you before. And I don't like that. I mean, I don't like being rude or mean. So there, I've said it, and I mean it. So, are we okay now?"

Lucas tipped his head to one side and continued to look at her with an amused expression. "I've no idea what you've just said, but if that was an apology, then I'll accept it." He crossed his arms while he stared at her, a slight smile still evident on his lips.

"Good. That's all I wanted to say. Right, I'm going now." Laura turned to walk away. The floor seemed to sway underneath her, and she grabbed hold of a table to steady herself.

Lucas cupped her elbow, gently guiding her to a nearby table and bench. "Something tells me you've had too much to drink."

Laura groaned and lay her head on the table. "I'm not drunk," she replied, sounding muffled. "Just tired and giving my feet a little rest."

She could feel the warmth of Lucas' leg next to hers on the bench seat. It felt so nice, so natural. Sitting close, she could see how toned his legs were, and she desperately wanted to move her hand and place it on his thigh, just to see how it felt, but she knew that wouldn't be a good move. Not tonight. Not ever! She didn't even like this man. He irritated the life out of her. But he looked so good, and God, he smelled so nice. Her traitorous body leaned against him, despite her head warning her to get up and walk away.

Lucas put his arm protectively around her shoulders. "The demon drink." He rubbed her shoulders as she shivered against him. "Let's go back inside where it's warm. I'll get you something to eat."

Laura snuggled against him, reluctant to move. It felt so good to have his arm around her. But it shouldn't feel good, she reminded herself. She shouldn't be here, sitting next to him. God, when had she leaned against him? Why did his hands feel so good against her bare arms?

"I'm going back into the bar now," she muttered, raising her head off the table. She needed to move away from Lucas and all these confusing feelings. As she raised her head, the world spun on its axis. She groaned and lay her head back firmly on the table.

"Okay, Nurse Nightingale." Lucas smiled. "I'm taking you home."

"No, you're not," muffled Laura from the tabletop. "I'm here to have fun, and you're not fun. You're very irritating. You're Mr Sour Pants."

Lucas laughed out loud, "Well, that's something I've never been called before. Where's your coat and bag, Laura?"

She heard Lucas come back with her belongings, Amy at his side.

"Oh, Laura! You're going to have such a hangover tomorrow. Lucas is going to take you home, okay? He's the only one with a car who's not been drinking."

"I want to stay," Laura mumbled. "I'm having a nice time."

"All good things come to an end. Come on, Nurse Nightingale, hold tight." Lucas lifted her up effortlessly and carried her to his car.

Laura laid her head against his solid chest, enjoying his closeness whilst breathing in the woody scent of his aftershave. "Why do you always smell so good, Lucas?"

"Oh, Laura," he replied quietly. "Take my advice and say no more. You'll regret it in the morning."

He unlocked the passenger car door and placed her inside, reaching over to fasten her seat belt.

"I'm not drunk, you know," she said, resting her head against the cool window. "Just tired."

"I know." Lucas smiled before jumping in the driver's seat and setting off down Harbour Road.

Laura tried to focus on the road, but her head spun so much she could barely see. She closed her eyes to stop the world from turning around and around, but the sound of the car engine combined with the movement made her feel worse. She felt her stomach lurch.

"Oh-oh!" Lucas noticed her expression. "Don't be sick, Laura! Hold on, I'm pulling over!"

He quickly turned into a layby, ran around the car and opened the passenger door, just in time for Laura to lean out and throw up in the grass. Lucas jumped back, but not quick enough to avoid his shoes being splashed. He knelt at

Laura's side and rubbed her back gently, while holding up her hair.

Laura started to sob and wretch, while Lucas continued to comfort her. She couldn't believe she'd found herself in this situation, with Lucas of all people. She'd tried so hard in the past few months to keep her defences up around him. She'd failed spectacularly tonight on that score.

Lucas pulled a bottle of water from his glove compartment, twisted off the cap and passed it to her. "Drink slowly. Just a few sips at a time."

Being sick sobered her up. Laura sipped at the water, glancing briefly at Lucas to gauge how annoyed he was with her. He handed her a packet of wet wipes to clean her hands and face. The wipes freshened her but did nothing to ease the flush of embarrassment creeping up her neck.

She pushed her head back against the seat and groaned. "Lucas, I'm so sorry. I can't tell you how embarrassed I am. This is so unlike me. I don't normally drink this much."

"I kind of gathered that," he replied, looking at her in sympathy. "That's the problem when you're not used to it. It goes to your head much quicker."

Laura nodded gently. Her head throbbed, and she started to shiver. Lucas took off his coat, placing it around her shoulders.

She smiled to say thanks, and he returned the smile shyly, sitting silently while she recovered. Laura wasn't used to this side of Lucas. The side that didn't try to wind her up or make her feel like an idiot. "Thank you. For this I mean."

"It's not a problem. I'll drive you home, then you can get warm and have something to eat. Just give me a sec while I change my shoes. I've got a spare pair in the boot."

"Oh no! Please don't tell me I was sick on you. I'm mortified."

"Only my shoes!" He laughed lightly. "Don't worry about it. I've had much worse."

"Really? Somehow I don't think so."

He pointed to his medical bag on the back seat of the car. "I'm a vet, remember. It comes with a lot of occupational hazards. I get weed and pooped on frequently."

"Oh, God. Of course. I forgot about that. I must admit, after the incident with Olly, I do tend to think of you more as a doctor."

"That was one hell of a night." He grimaced. "I'm glad I'm not a doctor, though. It's bad enough when you can't save a beloved pet. To think you can't save someone's child, or mum, or husband. That must destroy you after a while."

Laura appreciated his honesty. She didn't have him down as the type to share his feelings, especially not with her. His openness relaxed her a little.

"Lucas, can I ask you a question?" He nodded while he laced up his trainers. "Were you frightened the night of Olly's accident?"

"Frightened is an understatement." He smiled. "Remember when I said that the smell of cauterisation can be overpowering? I meant my bowels emptying if it all went wrong."

Laura laughed properly for the first time in a few days.

"Can I ask you a question, Laura?"

She nodded, wondering what he planned to ask. It seemed strange to be having such a civil conversation with Lucas.

"I know it's none of my business, but are you unhappy here in Lambsdale? You were so upset in the café a few days ago, and tonight, drinking so much. I can't help thinking the episodes are linked."

Laura didn't want to go into detail with Lucas. She suspected he already considered her a flibbertigibbet. She didn't want to give him further ammunition by telling him how Leon had so easily tricked and betrayed her. "I love it in Lambsdale. I'm unhappy because of a certain person."

"Relationship issues?"

"Yeah. That's more or less it."

"I thought as much," Lucas replied quietly. "Anyway, come on Nurse Nightingale. Your carriage will turn into a pumpkin very soon." He started up the car and headed back to the Harbour B&B.

Lucas walked her to the door of her annex, despite her protestations that she would be fine left at the gate. "Amy would kill me if I didn't see you inside. To be honest, I'm a bit scared of her, so I'm going to do as I'm told."

Laura unlocked her annex door, feeling uncomfortable about the next move. Should she ask him in for a coffee? After all, she had ruined his Friday evening. On the other hand, he may read more into the invite. She didn't need those kinds of complications.

Lucas seemed to read her mind. He deliberately turned to walk back down the garden as she opened her door. "Night, Laura. Drink lots of water tonight. You need to rehydrate."

"Wait, Lucas," she half whispered, aware of Olly asleep in the hut just a few yards away. "Would you like a hot drink before you leave? Just to say thank you for bringing me home."

Lucas stalled, seeming to consider the invite before shaking his head. "I'd best go. I've got surgery at eight tomorrow morning, but thanks for the invite. Take care, and I'll see you around."

Laura closed the door with very mixed emotions. Yesterday, she wouldn't have even tolerated being in the same room as Lucas. He'd always been so rude and abrupt with her. Tonight, she'd seen a very different side to him. A side she almost wanted to get to know better.

She climbed wearily into her bed, ignoring the Facebook message that just beeped on her phone. Instead she fell into a deep and much needed sleep.

CHAPTER 17

Her head throbbed as she unglued her tongue from the top of her sandpaper mouth. Even drinking water made her feel queasy. Brushing her teeth, she groaned as the full extent of yesterday's news came back to her. The B&B at risk, possibly being demolished. Rupert's sold to that bastard. The drunken apology in the beer garden. Being sick on Lucas' shoes and finally, the disappointment she'd felt when he left.

No doubt Lucas would be laughing at her now. She inwardly cursed herself as she remembered leaning against him. Where had that come from? What on earth must he have thought? Yesterday had been so stressful, she hadn't been able to think straight. Her hormones had been jumping around too. Must be that time of the month. That would explain it all.

But what about her B&B? If it had to be destroyed, what kind of financial position would she be left in? Would she have to pay for it to be demolished? That would surely be such a low blow, even for Leon to deliver.

She couldn't face a walk along the beach this morning. Instead, she headed over to Olly's hut while Bronte bounded happily around the garden.

"Hi," Olly said brightly as she stepped into the hut. "Come on in. Shut the door if you're cold. I've been enjoying the fresh air."

"I can see you've settled in." Laura noticed how cosy the hut looked and how tidy too, considering his disability. His bed had been made and the few pieces of cutlery and plates he'd used had been washed and stacked on the small worktop. "Did you sleep well?"

"I did," he replied, with one eyebrow raised. "Did you?"

"Yeesss," Laura replied, confused. "Why do you ask?"

"Oh, nothing. It's none of my business how late you come home, or who you come home with." Olly gave her a knowing look.

"You heard Lucas outside last night, didn't you?"

"Well, I may have been struggling to sleep. I was sat over there." Olly pointed to a bench under the apple tree.

"So, you'll know that he went home and didn't come in then, won't you?" Laura replied defensively.

Olly raised his hands. "Hey, it's nothing to do with me either way. Rough night?"

"Yeah, I got a bit drunk." Laura chewed her bottom lip as she tried to remember what Olly may have overheard. Nothing much as far as she could remember. "Lucas brought me home. I was sick on the journey, made a bit of a fool of myself."

"Nah, it happens to us all." Olly smiled. "At least you were with someone you could trust. Lucas is a good guy, no doubt he looked after you."

"He did, actually." Laura remembered the way he had stroked her back and held her hair. She shook her head again to get rid of those confusing thoughts. They shouldn't keep coming to the forefront of her mind.

"Tell me to mind my own business, but the way he talked about you after my accident, it made me wonder if there was something between you."

"Good God, no! That man irritates the life out of me!" Laura replied.

Olly smiled knowingly. "Well, like I said, it's none of my business. Anyway, stick the kettle on, and I'll do us a brew. John came down earlier. He brought me some milk and a newspaper, so I've had a busy morning, doing … not much, really." He laughed.

They sat outside with their hot drinks, watching Bronte snuffling around the garden. Cobwebs hung between garden flowers and branches, the damp morning dew making them sparkle in the sun. Bronte's ears were covered in little silver spinlets from the webs.

"This is a gorgeous place." Olly shifted his leg in plaster to make himself more comfortable. "I hope you don't mind, but John told me you'd come here following a breakup. That this place had been left to you by an aunt?"

"Not an aunt, my Godmother, Jemima. I never expected to inherit all of this, but I can't envisage another life now." Laura's eyes darkened as she thought about the ownership case. She had no intention of mentioning it to John or Olly, though. Let them live in blissful ignorance for a while longer. She would tell them when it became essential.

"You've done her proud, Laura. Lucky in business, hopefully you'll be lucky in love … after your breakup."

"Oh, I don't think so, Olly! I'm putting love on hold for a while."

"That's a shame." Olly looked directly at her, with a mischievous smile, "Lucas didn't look like he'd need much cajoling last night."

Olly laughed at her outraged expression as he tried to duck from a slap across his head. "Okay, I'm off before I insult you any further. Call of nature. I need to set off at least ten minutes earlier now on these crutches."

"Need any help?" Laura offered, thinking the path looked a bit frosty.

Olly turned to look at her with pretend shocked eyes. "Bad enough you saw me in just my underpants while I was unconscious. You don't want to see what's under them as well, do you?"

Laura picked up a small rock and threw it his way. He laughed loudly as it skidded past him towards the cliff face. She sighed as she considered Olly's words. Did she feel ready for romance? Quite frankly, she wouldn't have a clue where to start. She didn't know many men who were a similar age to her, other than Olly, Lucas and Sam, and all of them were out of bounds for obvious reasons. Nope, it would have to be Internet dating.

Her phone beeped with another message from Amy, checking up on her hangover. She replied with the basics. Amy didn't need to know about *'vomit gate'*. As she pressed send, she remembered the Facebook message that had popped up last night. She opened the app, then gasped as she recognised the name. Her hands shaking, she opened the message.

Dear John/Laura,

I can't deny I was surprised when I read your message. It's come at an upsetting time in my life.

To cut to the chase, I am an adopted child. This is something I've been aware of all my life. My adoptive parents never hid this from me, but they fulfilled every role in my life that a parent should. For that reason, I've never enquired, or felt the need to enquire about my birth parents.

My mother died two weeks ago, my father a few years previously. Your message arrived the day after my mother's funeral. I can't deny that if it had arrived before her departure, I would have deleted it and not looked back, but now that I'm officially orphaned, as they so delicately put it, my instincts are to respond to you.

The stars do seem to be aligned here, but I must warn you that my adoptive parents have been my world for over forty years, I'm not looking for any replacements. I will be happy to talk with John further, to put him out of his own misery more than anything, but I can't promise I will want to stay in touch if we do turn out to be related.

I'm aware my tone is harsh, forgive me, this is an unsettling time in my life. I just don't want to give a false hope that we will suddenly become happy families.

Please let me know how you would like to take this to the next step.

Kind regards,

Alice Rosendale.

Laura read the message over and over. She wondered how John would take this news. It really did sound as if they'd found John's daughter. There were too many coincidences. However, Alice didn't seem keen to start a relationship with her birth parents. This concerned Laura.

*

She found John in his kitchen preparing dinner for Olly and himself. John read the message, then took off his glasses and rubbed his chin. "Sounds like we've hit home, Laura," he said with surprising calmness. "But I get the impression she's not keen on meeting?"

"She does sound reluctant, but you must have considered this might happen?"

"Aye, I did. I've kept an open mind for a while now." John sat back in his chair and puffed out his cheeks. "What do you think we should do?"

"Well, I think you should suggest a telephone conversation, just to break the ice. If you both feel comfortable following that, then maybe meet for a coffee near where she lives or works. Her magazine offices are based in London."

"Oh, Laura, I don't know what to do. I knew it wouldn't be all hearts and roses, that she'd have questions, and it may also lead me to Lizzie, which would open another can of worms. Olly knows nothing about this, by the way. Not that I don't trust the lad, but I want to deal with this privately. So, if you don't mind, can we keep this between us?"

"Of course, John. I'll support you any way you wish. Look, shall I reply to Alice and arrange for you both to speak on the phone, then we'll take it from there?"

"Yes, that's a sensible plan. I think we have to take Alice's lead on this one."

CHAPTER 18

The remainder of the day dragged for Laura. She felt so lethargic after last night's drinking, but her first free Saturday couldn't be wasted feeling sorry for herself. DIY jobs on the B&B won in the end. No point letting it go downhill based on Leon's threats. Laura listened to her radio whilst she worked, her spirits lifting as the hours passed by.

A walk along the beach and into the village later that evening cleared her head. The sun had just started to set. The restaurants had all but closed their outside seating areas and had transferred their twinkly lights to their indoor areas, which were surprisingly full for this time of year.

She walked past one of the restaurants and looked through the slightly steamed windows. Laura recognised some of the diners inside from Lucas' cycling club. Facing the window, totally engaged in conversation with a petite dark-haired girl, sat Lucas. He tipped back his head and laughed with his female friend, their hands touching across the table.

The raven-haired beauty seemed to lap up Lucas' attention, her whole-body language suggesting laughter was only the first course. It had never crossed Laura's mind to consider Lucas might be in a relationship. She'd just assumed he was single. Now she had to accept this woman could be an important part of his life.

Laura carried on walking back to the B&B, feeling a little down. She really did need to get some romance in her own life, instead of watching everyone else progress in theirs.

By nine o'clock that evening her log burner and a few scented candles had been lit. She curled up on the sofa with Bronte and her laptop and three photos suitable for profile pictures on Lucky Cupid.com.

She took a deep breath and started to fill in the dating site details. First her profile name. She decided to go with 'HarbourGirl'. What age and gender should she look for? Well, male, not too young and not too old. She decided to go with the age bands of '30-50 years old'. How much did she drink? How often did she exercise? How would she describe her frame? Petite, sturdy, curvy? Petite, considering her height at only five foot one. Did she want children? Well, yes, someday. What was her annual income? *Hmmm...* She decided to leave that one as undisclosed, especially after the Leon incident. What made her stand out? Now that could prove to be the most difficult question of them all.

She went through her Facebook profiles from the past two years, trying to find posts or photos that made her sound interesting. Unfortunately, most of the updates were from other peoples' celebrations where she'd been tagged. There were no posts from interesting parts of the worlds. No photos of her skydiving in Dubai or skiing in Switzerland. There were no wild nights out in the city, or even photos of her looking happy, come to that. What had she been doing with herself? Is this all she had to show of her life so far? Photos of herself celebrating other peoples' successes and never her own?

Laura sighed. The last three months had been the most exciting of her life. Setting up her B&B business, meeting

Amy, helping John find his daughter, Olly's accident, getting drunk and being taken home by Lucas....

After a further half hour of dithering, Laura decided to go with the truth and build on the basics of a thirty something who enjoyed a busy lifestyle. She liked walking Bronte, good food and fine wines. She enjoyed socialising, films and reading.

Laura puffed out her cheeks. Now, what did she want from a man? This process felt almost cathartic in its experience. How tall should he be? Well, anyone taller than her really. Body type? Muscular, slender, toned, average, sturdy? Maybe average, she thought. His education? Well, intelligence was an absolute must, a deal breaker in fact. Laura quickly went through the other questions, then pressed submit.

What would happen next? Would it instantly give her details of potential matches? Would her mobile start to ring? She didn't have to wait long. The site pinged up a list of first matches and their photos.

Wow! So many, Laura thought, going through them and unticking those she already knew she wouldn't want to meet. Messages soon followed. Some were just too pervy, or too heavy. She excluded those immediately. Others were more like she expected, such as the one from 'JacketPotato', which simply said, *Hello HabourGirl, how's tricks this evening?*

Laura looked at his profile, deciding he looked perfectly normal and acceptable. She replied, *Been busy deciding if I wanted sturdy or slender, tall or short, educated or GSOH.*

I take it you also ticked athletic, handsome and successful in business, otherwise we wouldn't be talking :)

Laura laughed to herself. She liked 'JacketPotato'. He had a good sense of humour. She settled into her cushions, enjoying the experience of getting to know someone new. This is what she needed. Light-hearted chat. Someone who could make her smile.

Sounds like you're ticking a few of my boxes already, JacketPotato.

Shame there's no option for large penis, because I would have fitted that description too!

Arghhh! She hadn't expected that kind of a response. Not really her type after all.

She moved onto the next message but didn't like the profile. She knew she shouldn't judge just off a photograph, but really? There was no way he was a day under fifty. She scrolled through a few other messages, but nothing stood out. Maybe she shouldn't have unticked so many at the start.

Another message appeared. Thankfully, this one seemed more her type. *Good evening, HarbourGirl. I'm Riverwalks. So, what's your favourite genre of film?*

Rom-coms, thrillers, and horrors when I'm not alone! How about you? She held her breath, waiting for his reply.

I love horror too, and rom-coms when I absolutely have to :) Are you new on here, HarbourGirl?

Yes, I've just joined. So, tell me a bit more about yourself. What do you do when you're not replying to posts on Lucky Cupid?

I've got two red setters. They've taken over my house! We go walking quite a bit. Are you team feline or team canine?

Laura smiled. She really liked 'RiverWalks'. She told him about Bronte and how he'd wormed his way into her heart in such a short space of time. She didn't want to tell him too much about herself too soon, though. Surely part of the fun was getting to know each other.

'Riverwalks' didn't push her. His responses were a mix of funny, light-hearted and sincere. Nothing inappropriate at all. *I'm recently divorced,* he explained in one of his messages. *Thankfully no children to be caught up in the upset, but I'm ready to move on. It's been a relatively amicable split. I come with no unnecessary baggage, other than my dogs!*

Their messages became less formal as they chatted. He even made her laugh with quite a few of his comments. Who knew Internet dating could be so much fun? She didn't need to dress up to do it, wash her hair, or worry about makeup. They made each other smile just by talking. Laura knew she would look forward to getting to know this person better. They seemed to click.

She finally closed her laptop, feeling proud of herself. She had taken that first step towards finding romance. It had also been a good distraction from her worries and the dark-haired petite girl that Lucas seemed so enthralled with.

She let Bronte out for his nighttime snuffle around the garden. The faint sound of a radio drifted across the garden from Olly's hut, making her smile as she thought of him all cosy and warm. She whistled softly to Bronte, and he came padding back inside the annex, his bedtime routine as familiar as her own now.

CHAPTER 19

The smell of bacon and sausages made her mouth water. Laura plated up the hot food and switched on the kettle to make a brew for Olly and herself. With only one room occupied, she had given Amy the morning off, on the proviso she would come later to help clean the bedrooms.

Olly came hobbling into the kitchen with his crutches. Laura smiled at the sight of his cast, now covered in scribbles and drawings from his four-year-old son, Danny. He gratefully accepted his hot coffee after pulling on her pigtails.

"So, Laura, was your Saturday night as rock-and-roll as mine?"

"'Fraid so!" She wondered whether to tell Olly she had joined a dating website. He would no doubt tease her mercilessly. His reaction surprised her.

"Good on you, Laura. Found anyone worth chatting with yet?"

"Yeah, I did. We messaged each other for ages last night. He's around my age and likes similar things to me. I guess I can only see where it goes."

"So, Lucas is definitely off the menu then? I bet this will make him jealous."

"Oh, Olly, I'm not doing it to make Lucas feel anything. I sent him a text to say thank you for bringing me home on

Friday. He never even replied. That's just rude. I don't care what he thinks about anything."

Olly raised his eyebrows. "Fair enough. However, just say if you did like him, wouldn't it be great to turn up at an event with a fit handsome guy on your arm? That would really get him thinking."

"Olly, I know you hit your head hard a few months ago, but please hear me out. I don't like Lucas. I have no intention of making him jealous, okay?"

"Hey, I hear you loud and clear. You don't like him; he doesn't like you. No long-term relationship has ever started on that story, has it?"

Laura had to smile. He constantly teased her with his wicked sense of humour. He also had the knack of being able to read her like a book, which she found comforting and unnerving in equal measure. "Don't worry, Olly, this Elizabeth Bennet isn't going to fall for Arsey Darcy."

Amy arrived in the afternoon as promised, bringing with her a breath of fresh air, as she always did. "Guess what? I've booked a table for this Thursday evening at Papa Antonio's on the harbour for Sam's birthday. I've booked for twelve people. Are you coming? It's a joint party for Sam and Mia."

"Who's Mia again?" Laura asked. She had heard the name a few times but couldn't remember how she fitted into Amy's friendship group.

"Mia is Lucas' veterinary nurse. She's leaving to have a baby. I went to school with her. Actually, just thinking, Lucas will be there too. Will that be a problem?"

"No, why would it be?" Laura inwardly cringed. Even her social life had to revolve around people she disliked. Oh God, what if he turned up with his dark-haired friend? She would have to watch them being all loved up while she still had no significant other. He would no doubt love that!

"Cool. I'm glad you can make it. You'll already know most of the people coming from The Goose."

"Will I be the only singleton?" Laura asked, thinking this could be the ideal opportunity to get some answers on Lucas' friend.

Amy frowned while counting names on her fingers. "Nope. A few are not bringing their partners. Although I'm not sure about Lucas. I don't know what's going on between them two."

"Lucas and who?" Laura pretended not to be interested.

Amy couldn't be fooled that easily. She looked up at Laura, hands on hips, her curls all over the place after stripping two beds. "What does that matter to you, Miss Thompson? Is this a case of, 'you don't want him, but no one else can have him either'?"

"Good God, no," Laura replied nonchalantly, while smoothing down a bed sheet. "I'm just curious as to who would be daft enough to date someone with so little personality."

"Well, her name is Keely. She's one of the cycling team," Amy explained, evidently happy with Laura's response. "You've probably seen her around. She's quite small, long dark hair, fringe, fancies herself a bit. She's a physiotherapist at the hospital, quite high up in her department. Probably a good match for Lucas. He only seems to date women in professional roles."

Typical, thought Laura. He's an arse and a snob to boot. Maybe that's why he liked to patronise her, because she wasn't educated at bloody master's level. People like Lucas got on her nerves. He'd obviously had a good education to get to where he was now. No doubt his parents were snobs too, egging him on to find himself the perfect wife, one that wouldn't feed her dog cheap biscuits.

Well, she wasn't going to give him the opportunity to judge her. He would never find out about how Leon had so easily tricked her; she'd make sure of that. In fact, just to prove she too could be successful in all aspects of life, she just might invite a significant other along for this meal on Thursday. That would show him.

An idea suddenly formed in her mind. Would four days be enough to pull it off? She kept the thought in her head and decided to think about the feasibility of it later.

"I've got an appointment with Sam tomorrow morning." Laura needed to change the topic of conversation to something safer. "I hope he's got some good news for me."

"He's been working so hard on this case for you," Amy replied, shaking pillows into clean white cases. "He's stayed late a few nights, looking for loopholes. I hope he's got some good news for you too."

Laura smiled, grateful she had the support and friendship from both Amy and Sam. "I really am so sorry all this mess led to you missing out on Rupert's."

"Oh, Laura, don't worry about it. It wasn't meant to be. Maybe it would have failed under my lead. I'm more cut out for working for others."

But Laura knew Amy was wrong. She would have been perfect for Rupert's. She had the right attitude and friendliness to pull customers through the door and keep them coming back. It was such a shame. She could throttle Leon for everything he had done to them both. Worse still, he would most likely sell the shop as office space. That's what he normally did. That beautiful view of the harbour wasted on the back of a computer screen.

"He's just a knob head," Laura spat, throwing the pillows on the bed in frustration.

"Who is?" Amy laughed. "Leon or Lucas?"

"Both of them," Laura replied, laughing herself now. "Maybe I should have another year off men. Concentrate on other things for a while."

"What? A complete penis embargo?" Amy snorted with laughter. "I'd like to see you try. I'd give you another three months before you're dry humping every bedpost in this building."

CHAPTER 20

John laced his fingers while he spoke. "Alice came across as quite approachable on the phone. She doesn't know anything about her birth parents, where she was born, their nationality, nothing. We've not much to go on. But still, she's agreed to meet with me, so I'm going to London in three weeks."

"Are you nervous, John?" Laura asked.

"A bit. I've waited a long time for this. I wonder if she'll look more like Lizzie or me. It's hard to tell off a photo, isn't it?"

Laura nodded. She had to admit, John going to London on his own bothered her, especially if the meeting didn't go to plan. "Would you like some company when you go, John? I mean, just the train journey there and back. I quite fancy a shopping trip to London. I've not been in years. I could shop while you meet Alice, then we can get the train back together."

John rubbed his hands. "My pleasure, darling girl. That would be perfect, but what about this place if you have guests?"

"Well, I don't want to turn business away. If I've got guests booked in, I'll ask if Amy can sleep here the night before. She can keep her eye on Olly too. His cast is due off in two weeks."

John nodded slowly. "I just hope he still wants me in his life when that happens. I feel like I've found my soulmate."

Back in her annex, Laura logged into Lucky Cupid and sent 'RiverWalks' a message. He replied within five minutes. This bothered Laura. Why was he logged in and not messaging her? Although, she supposed he must be keeping his options open. After all, they'd not committed to anything so far.

Has your day been as lazy as mine? Or have you walked your dogs senseless around rivers all afternoon? Laura realised she'd chewed most of her nail while waiting for his response.

You've hit the nail on the head, HarbourGirl. How about yourself? Done anything interesting today?

Laura guessed this was maybe the perfect opportunity. She wondered what level of subtle to start with. Perhaps very subtle and build it up.

I've spent ages going through my wardrobe trying to find an outfit for this Thursday. I'm going to a friend's birthday meal. I'm a bit nervous. I find wearing the right clothes makes you feel more comfortable. Do you often feel like that?

Why are you nervous, HarbourGirl?

Laura grinned. Subtle seemed to be working so far. *Meals out generally involve couples. I'm a singleton.*

Are you not comfortable being out on your own with your friends?

Laura groaned, maybe subtle needed to be upgraded straight to a hammer. *Normally, yes. Would have been nice to be part of a couple, though…*

Well, maybe I could join you? It would be a good opportunity for us to meet up. Depending on where you live, of course...

Laura jumped up and did a victory dance on her rug. The almost-hammer had worked! Bronte raised his head off his paws and looked at her in confusion, before settling back down again with a big doggy sigh.

Her heart beat fast. She didn't want to appear too eager, yet she needed to keep her bait attached. *Seriously, that's a wonderful offer, but I know it's short notice and the distance between us may be too much. Could I ask where you live. We've not shared personal information before?* She chewed her already bitten nails while she waited for a response. Please, please let it be a feasible distance, she thought.

Hebden Bridge. Do you know it?

Laura breathed a sigh of relief. That was less than a few hours' drive away. *I live in Lambsdale, near Whitby. It's very beautiful here. Lots of lovely walks and amazing scenery. I believe it's less than two hours between us.*

'Riverwalks' replied within seconds. *I've heard about your village. Lots of friendly beaches for dogs. It looks like a very attractive place to live.*

They agreed to meet on Thursday evening at six o'clock at The Goose, giving them the opportunity to get to know each other before Sam and Mia's meal. Laura wanted the party to think her date was a natural finding. That maybe they'd met on a country walk, a romantic story, perhaps. She fell, he pulled her up. That kind of meeting. She didn't want to deliberately lie, just not to over-share.

Looking forward to meeting you, HarbourGirl. I'll wear my blue walking jacket so you'll recognise me. My name is Tony, by the way.

Hi, Tony, I'm Laura. I'll wear my mustard wool coat. I'm looking forward to meeting you too. Have a wonderful evening. See you Thursday.

CHAPTER 21

Monday morning brought ten new guests, all part of a rambler's club. The men, all aged around sixty, filled her B&B with laughter. Each morning they helped with breakfasts and even made her and Amy cups of tea once the plates had been cleared. Being such a large group, they struggled to find places to eat together during the day. Laura suggested she could pack them up with a picnic daily if they gave their orders the evening before. One of the group kissed her hands in gratitude. Laura knew they'd turn out to be some of her favourite guests.

Unfortunately, Monday also brought with it her appointment with Sam. Her Aunt Maria met her at the bottom of the stairs to the solicitor's office. "No point worrying about what you can't change," she said to Laura. "Come on, let's find out where we stand."

One look at Sam's sombre face and Laura's heart fell. She hadn't been expecting to hear that Leon had dropped his case, but she had hoped Sam would have some positive news. He invited them both to sit down opposite his desk.

"I wrote to Leon Finch's firm of solicitors to ask them what his intentions were following his initial letter," Sam explained. "They replied within a few days to say, and I quote from their letter '*The land on which the property lies can be purchased by the encroaching party to the value of £18,000. Failing that, we will start proceedings for the buildings to be either fully or partially demolished.*'

"What!" Laura stuttered, "I don't have that kind of money. Can he do that? Insist I pay for the land or have my B&B demolished?" Aunt Maria put her arm around Laura's shoulders as they both looked to Sam for support and answers.

"It's not in his interest to have it demolished," Sam replied. "Quite simply, reading between the lines, he's bought the land, so you are forced to buy it from him for a much higher price. Mrs Henderson sold it to Leon Finch for two thousand pounds. As you can see, he envisages making a tidy profit from your predicament."

"Bastard," Laura muttered. She wandered over to the window to allow herself time to calm down. "Is there anything we can do?"

"Ideally we need proof of the building agreement. The building would then remain separate from the realty and not considered a fixture. Unfortunately, it seems Leon's done his homework, as legal proof of agreement doesn't seem to exist."

"He's got me cornered, hasn't he?" Laura said quietly.

"Can we not have the land valued and insist he lowers the price?" Aunt Maria asked. "Surely it's not worth anything near eighteen grand."

"I've already arranged for that to go ahead," Sam replied. "I've also asked for copies of land rights back to the start of the 1900s from the town hall in Whiterham. They'll have the details there for this village and those surrounding it. They'll need to extract them, but I expect to have them within five working days."

"What will they tell us?" Laura asked. "Do you think they'll help?"

"I honestly don't know." Sam rested his hands on the desk. "But I do know that old laws have some strange traditions, and it's often within those we find loopholes. Did you know. for instance, that it's an offence to be drunk and in charge of cattle in England and Wales? We could earn a fortune off Farmer James Briar if we enforced that one on a regular basis! Leave it with me, Laura. It's the best I can say. I'm writing to Leon Finch daily now to try and find a compromise. I'm also researching for any minor detail that could contradict his request. Arrange with my secretary to see me a week from today. I should have more news by then. If I do find anything in the meantime, believe me, I'll be in touch. I can't be fairer than that."

*

Amy placed a large piece of carrot cake in front of her, "Drink your coffee, Laura, and eat. We won't let him win."

Laura stared outside the Harbour Café window. Why did she have to get involved with such a low life? Why couldn't she have met someone lovely and caring, like Sam or Olly?

"There's a van outside Rupert's now." Amy pointed through the bay window. "Looks like removals."

"It's such a shame." Laura sighed. "All those shelves and rows of sweets and that gorgeous old bicycle in the middle of the shop."

"I can't believe Mrs Henderson left the bike. Did you know it belonged to Jemima?"

"Really? I didn't know that."

"I'll go and get it for you." Amy jumped up excitedly. "I bet the removals firm won't give a toss who takes what. More room in their van. You could put it in the hallway at the B&B, a memory of Jemima."

Before Laura could even agree, Amy had used her feminine charms with the removals firm. Not only did she get the bicycle, but they agreed to drop it off at the B&B for her too.

An old red fiesta pulled up at the side of the kerb as they headed back into the village. Laura quickly turned around as she spotted the owner. "Oh no, Amy. It's Leon. Let's go."

"Don't give him the satisfaction of walking away," Amy whispered in her ear, as they watched the podgy figure approach them with a swagger.

"Well, look who it is." Leon sneered at Laura. "Yorkshire's answer to Alex Polizzi. You thought you were so superior owning that shed of a B&B, didn't you? Trying to make a fool out of me. Well, I hope you can cough up the dosh I want for that dump to remain on my land or ... boom!" He laughed at Laura's anxious face.

Laura felt such a tangle of emotions at his sudden arrival. Embarrassment being the strongest. She watched Amy take in his greasy face and arrogant stance. Laura could see her mind trying to compute what had drawn them together in the first place. Taking a deep breath, Laura took hold of Amy's arm and pulled her along the small street. The less time she spent around Leon, the better.

Leon followed them slowly. "Don't think I'm going to give up on this land case, Laura. I don't forgive that easily. I'm going to stay in this village and watch you go under, and I'll enjoy every minute of it. I hear you've got a gimp living with you now. Varied interests, I'll give you that..."

Amy turned on him. Her curls wired to match her anger. "Listen here, you little maggot. Do you really think you can get away with insulting my best mate while standing there in your cheap t-shirt and piss-stained jeans? I've absolutely no idea what she saw in you. Quite frankly, I see nothing but a middle-aged loser who needs to resort to making someone else's life a misery because they're not clever enough to make a success of their own. If you think you're going to get one over on Laura with this pathetic land case thingy, then you're a bigger fool than you already look. You are nothing but an ignorant little shit with an inferiority complex and, to be quite honest, friggin' awful breath."

With that, Amy pulled Laura down the road to a smattering of applause from the small crowd that had collected around them. Laura turned around briefly to see Leon push his way angrily through the door of Rupert's. Not quite the entrance he had planned on.

*

Adrenaline caused her to almost jog back to the B&B with Amy. They didn't speak. They didn't need to. Laura occasionally gave a little grin as she recalled Leon's reactions to Amy's outburst.

Jemima's bicycle had already been dropped off, complete with a basket-full of toffee and fudge. Laura opened the front door and propped it against the stair post. It might be breaking fire rules, but at this moment she didn't care.

"John and Olly know nothing about this land case," Laura informed Amy as they headed down to the annex.

They found Olly sat in his usual spot outside his hut. He laughed at their serious faces. "Jesus, it's the muffia. It's not personal, Sonny. It's strictly business," he quoted in a Marlon Brando fashion.

Laura took a deep breath and put on her brightest smile. "Hi, Olly, have you two been okay?" She pointed to Bronte, currently licking Amy's face in delight.

"Yeah, Bronte's been fine." Olly stared at her for a few seconds. "Are you okay?"

"Yeah, nothing to worry about. Do you want to join us for a brew?"

Olly grabbed his crutches. "Nah, I fancy a kip. Plus, I'm not into women's talk. It always makes me feel guilty for being a mere bloke."

Laura knew he had deliberately made himself absent. She sighed as she realised this wasn't a secret she could keep from him for much longer.

Amy grinned. "Did you see his face when I accused him of having piss-stained jeans? I honestly can't believe you lived with that toad, Laura. What on earth did you ever see in him?"

Laura thought for a few seconds. Compliments didn't come straight to mind when thinking about her first few months with Leon. "Well, he was funny and quite considerate at first. We got on well, chatted, went for nights out. He could be boring and arrogant at times, but he was safe, if you know what I mean?"

Amy shook her head. "You mean he always used a condom?"

Laura spat out some of her tea, laughing. "No, I meant he was always around when I needed him. If I wanted to watch something at the cinema, or needed a partner for the work's Christmas do, he always came. I knew, or should I say, I thought, he was loyal."

Amy shook her head in mock disgust. "You've just described a crusty old marriage, not a two-month-old relationship that should have been full of sex and lust. Were you seriously going to settle for that? Saturday night with a few pumps and a squirt."

Laura shrugged. "Yeah, as much as it pains me to say it. I guess I would have stayed if he hadn't left me first. I got stuck in a rut with him."

Amy threw her a dirty look, "Girl, I'm so glad you moved down here and met me. I bet you've had more fun in these past few months than you've had in the past two years!"

Laura cringed as she replied, "I was only thinking that same thing the other night. I've opened a B&B, met you, saved a man's life. Joined a dating agency."

"No way!" Amy shifted to the edge of the sofa in expectation of juicy gossip. "Have you met anyone yet? Is it that swipe left or right one?"

Laura laughed at her animated face. "No, it's called Lucky Cupid. And yes, I've met someone. He's coming to Sam's birthday party on Thursday evening as my plus one."

"Well, you have been busy. There was I thinking you were wallowing in your own misery over this land business."

"Well, actually, that's part of the reason I joined. Lots of other reasons too, but I thought it would be a good distraction for me."

Amy winked at her. "You're just jealous because Mr Sour Pants might have found himself a girlfriend."

"Oh, not you too! If Lucas were the last man on this planet, I'd still avoid him."

"Hmm, you weren't avoiding him Friday night. I saw your arms around his neck when he carried you to his car."

Laura cringed. "I was drunk. Also, I'd have fallen if I hadn't held on to him."

Amy gave a small smile. "Or you'd have fallen for him."

*

Olly took the top off a bottle of beer with his teeth and passed it to Laura. "What brings you to my humble abode, fair princess?"

"I've come to explain about earlier." She picked anxiously at the label on her beer. "I'm in trouble with the B&B."

Olly simply nodded. "Carry on, spill the beans."

"I didn't know the land my B&B is built on didn't belong to me. It has since been sold on to someone who, shall we say, doesn't favour me very much. They have demanded money or threatened to demolish the building."

"Your ex, by any chance?"

Laura nodded, grateful he'd obviously listened carefully to her accounts of Leon from previous conversations.

"Can I ask how much he wants for the land?"

"Eighteen grand," Laura replied, still picking at her beer bottle label.

"Ouch."

"I know." Laura sighed. "He's been making my life a misery lately, and now he's living in the village. He's bought a shop here too, so I guess he plans on staying for quite a while. I just don't know what to do, Olly. I feel like my life is on hold until all this is resolved. I can't relax, plan for the future, nothing."

"Bloody hell, Laura. No wonder you looked so stressed earlier. I wish I had that kind of money to lend to you, but I don't."

Laura choked on her beer. "Olly, I didn't tell you so you'd offer to pay."

"I know you didn't," Olly replied gently, "but if I ever had reason to lend someone money, it would be to you and Lucas."

"I've been so worried about telling you. I want you to stay here for as long as you need while you recover, but I just don't know what will happen now. On the plus side, legal wheels grind slowly and it's not in Leon's interests to have the B&B demolished. He just wants to make me sweat for as long as he can."

"Is this why you've not told John? You were worried about his reaction if I couldn't stay here?"

Laura nodded. "He's been so happy since you came to stay. It's like you're soul mates, cut from the same cloth. You both like fishing, the same TV shows, beer."

"He's been a good mate." Olly opened another beer for them both. "Shame he never married and had kids of his own."

Laura smiled. She had no intention of breaking her promise to John.

"Look Laura, if you need anything. Company, a shoulder to cry on, someone to come with you for any legal appointments, just shout at me, okay? I hate to see you so upset. No matter what happens, I'm here for you."

Laura leaned over and kissed his bristly cheek. He'd become like a brother to her. She knew he would always look out for her.

Laura eventually left Olly to his book while she headed back to check for any messages from Tony. There were none, but Laura didn't mind. She wasn't in the mood for trying to sound interesting and vibrant tonight. She just wanted to curl up with a book, her log fire, a cup of tea, and Bronte.

CHAPTER 22

Sorting out her washing, Laura came across Lucas' jumper he'd left the night of Olly's accident. She needed to give it to him, or it would stay in her annex forever. Her anxiety rose at the thought of seeing Lucas again. Would he mention Friday night? There had still been no reply to the text she'd sent him. Typical stuck up Lucas.

Laura hadn't been to Lucas' surgery before, but she had a vague idea where it was. Instead of heading left towards The Goose on the harbour front, she turned right and walked past the Italian, where they'd be eating on Thursday, carrying on towards the church on the village green. It didn't take long to find the surgery. She stood outside, admiring the large white Georgian building with its sage green front door and large windows on either side. A shiny brass plaque attached to the brickwork near the front door stated:

Chamberlain and Stokes Veterinary Surgery.
Lucas Chamberlain RCVS and Aiden Stokes RCVS.

Bronte started to whine as they approached the surgery door, pulling on his lead. He'd obviously been here before and didn't remember it with fondness. In the end, Laura picked him up and carried him inside.

Dogs of all sizes, cats in their baskets, and rabbits in small carry cases filled the small reception area. Their owners sat on the benches around the walls, trying their best to pacify their stressed and anxious pets. Behind the reception desk stood a man Laura had never seen before. She presumed it must be Lucas' partner, Aiden. She guessed him to be a similar age to herself. He wore a pair of green cargo pants and a grey t-shirt underneath his white coat. His hair, dyed blonde and cut very short on one side, suited his slim, friendly face.

"Apologies." He smiled as Laura approached the desk. "I don't use this computer system often. Our receptionist has gone on maternity leave, so you've got me, I'm afraid." Aiden didn't try to hide the fact he was gay and proud. Laura instantly took a liking to him. A wedding band shone on his left hand, obviously newly married.

"I've not come for an appointment," Laura replied, sympathising as Aiden failed in his attempts to unlock the computer. "I've just come to deliver this for Lucas. Can I leave it with you?"

One of the surgery doors off the reception area opened. Lucas walked through carrying a cat basket. Laura noticed many of the females in the waiting room seemed to sit up a little straighter. Phones were ignored while lipstick smiles suddenly became brighter. Laura had to admit, in his white coat, blue open-necked shirt and dark blue jeans, he did look very attractive. He walked to the desk and laughed as Aiden failed again to log into the computer.

"I don't get this system," Aiden bashed at the keyboard in his attempts to enter a code.

"Move over, matey." Lucas pressed a few digits on the keyboard, and the computer screen came to life. "He can perform open-heart surgery on a horse, but he can't work a PC."

All the women in the waiting room giggled over-enthusiastically at his joke.

Lucas turned to walk back into his surgery when he spotted Laura still carrying Bronte. "Laura? What's the matter with Bronte? Have you been seen by someone?"

Laura sighed and shook her head. She had hoped to disappear before seeing Lucas. "No, there's nothing wrong. I just wanted to drop something off that belongs to you."

"You don't have anything that belongs to me."

"Your jumper," Laura whispered quietly, keen not to attract an audience.

Lucas nodded his thanks, then glanced at his watch, "My four-thirty has just cancelled on me. Do you want to come into the surgery? I'll do a quick check up on Bronte while you're here?"

"Why, does he look ill?" Laura looked in concern at the quivering Bronte, his tail tucked firmly underneath him.

"No, he seems fine, apart from looking terrified. But I don't think we've seen him in the surgery for a while now. There's no harm in a quick consultation."

"Well, if you feel it's necessary." Laura followed Lucas into his surgery, aware that many females were currently throwing daggers in her direction. Still, he said he'd had a cancellation, so she wasn't putting anyone out.

Laura quickly registered the clean surgery and spotless table in the middle of the room. Walls were filled with posters containing advice on looking after many types of animals with warning signs of different illnesses. One section contained all his certificates. Laura had to admit they were impressive; he was obviously highly qualified. Thankyou cards were pinned to a cork board near the window. This surprised her. Lucas didn't strike her as a sentimental person.

If Laura expected small talk while Lucas examined Bronte, she would have been disappointed. He listened to Bronte's heart and lungs carefully, talking continually to calm the anxious dog, while gently running his hands all over the abdomen, feeling for lumps and bumps. By now, Bronte had started to act more like his normal self. He licked Lucas' hand before allowing him to examine his ears thoroughly. It seemed Lucas did have a way with animals, if not with humans.

"Full bill of health." Lucas stood up and walked to the sink to wash his hands.

"Are you surprised?" Laura couldn't help having this little dig, although she did regret it almost the minute it came out of her mouth. She picked up Bronte and scratched his ears while he licked her face, making her laugh.

Lucas chose either not to take the bait, or he hadn't picked up on her prickly response. "He looks happy. He's healthy. That makes me happy."

Laura stored that one up. At least something made him happy, other than little Miss Dark Hair.

Lucas diligently typed up his notes on the computer. It seemed to take forever, and the silence became awkward. Laura started to wonder if he'd forgotten she was there. She turned to leave the room when he spoke, "You're going this Thursday, I hear. For Sam and Mia's meal, I mean."

"Yes, I am." Laura stood in the middle of the room, holding Bronte's lead, shuffling her feet. Was that it? Conversation over? Should she leave now?

"Did you rehydrate?"

Laura shook her head, not understanding. She glanced at him briefly.

"Friday evening. I said you should drink lots of water. Did you?"

"Erm, yes, I did. I texted you, thanking you for bringing me home. You never replied."

"You sent the text to our emergency mobile number. Aiden picked it up initially. He passed the message onto me this morning."

"Oh, I hadn't realised. Sorry."

Lucas gave her an amused smile. It irritated Laura when he smiled at her like that. She felt patronised.

"Alcohol dehydrates you, Laura. That's what makes you feel ill and dizzy. Did you have anything to replace your salts after being sick?"

"I don't know," she replied, flustered. "Possibly."

"Just be careful. Most people are genuine, but some would have taken advantage of you being so vulnerable. It might not end well next time."

"What do you mean by next time? You make it sound like this is a habit of mine. I explained I'd lost track of my drinks and the fresh air made it all go to my head."

"Hey, Laura, I'm not criticising you. I've done it myself, drank too much and regretted it the next morning. Why do you always fire off at me when I try to give you advice?"

"Because you've not just given me advice. You've just lectured me, and that's not your place. I know how to handle my drinks. And for your information, I didn't regret it the next morning. There was nothing to regret. I didn't say or do anything I'm ashamed of."

Lucas sat back against his desk, an amused look on his face. "I never said you did."

Laura felt an angry flush creep around her neck and up her cheeks. She felt certain she hadn't said or done anything embarrassing, but by the way Lucas looked at her, his head cocked to one side, it seemed he thought differently. "Why are you laughing at me?" she asked defensively, putting a hand to her neck to cover the angry red flush.

"I'm not laughing at you, but you need to calm down. You've gone very red. Are you okay?"

Laura found herself fixating again on his deep brown eyes. She caught a trace of his aftershave as he came closer and she was momentarily taken aback by her reaction. Her heart skipped a few beats as her hands became clammy. A million butterflies danced in her stomach, but still, she couldn't stop looking at him. Her breathing became uneven and she started to shake. She took a few steps back as if to protect herself from these unfamiliar feelings.

None of this went unnoticed by Lucas. He stood still and watched her with curiosity. "I can see I've made you uncomfortable," he said softly. "I am sorry. It wasn't my intention. Here, drink water, it will calm you down."

"I don't need calming down. I'm not one of your animals. You don't need to stroke my body to stop me panting..."

Lucas bent his head to cover a smile as Laura turned a deeper shade of red. "I'll ignore that comment." He grinned.

"I didn't mean to say that. It came out all wrong. I'd better leave." Laura felt weak. She craved fresh air. "Thank you for examining Bronte. Do I pay at the reception?"

"You don't need to pay, Laura. It only took a few minutes."

Lucas didn't move his eyes from her, but the intensity had softened. Laura felt like she'd been in the room for hours. Her emotions had somersaulted and dived around the room in the space of just a few minutes. "I don't want favours. I'll pay like everyone else."

Lucas sighed. "Will you ever drop the defensive?"

"No." Laura closed the surgery door after herself.

*

Laura hated confrontation. She didn't know why, but Lucas brought out the worst in her. She didn't understand it. Okay, he could be rude and abrupt, and he enjoyed it when she made a fool of herself, but look what Leon had done to her. Yet, she could put Leon out of her head, but not Lucas He wound her up, got under her skin, irritated her beyond belief. That amused smile he seemed to reserve for her didn't help either. Mr High and Mighty, looking down on everyone else from his ivory tower.

So why the hell did people seem to think they'd be good together? Olly, for instance, even Amy. Okay, they had shared a life-changing moment together the night of Olly's accident. They had got along together then, but Olly had been their distraction.

Laura paused, attempting to see things from another angle, just as Amy had taught her. Technically, Lucas hadn't done anything to hurt her. He just wound her up, and he hadn't ignored her text. She'd sent it to another phone. He had also been kind to her on Friday night, bringing her home and not making a big deal of her vomiting on his shoes. Perhaps having wars with one male in this village was enough. Maybe she needed to be more tolerant towards Lucas. The next time they met, she promised herself she would be pleasant to him. She could do that, couldn't she?

CHAPTER 23

The next few days passed by in a blur of cooking breakfasts, changing beds, and cleaning rooms. The rambling group had promised to leave a good review on TripAdvisor. When Laura read it a few days later, it brought tears to her eyes. The words were so heartfelt and personal. News soon got around to other rambling groups and within a few days she had three large bookings. At this rate, she would find herself busier during winter than in summer!

Date night with Tony soon came around. She'd been through her wardrobe and changed her mind on what to wear three times already. Jeans, top and heels? Casual dress and heels, or dress and boots? What would give the right impression? She wondered what Lucas' girlfriend would wear. Last time she'd seen her through the restaurant window, she had been sporting a black strappy dress that scooped low at the front. Laura didn't have any dresses like that, and if she did, she certainly wouldn't feel comfortable wearing it tonight. But she did want something special. She wanted to look elegant and sexy. She wanted to show Lucas that she wasn't a flibbertigibbet who walked around in jeans, t-shirt and trainers, causing chaos with her wayward pup, but a confident, successful and sexy young woman. She also wanted to impress Tony.

In the end, Laura drove into the town where she frequently shopped with Amy and bought herself a black fitted dress that clung gently to her petite frame. It emphasised her tiny waist and curvy bottom whilst providing a little glimpse of cleavage via the respectfully low-cut neck. A pair of black velvet knee-high boots complemented the sexy dress.

She bought a nice bottle of brandy for Sam and three beautiful snow-white baby grows for Mia, then headed back to her annex to wrap her gifts. Tony had sent her a text message while she was shopping to confirm he'd be at The Goose at six o'clock. He'd ended his text with a smiley face.

Laura blow-dried her hair, using her curling wand to add some slight waves. Her makeup made her look glowing and fresh and, she had to admit, quite sexy. She lightly sprayed herself with a new perfume that promised to make her smell good enough to eat. Grabbing her mustard coat, phone and bag, she walked Bronte to the hut, so he could spend the evening with Olly.

"Bloody hell, it's Jessica rabbit!" Olly's eyes popped when she walked into his hut. "Seriously, Laura, you look as hot as hell."

"Is it too much?" Laura asked, pulling at her dress so it didn't cling as much.

"You look bloody amazing! Tony will feel like the cat that got the cream when he sees you tonight. Just stay safe, okay. Ring me if you feel uncomfortable at any point. I know I can't walk down to you, but I can ask John to come and get you."

"I'll be fine, thanks, Olly. Sam and Lucas will both be there, so there'll be plenty of support if anything turns uncomfortable."

Olly raised an eyebrow. "So, Lucas is going tonight, is he?"

Laura gave him the devil's stare. "And he's bringing his girlfriend."

"Ah, pity." Olly winked. "Don't do anything I wouldn't do."

*

No tables were free inside The Goose. Laura had a quick walk around to see if she could see anyone wearing a blue walking jacket. No one so far fitted the description. Still, it wasn't quite six o'clock. There was time. Sam and Amy waved frantically at her from one of the tables where they sat with many of their friends. Laura cursed herself. She should have known that most people would meet for a drink before the meal. Now she'd jeopardised her chance to get to know Tony on her own first.

She quickly surveyed the group, relieved to see Lucas and Keely were not there. Amy shifted over on the bench so Laura could sit between her and a very heavily pregnant woman, who she presumed must be Mia.

Laura liked Mia immediately. She had an open face and honesty about her that drew you in.

"I can't believe I've left work," Mia said, massaging her bump. "I've worked for Lucas for three years now. I hate to let him down, but I also want that special time with my baby."

"Has he not got a replacement yet?" Laura thought it was quite remiss of him not to have planned for this eventuality.

"Well, he did have, but she let him down at the last minute. She's been offered a job in a practice closer to where she lives. Lucas wasn't happy."

Laura didn't expect anything less of Lucas. Was he ever happy? Apart from when he was with Keely, it seemed.

"So, he's on his own until he can interview again, which takes ages," Mia continued. "It's a shame because he's such a lovely person. Do you know, from the minute I found out about the baby, Lucas was so supportive? He wouldn't let me lift anything heavier than a syringe."

Laura had to admit at being surprised by this. She would have thought Lucas would have viewed the news of Mia's pregnancy as an inconvenience to his lifestyle.

Mia whispered to Laura, "I had a bit of a bleed in my first few weeks. I was at work, and I felt so scared. In the end, I had to tell Lucas that I was bleeding. He cancelled all his appointments and drove me to the hospital. He even offered to come into the screening room with me because Joe, my husband, hadn't arrived. When I explained it would be, you know, internal, well, he stayed outside, but it was so sweet of him to offer."

Laura did not enjoy the jealous feeling that had just unravelled inside her chest. She knew she was being irrational. Lucas would obviously support Mia, being a member of his staff. Her mixed feelings were not helped by the heat, caused by still wearing her coat. Tony still hadn't arrived despite it now being half-past six. Her phone suddenly beeped. She opened the message, dreading a cancellation.

I've had to stop on the way down, I'm running a bit late. T.

Laura breathed a sigh of relief.

By ten to seven, Tony still hadn't arrived. Laura started to get tetchy. She checked her phone again, seeing another message from Tony. He was almost there. What did almost mean, though? Another ten minutes or another half hour. Not that it mattered, as they were starting to leave for Papa Antonio's.

The fresh air as they walked to the restaurant cooled down her cheeks but did nothing to calm the butterflies in her stomach. How would she deal with the seating arrangements in the restaurant? She'd have to ask for a seat to be left at her side, and if he didn't arrive, everyone would know she'd been stood up. It would also be obvious to everyone that this was their first date. *What a nightmare.*

Amy caught her up and pulled her to one side. "Where is he?" she whispered. "Is he still coming?"

"Apparently. He said he's stuck in traffic."

"Do you believe him?"

"I think so. I just know the next hour is going to be uncomfortable for me and everyone else when they realise it's a first date. I wanted to give the impression we were already dating, if you know what I mean?"

Amy nodded in understanding and squeezed her arm. "Don't worry. If he's intelligent, he'll figure that out himself and be diplomatic."

In the bar area of the restaurant, they found other members of their group, including Lucas and Keely. Laura felt nervous about seeing Lucas again. She hadn't fully recovered from the last time they had spoken. She wouldn't go as far as to say he intimidated her, but he had a way of making her feel self-conscious. She was never herself when she was with him. He got under her skin, full stop. However, she had promised herself she would try to be pleasant to him, starting with tonight.

Lucas currently had his back to her, facing his pretty girlfriend. Keely sat elegantly on a bar stool, wearing a tiny gold halter-neck dress that laced up at the back. It certainly suited her olive complexion.

Lucas turned on his bar stool to greet the new arrivals. He smiled and shook a few hands before spotting Laura. She pretended not to see him at first. It would give her time to think about how to greet him.

She headed to the bar for a drink with Mia, busying herself looking for her purse. Her curiosity eventually got the better of her. She glanced up and, by way of the mirror behind the bar, caught Lucas' eye. He gave her an awkward smile and wave. She returned it while sipping at her wine.

The bar area in the restaurant, being so small, soon became cramped with such a large party. Lucas gave up his bar stool for Mia, helping her up, and laughing as she referred to herself as an elephant. Laura held Mia's bag as she steadied herself on the bar stool, and she found herself standing next to Lucas.

"Hi." Lucas gave her a slight smile. "You look nice."

"Thank you." The compliment made her blush. She turned quickly before he noticed her flushed cheeks.

"Laura, this is Keely. I don't think you've met."

They shook hands politely, but Laura didn't miss the quick once over Keely gave her. It felt nice to be viewed as competition. It filled her with some much-needed confidence.

Lucas held a bottle of beer while he laughed with the group. She'd never seen him drinking alcohol before. Would he relax and be easier to talk to after a few drinks? She doubted he would ever get drunk. He seemed too much of a control freak to let his hair down completely.

Laura's legs shook with nerves as they made their way to the table. She sat down deliberately next to Mia, facing the door to the restaurant. On the chair to her right sat her handbag, with the explanation that her partner would join them in a short while. Lucas and Keely sat directly opposite her. Oh, God, not what she needed.

Keely draped herself around Lucas, reminding Laura of a fox stole. *Be nice*, she told herself. *Show him you are mature, smile nicely, and keep your thoughts to yourself.* Keely continued to show her affection for Lucas, causing Laura to look away, feeling uncomfortable. Lucas didn't seem happy with this show of affection either. He excused himself and walked to the bar, leaving Keely pouting. Laura thought she wasn't quite as attractive when she sulked.

She checked her watch again, then her phone. Where was Tony? Would he ever turn up?

"Who's the mystery guest?" Lucas nodded to the empty chair.

Laura had been dreading this question, especially from Lucas. "A friend of mine," she replied with an air of calmness she didn't feel.

"So, is your friend male or female?"

"Male, as it happens. Does it matter?"

Lucas gave her an amused smile. "And where is your male friend? Does he have a name?"

"His name is Tony, and he's stuck in traffic."

"Does Tony live in the village? Is that where you met?"

"He doesn't live in the village."

The restaurant door suddenly opened, and in walked a man in his forties wearing a dark blue coat. Laura half stood

165

to get a better look at him, but then sat down again when she realised he had a female with him.

Lucas following her gaze. He turned back to Laura and smiled knowingly, irritating her even more.

"Darling, I need another drink." Keely pouted her bright red lips at Lucas. "Do you plan on talking to everyone except me this evening?"

Laura checked her phone again and sighed. No more messages. He must be here soon. This was torture.

The waiter came and took their orders for starters. Laura had to leave out ordering for Tony, not knowing if he would arrive in time.

"I always find bruschetta is a safe option," Lucas said, sitting back down again.

"What do you mean?"

"I mean, if you're unsure what someone likes to eat."

The door opened again, and Laura lifted her head up like a bullet, only to be disappointed. She pulled at the collar of her mustard coat and sighed.

"Why don't you take off your coat? You look like you're cooking under all that wool." Lucas stared at her.

"I'd rather keep it on if you don't mind."

He leaned over and whispered, "Please tell me you've got more than a nightie on under that coat?"

Laura's face blushed to deep crimson. She picked up her drink and almost knocked the whole thing back.

Keely tutted and threw daggers at Laura. "Lucas, darling, did I tell you about the paper I wrote for the board last week on continued use of tramadol in patients over the age of sixty? It's being published in the journal this week. Isn't that amazing?"

Lucas nodded before taking a deep drink of his beer.

The restaurant door opened again. In walked a tall man with a beard, wearing a blue jacket and a beanie hat, but Laura took no notice of him. She'd given up waiting.

"Laura?" She looked up to see the bearded man standing between Lucas and Keely. He leaned over them both quite rudely to shake her hand. "I presume it is Laura. You said you'd be wearing a mustard coat."

Laura cringed. Despite sporting a lot of facial hair which she hadn't seen before, Tony did look like his profile picture. Tact, however, seemed to be missing. Could he have made their blind date any more obvious? He shuffled past the guests sitting on her side of the table as he made his way to the empty seat at her side. Laura realised he'd taken the term walking jacket quite literally. Not only that, but he'd teamed it with waterproof pants and chunky walking boots. Combined with the fluffy beard, he looked more like a man ready to hike up Mount Everest.

Laura glanced at Lucas, smiling into his beer. Oh, she guessed he was loving this. At least he had the grace to say nothing, unlike his girlfriend.

"Oh, my God!" Keely squealed, angling her long bare legs in Lucas' direction. "Are you both on a blind date? How incredibly sweet!"

Laura wanted the ground to open and swallow her up. Some of the group raised their heads, looking in her direction, particularly at Tony, who had now taken off his waterproof exposing a chunky blue fleece jumper.

"Blimey, Laura, you're a good-looking lass, I'll give you that. You're much prettier than your profile picture."

Tony summoned a waiter over by waving at him, ordering himself a glass of tap water and a main meal. Laura noticed he didn't offer to get her a drink, even though her glass was almost empty. She felt herself squirm further down into her seat.

The arrival of the first courses provided a distraction. Laura looked awkwardly at Tony's empty place mat. "Would you like some of my pâté? I didn't order for you. I didn't know what you would like."

"Oh yeah, ta. I'm starving," Tony took a huge cut off the pâté and most of her melba toast, "So, do you come here often?"

Laura lifted her head to respond, but instead caught Lucas' eye, his hand over his mouth, trying to smother a smile.

"Not really," Laura replied, with as much dignity as she could muster. "I've not lived here long. This is my first visit to this restaurant."

"Pity." He brushed crumbs off his beard and onto his fleece jumper. "Nice pâté here. I like pâté."

Keely, it seemed, had sharpened her claws. "So, where did you two meet?"

"Lucky Cupid," Tony jumped in, loudly. "Lucky me, I'd say." He looked Laura up and down again before taking another portion of her melba toast.

Laura continued to eat, even though the food stuck in her throat. She felt it would be safer not to respond. The least said, the better.

"So, what attracted you to Laura's profile?" Keely cupped her not-so-sweet face in her hands.

Tony chewed eagerly on his food. "Well, that's an easy question. She loves dogs, country walks, and she lives near the coast. Oh, and she desperately wanted someone to join her tonight. I was free, so here I am."

Laura put down her knife and fork and lifted a hand to her face with embarrassment. Tony continued to eat, unaware of her discomfort.

Keely lapped up her humiliation. "Oh, darling Laura. Why did you *desperately* want someone to join you tonight?"

Keely reminded Laura of a prowling cat. She had her prey in sight, and she planned to play with it before going for the kill. Laura floundered. She had no idea how to respond. Tony had just exposed her insecurities about tonight. She didn't know how to come back from this.

Lucas downed his drink and placed his empty bottle firmly on the table. "Laura, how's Olly?"

Laura smiled at him, grateful for the distraction. "He's doing great, thanks. His cast comes off on Tuesday. He can't wait."

"Laura saved the life of one of our fishing men this summer," Lucas explained to Tony. "She helped me to deal with his injuries."

"Was that you?" Mia asked. "Lucas told us about that night. He said he'd been lucky to have someone with common sense assisting him. Well done, Laura. I'm impressed."

Many other members of the group raised their glasses to her. Laura felt her shoulders begin to relax.

Keely, however, wasn't about to give up. "Lucas, it's so hot in here. I'm so glad I'm not wearing a big chunky dressing gown type thing, like Laura." She gently pulled at the front of her dress, exposing more of her breasts. Tony grunted appreciatively.

Lucas simply sighed and stood up. "Laura, would you like another drink?" He took her lack of response as a yes.

Keely pouted and sulked while Lucas stood at the bar. It made Laura smile. She'd obviously riled her. It served her right after her attempts to embarrass her tonight.

Lucas returned from the bar with another martini espresso for Keely and a large white wine for Laura.

"Lemonade would have been fine," she whispered.

Lucas shook his head. "Just drink it."

Their main meals arrived. Laura planned to eat quickly, then she could make an excuse and leave. Tony opened his napkin and started to fill it with bits of chicken off his plate. Laura watched, confused. "Do you not like it?" she whispered.

"Oh, no. It's not that." He tied up the napkin and stood up, causing everyone to look his way. "The dogs love chicken. I'll just give them a bit. Not be long."

Laura looked up at him in astonishment. "You've brought the dogs with you? Where are they?"

"They're asleep in the car after their walk along the coast earlier. Bloody good walks around here, Laura. We'll have to try some together. If our dogs get on, of course."

"You've been walking the dogs around here? Is that why you were late?" Laura asked sharply.

Tony looked at Laura, confused. "Well, I couldn't leave them at home on their own, and this is a beautiful part of the country. I got engrossed in the walking, then when we got back to the car, we hit traffic. Is that a problem?"

Laura didn't bother replying to his question. "You'd better go and feed your dogs."

Amy, throughout the evening, had been trying to catch Laura's attention. She came over, sitting down in Tony's vacant seat. "How's it going, chick? Not good, I gather?"

Laura shook her head and took a long sip of her wine. "I have a knack of pulling them. I wish I'd come alone, preferable to this humiliation." Amy kissed her cheek and gave her a big hug, returning to her own seat as Tony walked back into the restaurant.

"I'll have to take them for a quick run in about thirty minutes." Tony started to eat the rest of his food. "The dogs are getting a bit restless. I saw that lovely pub we were going to meet in earlier, The Fat Goose is it called? I reckon we finish up here, give the dogs a quick walk, then head there, just me and you. We can get to know each other a bit better. What do you say?"

Laura's heart fell. She couldn't think of anything worse. Inside her head she screamed, *Piss off back to your dogs. You've wasted my evening and humiliated me beyond belief.* Instead she drew on her polite upbringing and nodded in agreement. This had to be one of the worst nights out she'd ever had. She excused herself and headed to the ladies for a chance to calm down.

The toilets were upstairs on the second floor. She ran up them quickly, stamping out her frustration, almost running along the deserted corridor to burn out more anger. With her hand on the toilet door, she jumped violently as she felt someone behind her.

"I'm sorry. Did I scare you? I tried to catch you up near the stairs, but you raced up them and then ran down here." Lucas glanced at the door. "I'm sorry. Are you desperate to…? I didn't think?"

"No, I wasn't rushing for the toilet." She laughed. "I just needed to get away for a few minutes. I was trying to stamp out my frustration."

"Not the perfect match after all?" he asked gently. For once, he didn't seem to be taking amusement from her situation.

Laura sighed and held her face in her hands. "I just want the floor to swallow me up whole."

Lucas laughed softly. "Internet dating, I take it?"

"How did you guess?" Laura grinned. "I thought we covered it up so well."

"Erm ... your infatuation with everyone walking through the door. I guessed then." Lucas gave her a slight smile. "If you don't mind me asking, aren't you already seeing someone?"

"No." Laura shook her head. "Why did you think I was?"

"Just my misunderstanding, probably. Last week when you were upset, I thought it was over a man. I'm sorry, it's none of my business."

"I was seeing someone. Things are still messy, but I am single. However, after tonight, I'll not be dating again. This has really put me off."

"I apologise on behalf of all men." Lucas bowed in mock apology.

Laura laughed. He did seem more relaxed tonight. Maybe the alcohol had mellowed him. She could faintly smell beer on his breath. Combined with his aftershave, it wasn't an unpleasant concoction.

Lucas glanced at his watch. "I'm having a pretty miserable time here tonight. I guess you are too. Do you want an escape clause?"

"But you're not having a miserable time, are you? You're having a night out with your friends and girlfriend. Good food, beer, what's not to like?"

"My girlfriend?" he asked, raising his eyebrows. "Oh right, Keely." Lucas paused as if weighing up his next words, then seemed to change his mind. "Do you want a get-out clause, then?"

"I do. But nothing too obvious. I've had enough embarrassment for one night. I don't need anymore."

"Leave it with me. I can be discreet. Just give me ten minutes, okay?"

Laura nodded and agreed, grateful Lucas was being supportive. Not for the first time, she marvelled at the fact that she always managed to be at a disadvantage around him. No wonder her defences were always high in his company.

She freshened her face with a cold towel. Her face in the mirror looked red and blotchy from the heat and awkwardness with Tony. What a waste this evening had been. At this rate, she would be back in her annex before ten o'clock. *At least my dress looks good.* She turned in the mirror to get a better look at herself. The evening may have crashed and burned, but she'd managed to look good while it happened.

High spirits reigned in the restaurant as alcohol and food went down well. One of the waiters brought out a guitar and entertained everyone by playing popular music. Amy started to sing at the top of her voice while tears ran down Sam's cheeks listening to her version of the lyrics. Laura soon found herself joining in with the laughing and cheering. Life was never dull when Amy was around.

Out of the corner of her eye, she caught Lucas stand up, his phone to his ear. "Excuse me," he said to a pouting Keely. "There's a problem at the surgery."

Laura watched him leave the restaurant to take his call. A problem at the surgery could mean the end of her get-out clause. Typical, now what excuse could she use to leave early? Sickness? The classic headache? Oh God, just as she thought light could be at the end of the tunnel.

Lucas returned and shrugged in apology. "Sorry, Keely, I need to leave." He picked up his coat and quickly drank the remainder of his beer. Laura noticed he avoided eye contact with her. She knew she shouldn't have trusted him.

Keely flew into a temper at once. "You said you weren't on the Rota. Why can't someone else deal with the problem? You're with me tonight. You promised."

"I'm sorry, Keely. Aiden has been called out and one of the animals in the hospital bay is sick. I must go. You know the score; this is what I do."

"Well, I'm fed up of you and this bloody job," Keely spat as she threw down her napkin. "You always put that surgery before everything else. I'm coming back with you to make sure you don't waste time. You can take me straight to The Goose after. I'm not having all my night wasted by someone else's pet."

Keely made to stand up, but Lucas put a hand on her shoulder. "Keely, you may as well stay and enjoy your evening. This isn't a minor incident I need to get back for. Your dress will get ruined. No doubt there will be vomit and diarrhoea everywhere. I won't be going anywhere after this."

Keely pulled a disgusted face. "Fine," she sulked. "But I won't wait around forever." She turned in her seat, rudely putting her back to Lucas.

He sighed and rolled his eyes. "Mia, do you know where the rehydrating fluids are?"

Mia stood up. "I'll come with you and help."

"No, you will not! You've finished now for maternity leave. I'm not having you slipping on wet floors. I can manage on my own."

"You can't manage on your own, Lucas. It's hard work when an animal is sick, I know."

Lucas looked briefly at Laura, and the penny dropped. This was her get-out clause. "Mia, if it's worrying you, I'll help Lucas. I've cleaned up after Bronte. It doesn't bother me. We'll be fine."

Mia nodded gratefully, but Keely looked outraged. She turned on Lucas. "Why are you taking her with you? Why not Mia?"

Lucas replied patiently, "Mia is eight months pregnant. She should not be in contact with animal faeces. It's dangerous for the baby. You know that."

Keely seemed to absorb this, "I suppose Laura's more appropriately dressed than me for scooping dog muck."

Laura knew better than to retaliate. She picked up her coat. "I'm sorry, Tony. I need to leave to assist in the veterinary surgery."

"Very admirable. I like that in a woman. Giving up her evening to look after a sick animal. We must get together with the dogs. I saw a lovely café on the coast a few miles from here. I'll message you."

Laura nodded as she rushed out the door with Lucas. She gave Amy and Sam a quick thumbs up. Amy stared at her open-mouthed before wagging her finger as she guessed their motives.

CHAPTER 24

Laura shivered as she pulled her coat around her. Thank God she'd escaped. At least now she could go home and relax. Tonight had been excruciating!

Lucas grinned down at her. "Was I discreet enough?" he asked, zipping up his own jacket.

"Yes, thank you. I just couldn't face an evening with Tony on his own. He's slightly obsessed with his dogs, isn't he?"

"Only slightly." Lucas laughed. "I love animals, but even I wouldn't leave a pretty lady to feed a dog."

Laura blushed at this unexpected compliment. They reached the corner of the harbour walk. "I'll head off home now, Lucas. Thanks again."

"Whoa, not so fast, Nurse Nightingale. I really do need to check up on an animal at the surgery. One good deed deserves another, after all."

"You mean there really is sick and poo everywhere?" Laura said. Maybe staying with Tony would have been the better option.

Lucas laughed at her expression. "There's no sick or poo. Just a cat who's due to give birth very soon. We don't want to leave her alone." He suddenly stopped walking and turned to face her. "Sorry, Laura, I'm being selfish. I can walk you back home if you like. You don't have to come with me. I just fancied the company."

Surprised, Laura looked at him. He'd never given the impression he enjoyed her company. However, she did owe him a favour, and maybe spending time with Lucas wouldn't be a bad plan. They might even find some common ground. "I don't mind coming with you. I'd like to meet this feline mother-to-be."

She looked up at Lucas as they walked, suddenly feeling self-conscious. They'd never spent time in each other's company before, not through choice. She took a deep breath and tried to relax. "So, does Aiden provide you with a lot of get-out clauses?"

"Quite a few in the past, especially in our younger days. I've known Aiden a long time. We met at university, flat sharing and on the same courses together. We hit it off straight away."

"How long has he been married?"

"Only a year. He married his partner Martin last October. They've been together a long time."

"And you've stayed friends since Uni? Is that how you both came to own the surgery?"

"Kind of." Lucas lowered his head to avoid the wind that hit them as they walked onto the village green. "Aiden already lived here. It made sense to join him."

"Did you always want to be a vet?" Laura realised they were having a conversation without snapping at each other. The drink must have mellowed him.

"My dad was a vet. I helped as a child. I never considered I would do anything else."

Lucas opened the surgery door, and Laura stepped inside, grateful to get out of the cold October evening. She took off her coat and placed it on one of the benches in the waiting area.

Lucas turned to her and smiled. "Silence is golden."

Laura nodded, suddenly aware it was just the two of them alone. His cheeks were flushed from the cold outside and she could see the outline of his toned body through his fitted shirt. She glanced at him shyly, determined not to let those confusing feelings take hold again.

Lucas seemed to sense her shyness. "Relax, Laura, I don't bite. The animals are through here. Do you want to see?"

He led them into a room with ten large cages. Three were currently occupied. Lucas walked straight to the one containing a sleepy cat, curled up on a cosy blanket, eyeing them with big green eyes.

"This is our mother-to-be. She's called Nina." He opened the cage and scratched the cat's head as she purred. "It wasn't a total lie before about the vomit. She has been sick a lot lately."

"When will she have her kittens?" Laura walked along the cages, looking at the other sleepy animals.

"Anytime, really." Lucas leaned back against the door frame, watching Laura feed bits of hay to a baby rabbit. "She's having three kittens. I'll help her deliver them."

"Wow! That must be amazing, to see new life enter the world. Have you delivered lots of baby animals?"

"Many. Mainly foals, lambs and calves. Farm animals are Aiden's area of expertise, but I assist when I'm needed."

"Can you deliver a human baby?" Laura asked, thinking how easily he had transferred his vet skills to help Olly.

"I guess I could. Same principle, really. Although I think Mia may refuse my assistance, if that's what you're thinking."

Laura laughed. "Maybe that's taking employee benefits too far."

"Would you like to hold the baby rabbit?" He walked over to join her. "I found her near the beach." Lucas gently placed the baby rabbit in her arms. "Just hold her gently and stroke her head and down her back. She'll soon settle."

The baby rabbit snuggled against her. Laura enjoyed feeling its soft fur against her bare arms. "So, who's going to help you now that Mia has left?"

Lucas sighed. "To be honest, I've no idea. I did have a replacement, but she chose another practice. I've not had time to put out another advert. So now I'm chief feeder, cleaner, receptionist, vet and midwife all in one."

Laura smiled at him. "You need someone who can come into the surgery a few hours a day and help you out, don't you?"

"If you know anyone who's interested, I will snatch their hands off. Do you know anyone with a few hours to spare to take phone calls and book appointments?" He took the baby rabbit out of her arms and placed it back in its cage.

"Well, me ... possibly." Laura stopped. Why on earth had she just offered? They could only just about tolerate each other.

Lucas looked just as surprised. "You?"

"What's that supposed to mean?" she asked, feeling a little irked. "I can manage appointments and computer systems. I even tweaked my own website for the B&B. If you remember, I'm also pretty nifty with cleaning horrible wounds."

"That's an impressive list of achievements, Nurse Nightingale. I don't doubt your ability. My concern is you're already really busy with your B&B and looking after Olly."

"Olly should have his cast removed next week, and the main work at the B&B is in the mornings. I can make time in the afternoons to help you out. If you want me to, of course?"

"I have to admit your help would be brilliant. Mornings are normally okay. Aiden is around. I struggle in the afternoons when he goes on his farm rounds."

Laura needed another distraction to take her mind off her Leon problem. This seemed perfect. Naturally, she worried about friction between them. But they were getting on well enough now, weren't they?

"I can start this Monday if that suits you?"

"Please. Thank you, Laura."

Lucas stood so close to her she could see the amber flecks in his eyes. He held her gaze for a few seconds and then lowered his head with a slight smile. "Would you like a drink before I walk you home? My apartment is upstairs, it's warmer up there."

"Your apartment? You live here?"

"For the time being. It's close to where I work. That was a joke, by the way. I can be funny when I want to be."

Laura paused. Was this a wise move? They'd both been drinking, Lucas more than her. They'd got on well tonight, maybe too well.

He seemed to read her mind. "Come on, Nurse Nightingale. You must be tired. I'll walk you home."

"No, it's just, maybe it's not appropriate," Laura said, flustered.

Lucas grinned at her. "I planned on offering you a coffee, Laura, not sex. I think I can be a gentleman and resist you." He held his hands in imitation of a halo over his head.

Laura laughed, feeling silly for being hesitant. "Actually, I am quite thirsty. A drink would be great, thanks."

She followed him up a staircase and found herself in a large open-plan apartment overlooking the village green. The walls were plain and painted white, which contrasted with the original dark wooden floors. It was very Lucas.

"Where do you sleep?" she asked, seeing no bed as she looked around.

Lucas pointed to the large brown leather sofa. "It's a sofa bed." He held up two bottles. "If you're thirsty, would you prefer a beer?"

"Please." Laura looked at a few books he had stacked in a corner. The room had an air of bachelor pad. She wondered how many times he'd brought Keely back here, then shook her head. She didn't want to think about that. Shyness once again got the better of her. This isn't how she expected her evening to end. Especially given the fact her relationship with Lucas had proved to be so volatile. She sat on the end of the sofa, pulling at the hem of her dress, wishing it was closer to her knees than her hips. Lucas saw her and smiled with amusement.

"Your dress is fine. It's not too short." He handed her a beer and sat at her side. "I'm sorry it didn't work out with Tony. You must be disappointed."

Laura shrugged. "It happens, I guess. I shouldn't have had any expectations. I admit, I'm a bit of a novice at this dating thing. Some of them can be quite rude."

"Yeah, I've heard stories." He smiled with sympathy. "So, you've encountered some warped individuals then?"

Laura laughed. "Only a few. The usual comments around penis size and the like."

Lucas groaned. "I really feel I should apologise for my gender. We've not all got one-track minds, you know."

"Yeah, I know." Laura took a drink of her beer. "I'm not bothering anymore with the dating site. I realised tonight that I'm happy enough with the B&B and my friends. I just had a moment last week where I felt a bit, maybe lonely, I suppose. Amy and Sam are so loved up. I guess it made me want some of that, too. I now realise I was wrong. My life needs a rest from men, at least for the moment."

"How so?" Lucas asked, watching her intently.

Laura took a deep breath. He would find out sooner rather than later. "Well, do you know the new owner of Rupert's?"

Lucas nodded. "I've seen him around this week. Unpleasant chap, I've heard."

"He's my ex." Laura watched as Lucas raised his eyebrows.

He exhaled before responding. "Well, that is a surprise."

Laura smiled as she picked at the label of her beer. "That was a better response than I expected. It's okay, you can ask me what I was doing with that tosser."

"So, what were you doing with that tosser?" he asked, returning her smile.

"I've absolutely no idea."

Lucas grinned at her. "You know, Laura, when you're not being defensive, you're really funny."

Laura chewed her thumb nail, slightly embarrassed. "I just thought the same myself, about you."

Lucas sat back on the couch and sighed. "Yeah, we didn't get off to the best of starts, did we? But I hope we can put that behind us and start afresh, especially if we are going to be working together. What do you say, truce?" He raised his beer bottle. Laura clinked her beer against his, before sitting back with him on the sofa.

They sat quietly, side by side. Their closeness reminded Laura of the night at The Goose. The warm feeling she'd felt with his arm around her shoulders. She really shouldn't be feeling this way about Lucas. Despite their truce, he could still turn back into Arsey Darcy.

To distract herself, she stood up and walked to a photograph on the fireplace, the only photo in the room. Lucas stood between his parents at his graduation. Even back then, his dark hair, chocolate eyes and olive skin would have caused havoc with the females. "Your parents must be so proud of you, Lucas."

When he didn't respond, she turned around. His eyes were closed. "My parents died when I was thirty."

"Oh, Lucas, I'm so sorry." Laura sat at his side. "I didn't know."

"It's okay. You wouldn't have known unless I'd told you. No one around here knows, apart from Aiden. It's why I came here. My mum died suddenly after a short illness. My dad wasn't in the best of health himself at that point. He didn't cope without her. He gave up and died not long after. I sold my dad's practice in Devon. There were too many memories there and nothing to tie me to that area anymore. I'm an only child, you see. I came here to spend some time with Aiden. To recover, to grieve in peace, and well, the rest is history."

Laura tried to steady her wobbling lips. Lucas had been through so much in his life. No wonder he could be abrupt. He wouldn't want to be bothered with the lipstick brigade with their fake smiles and giggles. No doubt he just wanted to make his parents proud and continue his dad's vocation. Laura couldn't imagine not having her mum and dad in her life anymore. The loneliness and loss of unconditional love would be heart-breaking. Her eyes filled with tears. She flicked them away quickly before they could fall down her cheeks.

"Hey." Lucas placed his beer on the floor. "I didn't mean to make you cry."

He reached for one of her hands and held it while she composed herself. She watched him trace a vein softly with his thumb on the back of her hand, not saying a word.

After a few minutes, he asked, "Better?"

Laura nodded as she wiped her eyes. "I'm sorry. Your story really got to me."

"There's no need to apologise, Laura. I just want to know you're okay."

Lucas leaned towards her and gently wiped her tears away with his hands. The smell of his aftershave combined with the faint trace of alcohol on his breath was intoxicating. Their faces were only inches apart. Laura's heart banged painfully against her chest and her stomach fluttered with a thousand butterflies. She closed her eyes, waiting for his lips to find hers.

"You've a piece of hay stuck in your hair." Lucas gently pulled a piece of straw away from her blonde curls.

Laura opened her eyes and blushed with awkwardness. What on earth? Had she really expected him to kiss her? More importantly, had she wanted him to? Lucas, of all people. It must be the wine, his story, their holding hands. She'd misread the signs. Oh God, the shame.

Lucas took a drink from his beer and leaned back against the sofa, closing his eyes. He was drunker than she realised, but he'd hidden it well. Had he noticed what had just happened? She hoped not.

"I should be getting home. It's almost midnight." Laura stood up, annoyed with herself. Her feelings were normally so guarded, but Lucas had lowered her defences tonight. The frustrating thing being, she couldn't blame him for any of it. He hadn't led her on or given her any impression he found her attractive.

"I'll walk you home." Lucas picked up his coat. He looked shattered.

"No. I'll get a taxi. Thank you for tonight. I'll see you Monday. What do I need to bring?"

"Just bring yourself, Nurse Nightingale."

*

Laura made herself a cup of cocoa. She took out her laptop and deleted her Lucky Cupid account. Her dalliance with Internet romance had ended. She now understood all the mixed feelings she'd had recently. It seemed her heart belonged to someone else, and that someone else belonged to Keely.

CHAPTER 25

Laura had butterflies in her stomach for many reasons. She had a morning appointment with Sam, then her first day in the surgery with Lucas. She didn't know which made her more nervous. She hadn't heard from Lucas since Thursday evening. Many texts had been prepared to send to him—they all varied in their content. Some thanked him for getting her out of the restaurant, some apologised for wanting him to kiss her, and some basically said she'd had a great night and she'd see him on Monday afternoon. Regardless, they all suffered the same fate and ended up in her delete box.

Amy arrived with her usual bubble of happiness. She gave Laura a quick peck on her cheek, then got down to business.

"So, I saw you leaving with Mr Sour Pants on Thursday to deal with his emergency. Did you get to see his stethoscope?" she teased.

Despite herself, Laura had to laugh. She played along with the joke. "Yep, it was very long and very hard."

Amy swooned against the worktop. "I know he's a miserable sod, but he is gorgeous, isn't he? I've never seen him drinking before. Did he walk you home after leaving the restaurant?"

"We called at his surgery first to check on a sick animal. I caught a taxi home."

"Did he not offer to walk you home?"

Laura knew she needed to tread carefully. She didn't want Amy picking up on her feelings for Lucas. "Yes, but I was happy to get a taxi. It was late when I left."

"I thought you only went to check on a sick animal. You left the restaurant at nine o'clock."

"Yeah, but we had a beer first."

"I never saw you. Were you in The Goose? We all went there after the meal."

Laura avoided eye contact with Amy. She could tell her neck and face were beginning to flush. "No, we went to his apartment above the surgery."

Amy looked at her, confused. "Why didn't you come to The Goose instead? It would have been much more fun than sitting on your own with Arsey Darcy."

"I don't know, really. I guess we just started chatting. Then it was midnight."

"You started chatting, and then it was midnight?" Amy repeated; her eyebrows raised. "I'm no brain surgeon, but I can spot something fishy a mile off. What are you not telling me, Laura Thompson?"

Laura sighed and put down the packets of bacon and sausages she had in her arms. She didn't want to lie to Amy. "He's more approachable than I realised. He mentioned his concerns with Mia leaving, and I offered to help in the afternoons. That seemed to break the ice. He offered to make me a drink. I accepted, then I came home."

Amy pointed her pencil at Laura. "I'm just going to take these breakfast orders. Then I want the truth, okay?"

Laura groaned and looked down at her hands. Astute should have been Amy's middle name. Nothing got past her, but did she feel ready to share her feelings for Lucas? Nothing could come of them, after all. Lucas and Keely were a couple. Perhaps Amy would see sense and not fly off on a romantic mission to try to get them together.

Amy came back into the kitchen and started to prepare the eggs, sausages, and bacon. Once everything had been plated up and served, she sat back against the worktop and looked at Laura. "Well?"

Laura wrung her hands with nerves. "Okay. I'm going to tell you something, but I don't want you to do anything about it. I just want your advice and nothing else."

"You like Lucas."

"Oh my God! How did you guess? I only realised myself Thursday night."

"Oh Laura, it's so obvious." Amy rolled her eyes and started to count reasons on her fingers. "Number one, you talk about him all the time. Mostly in a derogatory manner, but still, you talk about him a lot. Number two, you seek him out everywhere you go. You say you hope he isn't going to be there, and then your face falls when he isn't. Number three—"

"Okay, okay." Laura held her hands up in defeat. "But he's with Keely."

"Keely is a stop-gap. She's temporary. There's no way Lucas is going to spend the rest of his life with someone who concentrates on her nails more than him. Granted, she's good looking and she must be clever to hold down the job she does, but Keely isn't going to get up at three in the morning to make Lucas a hot drink when he's been out all-night lambing. She's not going to cancel nights out because he's shattered. She's not going to comfort him when he can't save an animal. You'll do all those things, Laura."

"But I don't know how he feels about me. Apart from last night, we've always fired off each other. He's barely spoken to me previously. He looks at me with that amused expression, as if I'm his personal entertainment. He winds me up most of the time, and I think he finds me irritating."

"Laura, that's just his way. He's a gentleman and he's also very private. If he liked you, I very much doubt he would make it obvious. He wouldn't want to make a fool of himself. He's not going to try out loads of different chat up lines on anyone. He'll be slow and methodical. He'll want to get to know you first."

Laura nodded. "He is a gentleman. I've seen that already, but he's still with Keely. I can't get around that. I won't act on my feelings while he's seeing her."

Amy nodded with sympathy. "I feel for you, hon', I really do. I don't know what's going on between them, but I truly don't think Keely and Lucas are a forever couple. They're not right for each other. You'll just have to hang in there, girl, and see what happens."

"But it's so frustrating," Laura groaned. "I can't stop thinking about him since Thursday, and now I've agreed to work alongside him during the afternoons. That means I'm going to be around him even more."

"Do you think he knows how you feel?"

Laura nodded her head miserably and then shook it. "I don't know, possibly. I made a bit of a fool of myself Thursday night. I thought he was going to kiss me, but he didn't. I raised my head to meet his, but he didn't kiss me."

"Ouch. What did he say?"

"He didn't say anything," Laura cringed as she remembered the awkward moment. "He acted like it hadn't happened. It was awful, Amy. He obviously has strong feelings for Keely, or he doesn't like me in the romantic sense. Either way, I'm out of luck."

"Not necessarily. It means he respects you both. That shows he's got scruples. Most guys would have kissed you, Laura, and then admitted later they had no intention of ever leaving their girlfriend. He saved you that humiliation."

Laura nodded as she absorbed Amy's words. "I suppose so."

"Has he ever given you any impression he likes you? Has he ever flirted with you?"

"I don't know." Laura sighed. "Maybe, a couple of times. The nightie comment, possibly. Nothing for certain. He's never done or said anything definite to make me think he likes me in that way. We've always just argued."

"Who could not like you, Laura?" Amy gave her best friend a big hug. "I hope Lucas comes to his senses and sees what's in front of him. Until then, you've always got me."

Laura returned her friend's big hug and held her tightly. "What would I do without you, Amy?"

"You'd have a very sad and boring life. I bet by Christmas day, you two are madly in love, making me and Sam look like an old haggard couple."

*

Laura walked into the village feeling better now that she'd spoken with Amy. She'd moved here to relax, not to fall in love. Not that anything would come of it, despite what Amy said. Lucas and her, they were like chalk and cheese. What was that old song? *'You like potato and I like potahto, let's call the whole thing off'.*

190

Sam already had someone in with him, an appointment that had run over. Laura sat in the waiting area with the receptionist.

"Morning, Laura." Sam ushered a red-eyed and flustered lady out of his office, asking his receptionist to make her a cup of tea and phone her a taxi home. He held the door open for Laura to walk through and directed her to a chair.

"Bad morning?" she asked, seeing all the crumpled tissues on his desk.

Sam grimaced while he cleared his desk. "People can be cruel. Even after their death. Anyway, Mr Leon Finch and his land ownership claim." Sam pulled a folder out from his drawer. "I still haven't found anything legal on building permissions, and to be honest, I think we need to close the door on that one. I've considered other clauses instead. If he owns the land your B&B is built on, then he has a duty to maintain it, until at a point where he sells it on. You've already stated the proposed eighteen thousand is a ridiculous price, so let's go down the route of him continuing to own the land. My proposals are the following."

Sam pushed a list towards her. Laura read the contents and started to smile.

1. Upkeep of gardens, approximate quote of £35 per month from landscaping services.

2. Uneven paths in garden, causing trip hazard. Approximate quote of £350 for a new path.

3. Waterlogged garden, left-hand side of Bed and Breakfast property, risk of damp. Approximate quote of £90 for initial work and £1,000 for damp-proof course if treatment fails.

4. Broken manhole cover to rear of property. Approximate cost of replacement and new frame £250.

5. Large apple tree leaning towards main building, causing possible foundation disturbance. Felling cost of £500.

"How do you know all this?" Laura asked Sam, still smiling.

"You signed a form giving me permission to walk around the B&B. I took the liberty of doing that one afternoon. I think you were out. I did knock first. I hoped to find faults around the property. The notes I took are what you have in your hands. I've always been aware of this clause, that if you own land, you have a duty to maintain it. That apple tree, though, did concern me. You may want to consider having it felled, regardless."

Laura added up the approximate cost in her head. "That's over two thousand pounds already! Are we going to ask him to pay for these jobs?"

Sam shook his head, "No, Laura. We are not going to ask him. We are going to demand it. I will also insist on a completion date of eight weeks for all work to be completed."

Laura stood up and hugged Sam. "You are amazing!"

Sam laughed, "If Leon wants to play dirty, he can play dirty. I'm ready and waiting."

Sam had really surprised her with his new tactic. No way would Leon agree to all this work. Best of all, Sam seemed unlikely to back down. "I really wouldn't like to be on the wrong side of you, Sam."

"I'll have this list emailed to him immediately, with a request that he agrees to either arrange for the work to be done or pay you the money to have it done yourself. I'll be chasing up his response before Wednesday. I'll also include with it a summary of legal responsibilities when you own land. No doubt that will frighten him. The items on my initial list are only the start. The big items, such as drainage, fencing and flood defences are not yet named, but they are all relevant. If he's as smart as he appears, he will research this himself. My guess is, before Friday, he will regret purchasing that piece of land. I expect he will want rid of it immediately. Now, I'm afraid that may mean us agreeing to buy it back, but I would imagine he will only want what he paid for it, which is a lot more agreeable than the eighteen thousand he first quoted. Don't you think?"

Laura breathed a sigh of relief, "I don't know what to say, Sam, except thank you."

Sam stood up and shook her hand. Laura loved the fact that when they were out socialising, he would give her a hug and a peck on the cheek, but when in work, he returned to a professional. It made him even more adorable. She envied Amy so much, having this man in her life.

Laura left the solicitors feeling lighter than air. This had to be a step in the right direction. She stood on the harbour wall and took a deep breath of fresh air, while admiring the view of her beautiful B&B, standing strong on the edge of the cliffs. Even in autumn, when the flowers were no longer in bloom and the wisteria and roses had lost their leaves, it was still the most beautiful house in the village.

Laura called in at the Harbour Café and bought three cups of strong coffee, then headed to the surgery. The butterflies returned to her stomach as she rounded the corner onto the village green. She felt excited about seeing Lucas again, but also nervous. Over the weekend, she'd thought about Thursday night a lot. Lucas had been quite drunk. Maybe he hadn't noticed the bit where she'd lifted her head for a kiss. She preferred this version of events. It gave her the courage to knock on the surgery door.

"Come in, come in!" Aiden led her into a small kitchen at the back of the reception area. "We keep the front door locked during dinner time, otherwise we get no rest. Welcome to our little team, Laura. Can I say how pleased we are to have you join us? We need all the help we can get at the moment, don't we, Lucas?"

Laura's heart beat fast as Lucas raised his head and nodded to her with a brief smile. His face remained completely passive as he read through a file of notes. *Okay*, thought Laura, *he's back to being distant.* But this didn't annoy her anymore, knowing that underneath his offhand exterior lay a different person. She sat down on a chair and handed around the takeaway coffee.

Aiden took his gratefully and pulled the lid off straight away, inhaling the strong aroma. "I love her already, Lucas. Look after this one. See you later."

Lucas gave Aiden a warning look, then returned to eating his salad box.

"Where's Aiden going?" Laura felt awkward on her own again with Lucas. She hoped they could get back some of that friendly banter they'd had.

"Farm rounds," Lucas replied, not giving her much eye contact. "He'll be back in a few hours if everything runs smoothly."

"Oh, okay." Laura sat on a chair, wondering what to do or say next. She watched Lucas as he cleared away his plate and washed the few bits of cutlery. His white t-shirt clung to his chest. She'd never realised before just how broad his shoulders were. His light blue jeans fit his frame snuggly, and she blushed as she tried to avoid looking at how they outlined his lower toned body.

"Have you eaten already?" He turned around suddenly, making her jump. "I can make you something if you like. A ham sandwich or chicken? There's normally something in the fridge."

Laura shook her head as she sipped her hot coffee, "I had dinner earlier, but thank you."

"Okay then. Let's get started."

He ran his eyes over her body as she stood up. She looked down at herself, then back at him. "What? Is there a problem?"

"No, not at all. I'm just thinking that Mia's uniform should fit you. Do you want to try it on? She stopped wearing it when she discovered she was pregnant."

Laura hadn't considered she might need to wear a uniform, but she agreed regardless. His house, his rules. He led her into a small clean bathroom and handed her a white uniform which fastened down the front. Without a word, he closed the door, leaving her alone to get changed.

Laura tried to pull the uniform on over her jeans and t-shirt but failed. Should she wear this instead of her clothes? It seemed so. She stripped down to her bra and knickers and pulled the uniform on. It fitted snuggly around her full bottom. Laura pulled at the material, but it remained tight to her frame.

The image in the bathroom mirror made her laugh. This outfit didn't exactly go with her converse, but it would have to do. At least she'd shaved and moisturised her legs this morning. Things could be worse. She gathered her clothes together, then joined Lucas at the reception desk.

He lifted his head and glanced at her as she walked self-consciously over to him. As he caught sight of her converse, the corner of his mouth lifted in a slight smile. Two months ago, this would have infuriated Laura. Today she humoured him.

"You didn't warn me about a uniform. I'd have worn more appropriate shoes."

"It suits you," he replied, "apart from … sorry, but you seem to have missed a button."

Laura looked down to find her pink bra on show through the gap in an unfastened button. Her fingers fumbled to close it as Lucas looked at the computer screen.

"I should have said this before, but tomorrow, could you tie your hair up? Just for feeding and cleaning the animals?"

"Of course. Where should I start?"

"Well, we can deal with all the boring red-tape. I just need you to sign a few forms, then I'll give you a quick run through the database. It's not complicated."

Lucas sat at the side of her as he explained the system. Laura found herself examining his face. His dark eyebrows, stubble, and long eyelashes. His hands were scratched, most likely from fighting feline customers. Laura could feel his breath on her cheek as he leaned over her to type in a password. She felt herself shiver in response.

"Are you cold? I have a fleece upstairs. Do you want to borrow it?"

"No, I'm fine, thanks. Just nerves, I presume."

"Why are you nervous?" Lucas examined her face, his eyes trained on hers.

"I don't know, really. Probably just first day heebie-jeebies." God, she wished he wouldn't keep looking at her like that. Her temperature seemed to change by the minute around him.

"As long as it's not me that makes you nervous. Would you tell me if I did?"

Laura nodded. She had no intention of telling him anything.

Lucas led her back into the hospital bay. Nina lay peacefully on her blanket, her large stomach indicating the kittens were still on board. At the front of each cage were notes regarding medication and feeding patterns. He explained the basics to her.

"It all sounds simple," Laura replied. "I'll let you know if I have any problems, but I'm sure I'll be fine."

"I'm sure you will be, Nurse Nightingale. I have absolute faith in you. I remember your cleaning skills the night of Olly's accident."

Laura blushed as she recalled what else he may have remembered. Her clothing hadn't exactly been appropriate for a start.

Lucas seemed to read her mind. "Hopefully today will be less stressful than the last time we worked together. We're back open in a few minutes. Will you be okay if I leave you to it? Your main duty is the reception area. If you do get a chance to feed and change the animals, that would be great. If not, your help with the phones and appointments will be appreciated."

Afternoon surgery started. The constant stream of customers and phone calls made her wonder how Lucas had coped on his own last week. Sometimes he would come to the reception area to query an appointment, but mainly he stayed in his surgery, much to her disappointment.

An elderly man walking through the door with a whining Alsatian broke her reverie. "It's an abscess under her tooth," he explained. "She gets them all the time. I've no appointment, though."

The suffering dog lay on the floor and continued to cry. Lucas opened his surgery door and popped his head around the corner. "I thought I heard a desperate cry for help. Another abscess, Fred?"

The dog stood up and raised her hackles at the sight of Lucas. Her teeth bared in anger. Laura watched in fascination as Lucas approached the poor animal and started to talk to her gently, before finally managing to stroke her aching and throbbing head. Lucas kneeled and with little effort, picked up the heavy dog and carried her into his surgery, kicking the door shut with his foot as he went.

He appeared ten minutes later with his jeans sopping wet. "Didn't quite go as cleanly as I'd hoped." He winced. "Told you my job has many drawbacks." The Alsatian came through the door wagging its tail, looking around the reception area with interest.

"What did you do?" Laura asked. "That dog is a different animal."

"I just drained a dental abscess. It's a simple enough procedure, but I always count my fingers before and after." Lucas wiggled his scratched hands in front of her, making her laugh.

Laura found she really enjoyed herself. Many of the customers she already knew from the village. They chatted to her freely as she made their appointments and asked about their pets.

Lucas came out of his surgery and glanced at his watch. "You still here? You're only contracted to work four hours."

Laura gasped as she checked her watch. "I had no idea of the time. I can stay longer if you need me?"

Lucas shook his head. "Aiden has rung to say he's on his way back. We close in two hours anyway, but thanks for the offer."

Laura went into the bathroom and changed back into her own clothes, suddenly reluctant to leave. This time last week she would never have considered working in a vet's office, especially not alongside Lucas, but it had gone well.

"Are you coming back tomorrow?" Aiden walked in via the back door, smelling of manure and covered in mud. "As you can see, Lucas gets the easy jobs."

Laura giggled. "Yes, I'm coming back tomorrow."

"Good. Does that mean Lucas behaved nicely?"

"I'm always nice," Lucas replied. "See you tomorrow afternoon, Laura."

CHAPTER 26

Laura went back to her annex feeling drained, but strangely happy.

Could she cope with this? Working alongside Lucas, knowing nothing would ever happen between them? Spending time with him today had been amazing, but would she still feel like that in a few weeks? If her feelings for him grew, she would have to consider leaving. Unrequited love wasn't on her plan for this year. She had enough to deal with.

Her pyjamas were warming near the log burner. She pulled them on and sat down with something to eat. The scent from her lavender candles started to relax her. Whatever happened, she would cope. After all, wasn't there meant to be a soul mate out there for everyone? She would find hers, in time. If someone else didn't get there first.

Bronte started to paw at the door. Laura smiled, hearing the familiar clunk of metal crutches. She drew back the heavy curtain and unlocked the patio door, shivering as the cold air hit her.

"Hmmm, Indian." Olly sniffed the air as he sat on a chair near the fire. "Shall I come back later?"

Laura smiled. He seemed to have settled in already. "Let me get you a plate. There's enough food for two."

They ate in companionable silence. Olly stretched and patted his stomach. "I'll have to start exercising again after tomorrow. I've put on tons of weight."

"You haven't," Laura lied, thinking to herself how much he suited the extra weight around his face. John's home cooking obviously agreed with him.

"When do you go to London with John?" Olly carried their plates into the kitchen, hobbling as he went.

"Next Monday." Laura wasn't sure how much John had told Olly about Alice, his potential daughter.

"He's alright, though, isn't he?" Olly looked worried. "He's not visiting a specialist there, is he? He's not ill?"

"No, I don't think so," Laura replied, trying not to give too much away, but also keen to offer reassurance. "I'm pretty sure he's meeting a family friend. I'm going with him to start my Christmas shopping. We'll be company for each other on the train. He's not ill as far as I know, Olly. There's no need to worry there."

Olly breathed a sigh of relief. "I'm glad. He's been a bit quiet about this trip, and I didn't want to pry. Anyway, on a more positive note, my cast comes off tomorrow. I'll need lots of physiotherapy, then hopefully I can get back to work. Speaking of work, how did your first day go at the vet's?"

Laura wished she had a script to read from. At least she had Amy's feedback. *Don't talk about Lucas. Not even in a derogatory way.* "I enjoyed it. It's really busy in there. Aiden is friendly, and the customers chatted away to me. I'm looking forward to going back tomorrow."

"And how about the main man himself? Did he make you feel welcome?"

"Who, Lucas?"

"Who else?" Olly raised an eyebrow. "Did you argue?"

"No. We got along just fine."

"He's got a good reputation around here as a vet. Lots of people respect him. I know the ladies like him."

"Hmm. I have noticed the surgery has a lot of female trade," Laura replied.

"Does that bother you?"

One thing about Olly, she thought, *he doesn't mince his words.*

"Why would it bother me? I'm not his girlfriend. He can talk to whoever he wants to."

"Oh yes, the sultry Keely. I've seen her in The Goose a few times with Lucas and his cycling group. Is she one of them?"

"Yeah, they met through that group. She's also a physiotherapist. Head of her department at the hospital."

"Physio?" Olly wriggled his eyebrows. "I hope I get her tomorrow then!"

Laura threw a cushion at him, which he caught, laughing.

"You know, Lucas asked me about you a few nights after my accident. He wanted to know what brought you here."

"Yes, we've had that conversation. He knows about Jemima."

"Does he know about Leon?"

"No."

"Why not? It's a big part of your life."

Laura paused before replying. If Olly knew how she felt about Lucas, he would tease her mercilessly. "Lucas is more of an acquaintance. I don't know him well enough to talk about my personal life."

"But you know him well enough to invite him into your annex after you'd been drinking."

Laura blushed. Deception didn't seem to be a skill of hers. Her mum had always said she wore her heart on her sleeve, left herself open for people to see the vulnerable side to her. "That was different. I wasn't thinking properly that night."

"Oh, Laura. If you want something, get up and get it. Don't be one of those people who wake up and realise they've missed their chance."

Laura's cheeks burned. "You're talking nonsense."

Olly sighed. "I know you're attracted to him. I'm just a humble bloke, but I've seen the signs."

Laura looked down at her hands. Bronte lifted his head and placed it on her knee, sensing her upset. She stroked his silky ears as she thought. Her feelings lay deeper than attraction with Lucas. She was falling in love with him and that scared the hell out of her. He could be rude, abrupt, argumentative even, but she had seen another side to him recently. A side she wanted to see more of. However, it all came back to Keely. With her on the scene, Lucas was out of bounds.

Olly took her silence as admittance. He pulled his chair around to face her. "If you want my opinion, make him see what he's missing out on. You know what guys like, don't you? I'll give it to you straight. We are simple creatures. We like the female form in whatever shape it comes in. We like boobs, bums, legs. We are fascinated by how women walk, talk, sit, move and dance. But what attracts us most is what's inside, like kindness and confidence in yourself. Show him you are a strong woman who will stop at nothing to get what she wants."

Laura absorbed his words. It sounded so easy, being confident. However, the truth had to be acknowledged. She wasn't that sort of person. She couldn't imagine ever flirting with Lucas. If he ever got wind of her feelings for him, he'd either laugh hysterically, or cringe with embarrassment. Lucas did seem to go for strong women, like Keely. He obviously felt attracted to that kind of person. The complete opposite to Laura. Her feelings were doomed before they even began.

"Olly, can you imagine me flirting with Lucas? Short dresses, sashaying around the building like a model? Making him laugh with my witty repartee. It's just not me."

"You don't have to make it so obvious. That would be a turn off for most men. Be subtle. Let me tell you about how I met my Katie. She worked in a book shop. Each day I would go in with the excuse of being interested in American history, of all things. I bought pretty much every book in that section over a series of a few months, just so I could talk to her. One evening I opened one of the books. A few numbers were written in pencil at the top of the first page. It intrigued me. I looked at each book. All had a few digits scribbled in them. I remembered the order I'd bought them in, put the numbers together and rang them. She answered."

"That's so cute, Olly. Where did she get the idea from?"

"A book, apparently. We've been married for four years now. I love how she picked up on my reason for visiting her shop, but dealt with it so subtly, yet with such confidence."

Laura nodded. She understood the message.

"I'm going." Olly stood up and hobbled to the door. "By the way, John and me are going to The Goose tomorrow night to celebrate my cast coming off. Are you joining us? Drinks on me?"

"Try and stop me."

CHAPTER 27

Laura went through her underwear drawer and pulled out a white lacy bra and a pair of matching knickers. With Olly's words in her head about being more confident, she dressed, curled her hair, and added a slight touch of bronzer to her already sun-kissed cheeks. Who said you had to look drab when suffering from unrequited love?

As good as her promise, Amy didn't tease her about Lucas as they cooked breakfasts together. She listened without judgement and offered bits of advice where she could.

"So, given Olly's story, what's the plan of attack for today?" Amy struggled with pillowcases and fresh duvet covers.

"Be more confident. I'm going to engage him in conversation. Maybe find some common ground between us. Whatever I do or say will be subtle and light-hearted."

"So, you don't plan on having sex on his surgery table?"

"Amy, no! But I am going to make sure I give him no reason to laugh at me. I want him to see me as an equal in his social and professional life. So far, I feel like I've always been at a disadvantage around him, but not anymore."

"Laura, you make it sound as if you're batting out of your league with him. Believe me, he'd be lucky to have a girl like you. Intelligent, beautiful, successful…."

"Yeah, with a land claim debt hanging over me, a loser of an ex-boyfriend living down the road and short stumpy legs. Do you know he's over a foot taller than me?"

"Don't underestimate a short girl! They are normally stronger than us all. Olly's right. Just be yourself. He'll be cricking his neck to kiss you in no time."

*

"You don't need to buy us coffee each day." Aiden opened the door and guided her into the waiting room. "I may grow accustomed to this treat on a daily basis."

"There's a method in my madness. I keep you both sweet, you won't make me clean out the guinea pigs again."

"Did Lucas make you do that? That's the worst job of them all. I'll have words with him later." Aiden grinned to show he was joking.

Laura walked into the kitchen to find Lucas eating his dinner. She sat down at the side of him and opened her own sandwich. Lucas opened a packet of crisps and pushed them her way, ripping open the bag, so they could both take their share.

"Did you enjoy yesterday?" Lucas finished his sandwich. He looked at her intently as she ate.

Laura mumbled, pointing to her mouthful of crisp, trying to swallow them quickly so she could speak.

"Just nod or shake your head." He laughed. "I don't want you choking."

Laura nodded. Not a great way to impress him, she thought, already at a disadvantage.

He stretched his long legs under the table. "I'm glad you enjoyed it."

Laura sipped her coffee, watching him read case notes. His eyes scanned the document quickly, and he bit his lip as he absorbed the information. He looked tired. Laura wondered if he'd spent the night with Keely. What if they'd stayed up most of the night making love? No, she shook her head. Confident thoughts only. Engage him in conversation. Now seemed as good a time as any.

"So, what does a vet do when he's not looking after animals?"

He put his paper down. "Do you mean, what do I do when I'm not working?" He smiled.

"Yes." She inwardly cringed. It was a random question. Regardless, she held his gaze confidently.

"Well, I cycle a lot. Sometimes I swim or surf. I like being outdoors when I'm not working. How about you?"

"Erm ... I like walking. Hills, fields, streams. That kind of thing." Her cheeks started to throb as they went pinker. He must think her so boring.

"But not with hairy-faced dog owners?" He grinned.

Laura had to laugh. "Thank God I escaped." She fanned her face with a magazine on the table to try to reduce the heat in her cheeks.

"You're hot?"

"Pardon?"

"Sorry. It was a question. You look hot. Overheated. Are you too warm?"

"No, I'm fine, thanks. I'm not hot."

He looked at her out of the corner of his eye. "I'd disagree with that statement." He stood up and poured her a glass of water.

Laura took the glass with a shaking hand. She really needed to get a grip of herself. What happened to being witty, funny, confident? Right now, she felt none of those, and he was still looking at her with that amused smile.

"I'll go and get changed." She walked into the small bathroom, feeling frustrated with herself. Why couldn't she be more like Amy? Confident and outgoing. Why couldn't she just relax around him? The answer being, she liked him too much, and she really didn't want him to know.

Uniform on, and Laura instantly regretted her choice of underwear. The lacy bra didn't pose a problem. You couldn't see it through the uniform. The tiny lacy knickers, however, were a different matter. The uniform clung tighter than she'd remembered around her bottom. She turned around, looking at herself in the full-length mirror, and groaned. Well, she had two choices. She could either wear the tiny frilly bit of lace and hope he wouldn't notice the outline, or she could take them off and risk not falling over. As luck was never her strong point, she opted to stick with the knickers and hope for the best.

She walked into the reception area, feeling very self-conscious. Five minutes to opening time.

Lucas sat on her chair, reading something on the computer. "You've not tied your hair up." He pointed to her wavy curls.

Laura cursed under her breath. "I had to buy a bobble from the shop. It's not my usual style. I forgot to use it." She pulled the hair bobble off her wrist. It pinged under the desk and disappeared.

"Bugger," she whispered.

Lucas looked at her and laughed. "It's not a problem, I'll get it." He got down on his knees and retrieved the pink sparkly bobble with a plastic unicorn attached. He looked at it in surprise.

"It's all they had in the shop," she replied with a sigh. It seemed confident and sexy were not going to be on her agenda today.

"I think it's kind of cute." He twisted the bobble around in his large hands. "Turn around. I'll do it for you."

"Sorry? Do what?"

"I meant, I'll put your hair up for you. I'm intrigued by this pink unicorn bobble."

Laura turned around, conscious of the tight uniform, her lacy knickers, and how close he stood to her. She felt his hands as they scooped her hair up away from her neck, gently and carefully. She breathed in his aftershave deeply. Her legs felt like jelly.

"There we go." He turned her around to face him. "I've now mastered how a hair bobble works."

He looked into her eyes fleetingly as her heart began to race. She felt like a love-struck teenager, incapable of talking to her crush, just mumbling and making a fool of herself. Laura let her gaze drop to the floor. He had Keely. He was not hers to stare at, regardless of how beautiful his eyes were.

"Back to work, Nurse Nightingale. If anyone compliments you on your hair, remember, I didn't do it. I have a reputation to keep." He headed into his surgery and closed the door.

Laura stood behind the reception desk and blew out her cheeks. She was not cut out for this.

Lucas wandered between his surgery room and the reception, dealing with anxious pets and equally anxious owners. She had just finished a phone call when he opened his door and caught her attention.

A mother and her small son stood in one corner of his surgery room, looking sheepish, a small empty cage on the floor. From under one of the desks came the unmistakable sound of a guinea pig whooping.

"I can hear, even though I can't see your problem." She smiled sympathetically, shutting the surgery door behind her.

"My son opened the cage. The guinea pig ran out," explained the mother, cuddling her sobbing son.

"I can't get to it. Can you help me?" Lucas looked flustered. His hair stuck up as if he'd been running his hands through it, his cheeks flushed.

Laura smiled to herself, enjoying seeing the normally cool Lucas looking so ruffled. She stood at the other side of the desk and gently pushed it away from the wall. Lucas cupped his hands to capture the escapee, but he wasn't quick enough. The small animal scuttled across the floor and under the other desk. Lucas, in his attempt to capture it, slid along the floor and landed full length, empty handed.

"What I wouldn't give right now to be stocking shelves in a supermarket." He stood up and brushed hair and dust off his knees, while Laura smothered a grin.

She walked over to the computer desk and looked underneath. The escapee cowered against a stack of papers. Blocking most of the space under the desk, she knelt and tried to reach underneath.

Lucas knelt at her side, his voice barely distinguishable above the sound of the crying child. "This would be quite funny if I didn't have that big retriever in next. Rory will eat this guinea pig for its supper." He looked at her, then started to laugh.

"Stop it," she nudged him, laughing herself.

She twisted her arm under the desk, aware of her bottom stuck up in the air. "This isn't in my contract," she muttered, as she turned to look at Lucas. She caught him glancing briefly at her backside, then averting his eyes, his cheeks going pinker by the second. Laura smiled to herself. Maybe the lacy knicks hadn't been a mistake after all.

The guinea pig bit her a few times before she managed to get a hold. Lucas breathed out a sigh of relief and took the animal off her.

"I've rescued two pets for you now. Remember the kitten at The Goose, under the summer house?"

"How can I forget?" He checked Laura's bleeding hands. "Go and wash them straight away in the kitchen. I've got something to cleanse them with. I'll just finish up here. Give me a few minutes."

Laura headed into the kitchen, laughing under her breath. Each time she pictured Lucas, flying across the floor full length, she laughed even more. By the time he joined her, tears were rolling down her cheeks.

"I'm glad you find my occupation so amusing."

"It's just your face … I can't speak…"

Lucas started to laugh too. He shut the kitchen door and put his finger to his lips, "Ssshhh. I've a waiting room full of customers. They'll wonder what's going on, hearing us giggling like a pair of teenagers."

"How are your knees?" Laura wiped her eyes, trying to calm herself.

"They're killing me after that slide dive. Come on, we need to get back. Show me your hands."

"They're okay. I've washed them."

"Show me," he ordered. He held his large hands out to take hers and examined them carefully, turning them over slowly. "Wash your hands in this antibacterial wash."

"I'm okay. Honestly, it doesn't hurt."

"That doesn't matter. You're my staff, and it happened in my surgery. I'm responsible."

She washed and dried her hands. One of the bites started to throb. He rubbed antibacterial cream into the wound. The sharp sting caused her to wince.

"Sorry," he whispered.

Laura savoured the feeling of her hands in his. He looked so cute with his hair all ruffled, and his cheeks still flushed from laughing.

"All done." He placed her hand gently at her side.

"Do I get a sticker for being brave?"

"No, but you get a kiss." He bent down and briefly kissed her cheek, before opening the door and walking back into his surgery.

Laura's legs shook. She placed a hand to her cheek. Did that just happen? It was obviously a kiss from a friend to a friend, just a peck on her cheek, but she savoured the feeling, nonetheless.

CHAPTER 28

Her cheek had burned all afternoon, but there was nothing to see. Laura sighed as she left the surgery. This could get very complicated, for her at least.

She headed straight to the hut to see Olly, and found him on his bed, reading. Both legs were free of plaster.

"You've got one brown leg and one white leg," she giggled, kissing him on his bristly cheek.

"I know. I've some serious sunbathing to catch up on. I'm so glad to be free of that cast though. At least now I'm on the road to recovery. You've never seen me with two functioning legs before."

Laura gazed at the still vivid scar from his operation. She couldn't believe she'd seen the bone protruding from it, covered in dark red, sticky blood.

"How's your day been?"

Laura smiled. "Good. I'm still enjoying it."

"But I take it you're no closer to declaring your undying love to the good vet?"

Laura screwed up her face in frustration. "I can't, Olly. He doesn't feel that way about me."

Olly sighed and sat her down on his bed. "I don't know what to say, Laura."

"It's okay." She puffed out her cheeks. "I'll just have to get over it. Working alongside Lucas is wonderful.

However, in hindsight, knowing how I feel now, I'd never have agreed to it."

"So, are you going to pack in working for him?"

"I don't think I can. I must work for him for a whole month. It's part of our agreement."

"Oh, Laura, what a situation to be in. Come out with John and myself tonight and get sozzled!"

Laura smiled. "That sounds very tempting."

*

Laura offered to buy the drinks. She stood at the bar, taking in the posters advertising bookings for Christmas. Laura groaned, realising she only had two months to go. So much to do, so little time.

Out of the corner of her eye, she spotted Lucas and Aiden walk into the pub, deep in conversation. Lucas seemed frustrated, his arms gesticulating angrily. Aiden was doing his best to calm him down. Laura wondered if something had happened at the surgery after she'd left.

Aiden spotted her first. He patted Lucas' shoulder and pointed in her direction. Lucas sighed and rolled his eyes, his face a picture of irritation.

Aiden eventually broke the ice. "Who are you here with, Laura?"

"John and Olly," she muttered, still staring at Lucas' taut expression. "What's happened? Are you okay?"

"I'm fine," Lucas replied wearily. He took a deep breath. "How's your hand?"

"Good. It's healing well. Lucas, what's wrong? Have I done something to upset you?"

"No." He pinched the bridge of his nose, looking uncomfortable. "You haven't upset me."

Laura felt confused. Lucas could be abrupt when he wanted to be, but this was on another level. Almost as if he didn't want to be in her company. Then it dawned on her. He'd obviously figured out how she felt about him. Olly or Amy wouldn't have told him. He must have guessed. This must be his way of letting her know her feelings were inappropriate. Cruel to be kind, that kind of thing. Her heart constricted.

Lucas still refused to give her eye contact. Her heart beat faster against her chest.

"Lucas, do you want me to leave?"

He sighed. "No. I don't want you to leave."

Laura turned to Aiden, confused. He simply shrugged.

Keely broke their awkwardness. She walked into the pub wearing a tight black top and leggings, looking every bit the fit and healthy girlfriend. She motioned for Lucas to join her.

"I need to go." Lucas raised his eyebrows at Aiden. "I'll see you both tomorrow."

CHAPTER 29

Laura sensed an unusual mood in the surgery. Aiden greeted her, wearing his theatre scrubs instead of his usual waterproofs.

She had barely slept last night. A mix of hurt and embarrassment had filled her heart. She had considered not turning up today, but a part of her needed closure on Lucas' reticence last night. Maybe he would pull her aside today and explain that her services were no longer needed. That might be for the best, for them both.

Lucas finally appeared, encased in overalls and wellies. He gave her his customary nod, his face pale and drawn.

Aiden stood up and squeezed Laura's arm, sensing her discomfort. "Come on, let's wave Farmer Lucas off for the day. We swap duties every so often to keep our hands in. Literally."

"What's going on?" Laura looked at them both.

"Lucas is going to deliver a calf over at High Gate Farm, and I'm going to cover his surgery. This afternoon, my gorgeous Laura, you have me for company."

Lucas smiled at her wearily before picking up his medical bag.

"Are you okay?" she asked him quietly.

He nodded and gave her a thumbs up.

"Of course, he's alright. Aren't you, my darling boy?" Aiden slapped him on the back. "Just remember, the fat end is where the calf comes out."

Lucas gave him a black look as Aiden waved him out. "Be gone with you, man. Ring me if you've any problems."

"Can he really deliver a calf on his own?" Laura asked after Lucas had left.

"Of course, he can." Aiden laughed at her worried expression. "He's a very experienced vet. It's bloody hard work, mind you, especially if they get stuck or present breach. You always need calving chains or a rope for a calf. Cows can't deliver on their own, but he's done plenty of those unassisted."

Surgery that afternoon felt different without Lucas. Laura missed him desperately, but she put a smile on her face and made the best of it. Aiden turned out to be a humourist. He had the waiting room in an uproar, telling them tales of his training days with Lucas. He reminded her of James Herriot, even down to the flat cap he always wore on his farm visits.

At two o'clock, they experienced a rare break in appointments. Aiden invited her into the kitchen and made them both a cup of coffee. He encouraged her to sit down before pulling a chair up next to her.

"Are you liking it here?" he asked, blowing on his cup of coffee. "You don't find Lucas too overbearing?"

This was it. The conversation where Aiden would tell her Lucas wished for her to leave. She braced herself for the pain.

"I don't find him overbearing. Has he said something?"

"Nope. You know Lucas. He doesn't say much."

Laura paused. She needed to know the truth. "He was annoyed about something last night in the pub. I can't help thinking I caused that."

Aiden hesitated before answering. "Lucas has a lot going on in his personal life. He needs to reassess a few things. I know why you're asking was he annoyed with you. The answer is no. He's tired and weary. I was encouraging him to take a break from the surgery. It's me he's annoyed with. That's why he's on agricultural duties today. A change is as good as a rest."

Laura felt her shoulders slump with relief. Maybe her secret remained safe after all. Still, something had upset him. If it wasn't her, then what could it be?

"Is he okay, though? Lucas, I mean?"

"He'll be fine. He'll come up smelling of roses, like he always does. He's just messaged me, actually, speak of the devil."

"Is everything okay?" Already she worried about him. He wasn't even hers to worry about.

"He'll be fine. The calf is breach. He was just letting me know. Lucas can handle it, but his arms will bloody hurt tomorrow, all that pushing and pulling."

"It sounds unpleasant."

"Yeah, it can be. Sometimes you need to push the calf back into the birth canal to get its feet out. It's not a glamorous job, being a vet."

"You've known Lucas a long time, haven't you?"

"Yep, since Uni. We were in halls together. He was my roommate. I thought I'd died and gone to heaven when I saw him. However, my gaydar failed me. He's completely straight."

"Did you know his parents?"

"Ah, yes, he told me he'd had that conversation with you. Yes, I did know them. They were very good to me when I came out. It wasn't as common in those days to be gay. Lots of people judged me, including my parents. They didn't speak to me for a while, though we're fine now. Lucas never wavered, though. He stood by me through it all. Even when word went around that he was my partner, he never faltered."

Aiden took a sip of his coffee while he thought. "When his parents died, his world fell apart. He rang me after his dad's death, and I invited him to stay with Martin and myself. I held him like a baby while he cried. In fact, I'm not ashamed to admit that more than once, I sat up all night and cradled him until he slept. Nights always got to him. During the day, he would slap on a smile and come and drink with us, but the minute he crawled into his bed, I would hear the painful sounds of him sobbing. I never left him to cry alone. You see, me and Lucas, we are the same age, only a few months between us, but I became a father figure to him. I had to be strong after coming out, and I remained strong for him. We've maintained that relationship ever since."

"He speaks highly of you," Laura replied, feeling choked after listening to Aiden's version of events.

"Aye, well, the same in reverse. He just needs to sort his life out, that lad does. He needs to start living again. He's done his duty to his parents' memory. He owns this practice; did you know that? I'm a partner, but this belongs to him. I've not told you any of this though, okay? Lucas is very private. He won't wear his heart on his sleeve. He won't tell you when he's breaking inside. He'll just run himself into the ground trying to keep up. He needs the love of a good woman to support him."

"Well, he has Keely." Saying her name felt like a knife going through her back.

Aiden downed his cup of coffee and stood up, indicating their chat had ended. "Now that, young lady, is a part of his life I try to stay out of. Come on, let's get back to surgery. Lucas won't be happy until I get peed on at least twice today."

Without Lucas around, four o'clock came around slowly that day, despite Aiden's good company.

"Ha, the wanderer returns," Aiden boomed from behind the reception desk.

Laura's heart almost skipped with delight at the sight of a very dishevelled Lucas, rubbing his shoulder and grimacing in pain.

"Well, pink or blue?"

"Blue, another bull. I'm covered in cow muck and amniotic fluid and I'm sure I dislocated my shoulder and simultaneously put it back in, skidding across the floor trying to pull the calf out. I'm going for a shower. Has Nina had her kittens yet?"

Aiden shook his head. "Nah, she's showing no signs."

"I'll keep my ears open then. I'll see you tomorrow."

He gave Laura a brief smile. "See you tomorrow, too."

*

Laura headed back to her annex with mixed emotions. She tried to absorb everything Aiden had told her that afternoon. The more she thought about it, the more she fell in love with Lucas.

Not being able to act on her feelings felt like pure torture. Could she continue working with him while he belonged to someone else? But how would she cope with not seeing him every day if she left? It wasn't just the physical feelings, they were strong enough, but the emotional side too. The more she learned about him, the more she related to him. Whatever love she thought she'd felt with Leon was nothing in comparison to this. This thing with Lucas, it took over her heart and soul. She could barely look at him without wanting to hold him and kiss him and tell him everything would be okay. But that was not her place.

Darkness had fallen by the time she reached her annex. The clocks had gone back, throwing her out of rhythm.

A little bloom of smoke came from the log burner John had installed in Olly's hut. He waved from his small window as she unlocked her patio doors.

"Evening, Miss Thompson." He grinned, following her into her annex. "I've been waiting for you to come home."

Laura held her tongue. She wanted to spend the evening on her own, coming up with a plan for a life that would offer some happiness without Lucas in it. If such a thing existed.

"I've got some news." He sat down in her chair, smiling like a Cheshire cat. "And you're going to love it!"

"Really?" she hung up her coat on the back of the patio doors, while scratching Bronte's ears.

"I've been to the hospital today for more physiotherapy. Guess who my therapist was?"

Laura sighed. "Keely, perhaps?"

"Yes." Olly leaned forward in his chair, looking at her intently. "I have to admit, she was quite good, considering her bad news."

"What bad news?" Laura didn't want to know the ins and outs of Keely's life. So what if she'd broken a nail before therapy or been given a speeding ticket on her way to work.

"Oh, very bad news. Very, very bad news."

"Out with-it, Olly. I'm sorry, but I'm tired. I'm feeling emotional, and I might just break your other leg if you carry on winding me up."

Olly did a drum roll on the chair arms. "She's been dumped."

"What?" Laura turned around to look at him. "You mean she's broken up with Lucas?"

"Nope," Olly replied, relishing telling his tale. "He's broken up with her."

Laura sat down on the sofa with a thump. "How? When? Why?" she stuttered. "I didn't know any of this. He never said."

"I don't know all the details." Olly sat on the edge of his chair, glad that he had her full attention. "I couldn't hear much from the waiting room. I saw her run inside one of the treatment rooms, and I overheard her crying to one of her colleagues. I shouldn't have listened, but when she mentioned the name Lucas, my ears pricked up. Anyway, it turns out he went to see her last night, and he ended it with her."

Laura thought back to his strange mood this afternoon, "That explains his quietness today. I did wonder what had caused it. Why has he finished with her?"

Laura held her breath. Please, please, let it be because she'd been unfaithful. Something that would stop them from getting back together. Lucas didn't seem the type to end a relationship without consideration. Despite all his faults, he had treated Keely with respect. Something serious must have happened.

Olly grinned at her. "That's for you to find out. I have no idea why he's ended their relationship. It appears neither does Keely."

Laura sat back on the sofa and puffed out her cheeks. "I'm shocked. Of all the reasons for his strange behaviour today, I didn't expect this."

"Don't you see what this means for you, Laura? He's free for you to make your move. He's single and so are you."

That thought hadn't passed her by. However, given Lucas' low spirits today, replacing Keely may not be in the forefront of his mind. In hindsight, heartbroken seemed a better description.

Laura sighed and put her head in her hands. "I thought I'd be pleased, but now I just feel more confused. Plus, I feel sorry for Keely. I got the impression she liked him very much."

"Ha, would Keely feel sorry for you if the boot was on the other foot? I don't think so. Make your move, girl. Get your glad rags on and show him what he's been missing. This is what you wanted, Laura. You're both free agents and both adults. Use your feminine wiles and capture him before someone else does."

Laura twisted the rings on her finger. As if he'd be interested in her. He would hardly want to date a girl that wore her hair up in a pink, sparkly, unicorn bobble.

Olly sighed. "Look, Laura, I need to go. I'm due at John's. My mum is ringing me on his landline. She wants to come and stay with me over Christmas. Think about it, Laura. Spend some quality time with Lucas tomorrow and see how it goes. Look for the signs. If it's going to happen, it will happen, but you can help it along a bit. He's single. There's nothing standing in your way. Show him you love him."

How do you show a man you love him? She thought. If you're already a couple, there's a hundred things you can do. Cook him a nice meal. Take him for a romantic weekend away. Buy sexy underwear.

But if you're not together, if you love someone from a distance, then what? Laura rubbed her tired eyes. The Internet would tell her to listen to his dreams, compliment him on his looks. Laugh at his jokes. All the things Laura knew she wouldn't do. She couldn't even write her phone number in one of his books. His reading material stayed in his apartment and it was unlikely she'd be invited back up there again, not after last time. She had no option but to be herself and pray for the best.

CHAPTER 30

John brought in extra kindling for the log burner. He stoked it up before sitting back down with Bronte on his knee.

"I'm sorry, Laura," he apologised. "I know it's late, but I wanted to give Olly a bit of privacy while he's talking to his mum. I also wanted to check on arrangements for London on Monday. Are we still on for that?"

"Of course we are, John. I wouldn't let you down on something as important as this. Have you spoken to Alice since?"

"I've not spoken to her directly. I wanted to give her some breathing space. She did text earlier today to ask if we are definitely still meeting."

Laura thought John cut a lonely figure sitting on her sofa. She so hoped Alice would welcome him into her life. She understood Alice's adoptive parents had been her world, but John had so much to offer. He would be a good supportive friend to her, if nothing else.

Laura boiled the kettle and made them both a cup of tea while opening a packet of their favourite biscuits.

"Are you taking anything with you, John, when you meet her? Any photos of Lizzie, her birth mother? That photograph of her in the pink blanket, perhaps?"

"Yes, I'm going to take both, but I'll only show her if she asks if any such thing exists. I don't want to scare her off. I don't want to be a dad to her. I just want to get to know her. I want to see a piece of Lizzy..." John steepled his fingers and raised them to cover his trembling lips.

Laura didn't say anything. She knew John would be too proud to let her comfort him. Instead, she sat silently, nursing her cup of tea while John composed himself.

"I'm sorry, lass," he said at last. "I've thought about this and nothing else for the past few weeks. I just hope she's made a good life for herself. I'd like to hold her hand, I know that much. I'd feel like I had my Lizzie for one last time if she let me do that. Do you think that's inappropriate?"

Laura swallowed her tears and shook her head, not trusting herself to speak. "I think that's perfectly acceptable." She raised her cup of tea to cover her own trembling lips.

Laura had always appreciated her own mum and dad. Even now, in her thirties, living her own life and running her own business, she still rang them every week. Admittedly, they received an edited update. They still didn't know about Leon's land ownership claim, but they did know she was happy, healthy and financially comfortable. They didn't know about Lucas, either. Ignorance was bliss in some cases.

"Does Olly know about Alice?"

John shook his head. "He doesn't, lass. I want it to stay that way. Olly has been a new chapter in my life. He's like a breath of fresh air. I don't want to mix the two. When I'm with him, Katie and little Danny, I don't think about Alice, that's how I want it to remain."

Olly interrupted their conversation. He rubbed his cold hands and joined John on the sofa.

"All sorted. My mum is going to come down nearer Christmas and spend the festive season with us here. If the house is finished, of course. John, you've done loads while I've been laid up, but I need to start on the big stuff, like the roof and the damp proof course. Then I can start furnishing it and move us all here."

"Will your mum move here, too?" Laura asked.

"No, I can't see it," Olly replied. "Although we'd welcome her. She's got so much going on where she lives. She needs familiarity since her operation over summer. It was a cancer scare. She's fine now, just exhausted. To add to her problems, Alan Dearden, my stepdad, died only a few years ago. They married when I was five. Alan adopted me, and I took his name. My real dad died before I was born. Anyway, Mum goes dancing on Monday. Bingo on Tuesday. Soup kitchen on Wednesday. Blathering in the church hall on Thursday, and God knows what else Friday, Saturday, and Sunday."

"Busy lady." Laura giggled. "That's more than I do in a month."

Olly laughed. "Alan had a nickname for her, Busy Bee. Always buzzing around, going somewhere, doing something. In fact, the name stuck. For as long as I can remember, everyone has called her Bea. Most people think it's short for Beatrice. She'll enjoy coming here for Christmas, though."

CHAPTER 31

Laura awoke with a banging head. She had slid into one of those sleeps where nonsense trailed through her brain nonstop. Lucas With Keely. Lucas not with Keely. And a bit of Leon bulldozing buildings thrown in. *Why not?* she thought.

Only two rooms were occupied this morning. Laura had given Amy the day off to spend with her nieces and nephews, shopping for Halloween.

With Christmas around the corner, Laura needed to think about her plans for the festive season. So far, she'd received a lot of interest from people wanting to stay, but she hadn't confirmed anything with anyone. Ideally, she'd prefer to close the B&B and spend Christmas relaxing in her annex. Her parents understood her desire to rest and not return to Manchester. Anyway, they normally spent Christmas with their friends in a country cottage, somewhere remote. No doubt they already had this year's cottage booked.

Midday soon came around. As she walked to the surgery, her heart leapt into her mouth. Would Lucas talk about his split from Keely? Would he be upset? Would he be a broken man? Would his eyes be all red and swollen from crying all night? Would he break down and cry in front of her? Or would he simply retreat into himself and become even more rude and abrupt?

She found Lucas sat at the kitchen table in his usual chair, smiling at something on the radio.

He stood up when she walked in, opened the fridge, took out a sandwich and slid it her way across the table.

Laura looked at it in surprise. "What's this?"

"Ham sandwich," he replied with his usual amused smile that Laura had missed so much.

"It's chicken, not ham." She lifted the bread and peered inside to double check. His good mood confused her. She'd expected a sullen Lucas, not a seemingly happy Lucas.

"You've learnt fast, Laura. First test passed. I made myself a sandwich earlier and made you one too. I know you like chicken. You had it at the Italian. Remember?"

"How can I forget? This is really nice by the way, but I don't expect you to make my dinner."

"I made it because you don't expect it."

Aiden stood up and rolled his eyes. "I'll leave you two to it." He shook his head, smiling at the same time.

Lucas ignored him.

Laura ate her sandwich, her mind whirring. Lucas watched her. He laughed as mayonnaise smeared down her chin, and she wiped it away with her finger, smiling.

"Eat it all up. You're going to need some energy today. You'll have to assist me in surgery while my shoulder is bad. Don't worry, you won't be doing anything complicated," he assured her, as her eyes widened with uncertainty. "Just help lift baskets and hold animal's safe while I examine them. I won't ask you to do anything beyond your skill, or anything that would jeopardise your safety."

Laura spied her chance to quiz him about his gloominess yesterday. She looked him directly in the eye. "You were unhappy yesterday. I could tell."

Lucas puffed out his cheeks and stretched out his legs. "Yeah, I had a lot on my mind yesterday. It was good to get out of here and clear my head a bit. However, in clearing my head, I gained a sprained shoulder." He tried to move his shoulder, grimacing with pain.

"Anything you want to talk about?" She held her breath. *Please, please, please tell me you found Keely in bed with another man and you hate her and never want to see her again.*

Lucas shook his head. "It's fine. It's sorted now. I had to make a difficult decision, but I know I've done the right thing."

Laura let some of her breath go. *He'd done the right thing.* That had to be positive, didn't it?

"How was the birth? Bad, I take it, judging by your pain."

He laughed. "They're hard work. Stressful at times. I've done plenty of calvings before, but I don't like them."

"Why not? Because of the mess?"

Lucas shifted slightly in his seat, then mumbled, "Because I'm scared of cows."

Laura leaned forward, not sure if she'd heard right. "Come again?"

Lucas took a deep breath, then said more clearly, "Because I'm scared of cows."

Laura started to laugh. Surely not? The big, abrupt Lucas. The man of few words.

"Okay, okay." He raised his hands in admittance as Laura collapsed into fits of giggles. "It's always been a fear of mine. I could have murdered Aiden yesterday when he sent me on a calving. Horses, sheep, goats, pigs; not a problem. But cows, urgh. They are going to take over the world, with their giant udders and great big lumbering feet."

He did an impression of a zombie, making Laura laugh even more. "Was that the difficult decision you had to make? Whether to attend and deal with the calving on your own?" *She needed to know. She needed answers.*

Lucas stood up, wincing with pain. "No, unfortunately not. I would rather have delivered ninety cows, then milked them all after. Come on Nurse Nightingale, get your overalls on. We'll have a waiting room full of fluff and teeth to negotiate in a few minutes."

They barely had five minutes to themselves. The amount of knowledge a vet needed to know amazed her. Rabbits, hamsters, iguanas. He had answers for most people. The animals trusted him, and the owners respected him. No wonder his practice had such a good reputation.

The lipstick brigade were the only customers he became short with. Even Laura had to admit their reasons for appointments were questionable. Nevertheless, Lucas checked their pets and offered reassurance, without the smile.

As four o'clock approached, Lucas checked his watch and frowned. He had commented a few times now that Aiden hadn't come back.

He picked up his phone. "I've had a few missed calls off him. I'll be back in a minute."

He apologised to the customers in the waiting room and headed into the kitchen to ring Aiden. He returned, looking concerned. "I need to go to Cloverfield's. It's a farm on the other side of the village." He checked the contents of his medical bag. "A bull calf has collapsed on one of the farms. Aiden fears it's pneumonia."

"What about the surgery?" They still had a waiting room full of customers.

"We'll have to cancel their appointments and rearrange based on priority need. Leave it with me. I'll open up a late evening surgery, if needs be."

Laura changed out of her uniform, noticing as she came back that most of the customers had left the surgery.

Lucas bent down to pick up his medical bag, wincing as his shoulder jarred. He rubbed it with his spare hand.

"I'll get your bag for you. Have you taken anything for the pain?"

"Yeah." Lucas tried rotating his shoulder. "I can't take anything else for a while though."

Laura looked at him in concern. "Can you drive like that? I mean, you can barely move your arm."

Lucas rubbed his hand through his hair. "I'm not sure," he admitted. "I don't need this today."

Laura thought about what she needed to do that evening. Nothing that couldn't wait. "I can drive you. I'm insured to drive another car."

Lucas puffed out his cheeks, considering his options. He eventually nodded and passed her his car keys.

*

"What will happen to the bull?" She drove carefully along the country lanes, following the sat nav, trying to avoid the potholes. Nerves jingled around in her stomach, her usual reaction to being so close to Lucas.

"Depends. If it's advanced pneumonia, then quite often we must put them to sleep. I'm guessing Aiden already knows this is the case, and he wants me there for a second opinion, to reassure the owner."

"That's sad." Laura navigated the twisty roads, both grimacing as they hit a cattle grid. "Is it easier, knowing you are doing the right thing for the animal?"

"Sometimes. It's never easy to put an animal to sleep, regardless of the situation. My first few were horrible; it really tested my wish to follow this career. After a while, you realise it's the kindest thing to do."

Laura parked at the side of Aiden's car in the farmyard and walked with Lucas to the main barn, flooded with light.

Aiden welcomed them at the door, shaking his head sadly. "It's not good news, Lucas. I just need you to look and confirm my diagnosis. Then I'll do what's needed."

Lucas pointed to the main entrance of the farmhouse. "Go in there, Laura. We won't be long. I don't want you seeing this."

Laura waited patiently in the farm kitchen. So, this is the life of a vet. Long hours, unpredictable, always on call. Even with a sprained shoulder. It made her love him more.

*

"Bad news, I take it?" She joined Lucas back in the car.

"There was nothing we could do. It's nobody's fault. These things happen."

"Where's Aiden? Has he stayed behind?"

233

"No, he went home straight away. This kind of thing upsets him. We can't let the owners see it, though. We need to be strong for them, reassure them it's the right thing to do."

Laura nodded. "Have you ever cried over an animal? Putting it to sleep?"

Lucas cringed. "Only once. A dog belonging to an old man. If you've never owned a dog, it's hard to understand how strong the bond becomes. Anyway, he cried, I cried."

Laura smiled sympathetically. She understood the bond now that she had Bronte. God forbid anything should happen to him. "I would have sobbed my heart out for weeks."

Lucas gave her a slight smile. "It shows you care. Never hide behind your feelings. It gets you nowhere."

Laura raised her eyebrows. *If only you knew.*

"Have you eaten anything since dinner?" Lucas pointed to a cosy country pub. "I don't know about you, but I'm hungry. Pull in here. I've checked my messages. There's no need to run a late evening surgery."

They found a secluded booth near the back of the busy pub. Lucas slid into the seat opposite her and passed over a menu, "I'll get us some drinks."

Laura watched him walk across to the bar. *Did he have to be so good looking?* She watched as a few heads turned to get a better look at the tall, dark-haired man. *Make the most of these moments. If he ever found out, he'd run a mile.*

Lucas placed a latte in front of her. "I'm sorry it's nothing stronger."

Laura placed her hands around the warm cup gratefully. "I don't mind. It's been a long day. Alcohol isn't the top of my priority list."

Laura sipped her latte while glancing at Lucas. She'd had no idea that being a vet in a small village practice could be such hard work. He really did go above and beyond every day. He looked vulnerable, too. She wanted to take him in her arms and comfort him, but until she knew how he felt about Keely, she had to hold back.

Their knees touched under the table. Instead of moving, she left them to rest against his. Lucas didn't move his legs either. Their closeness caused a warm feeling to rise through her. She wondered if Lucas felt it too, but his face remained passive.

Eventually, she could hold back no longer. She needed answers. "Have you told Keely about tonight? She may be wondering where you are."

Lucas stirred his latte as if he hadn't heard her.

"Don't you think you should ring her?" She held her breath.

"We broke up," Lucas replied, still stirring his latte.

Laura didn't react. She didn't think she could pull off an Oscar nomination for feigning ignorance. She remained quiet, waiting for him to speak again.

He shifted awkwardly in his seat. "We wanted different things from life. It wasn't going to work. Best to move on quickly."

"Is that what upset you yesterday?"

He nodded his head. "It's never nice to let someone down. It wasn't pleasant. I don't take comfort from upsetting someone."

"She'll probably respect that." Laura didn't know what else to say.

"I don't think she did." Lucas winced. "She threw a dining room chair at me. It caught me on my shoulder, my sprained shoulder."

"Oh,"

Laura managed to keep a straight face. Lucas didn't. His lips eventually raised in a genuine smile. "Go on, tell me she was too high maintenance for me."

Laura didn't say anything. She knew better than to mock the end of a relationship. They could get back together tomorrow, and she would be the only one with egg on her face.

Their food arrived. Every so often, Laura looked up, watching him eat. He was so hard to read at times. "How long were you with Keely?"

"Not sure really. Maybe a few months. To be honest, I don't remember a time when we officially began. We started seeing more of each other, then one day she announced me as her boyfriend. I didn't want to embarrass her by denying it. It kind of went from there. How about you, with your ex? How long were you together?"

"Two years."

Lucas raised his eyebrows in surprise. "Wow! So, you know what it's like to be in love?"

Laura shook her head. "No. Looking back, I was never in love with him. My feelings were more of a desire to be part of something, to be needed."

"How do you know it wasn't love?" Lucas stared at her so intensely that she started to feel uncomfortable.

"I just know," she whispered.

Lucas picked up his half-eaten burger, then placed it back on his plate, his appetite done. "Have you ever been in love?"

Laura didn't know how to respond. She couldn't tell him the truth. If she explained she already loved someone, to the point where she felt incapable of breathing, then he would want to know with who. Telling him would jeopardise everything they had. Their friendship, working relationship, all the things she'd come to cherish. Her reply needed to be as vague as possible.

"There is the dream of being in love with someone." Laura placed her knife and fork down, keen to change the topic of conversation.

Lucas smiled gently. "I know what you mean. Anyway, it's getting late. I'll just pay for our food, then we'll head back home."

How could she tell him? Surely that had been the perfect moment? *You're the one for me. The one I dream about. The one I want to hold and kiss, until death do us part.*

Lucas returned, his face strained. This break up had obviously affected him more than she realised.

The cold air hit them both as they stepped outside. Laura pulled her coat around her tightly.

"I want to show you something." He cupped her elbow and guided her off the car park onto a small country lane. They came to a break in the hedges. Looking down over fields and hills, the coastline lay before them, its edge outlined by millions of twinkling lights from towns and villages. The stars above them lit up the sky like a shower of diamonds. Laura drew in a gasp as her eyes took it all in.

"I know," Lucas whispered. "It reminds me of my home in Devon. This is one of my favourite places. Sometimes you can see the aurora on a clear night. I'll have to bring you up the next time there's a known sighting. We can take a chance; hope we see it."

Laura couldn't think of anything more perfect than spending an evening alone with Lucas, up here, where no one could interrupt them. She could feel his presence so close to her, yet so unreachable. It caused her to shiver, partly with want of him, partly with the coolness of the night air.

"Are you cold?" He unzipped his jacket and pulled her towards him, her back flat against his chest. He wrapped his jacket around them both, his arms enveloping her to keep them close. She felt his hands come to rest just under her breasts. She ached for him to lift his arm and touch her.

"Better?" he whispered in her ear.

Laura didn't trust herself to speak. She simply nodded. The feeling of his arms wrapped around her were both agony and ecstasy. So close, yet so far away. She could feel his breath against the back of her neck. To turn around and kiss him, that's all she wanted. But she could imagine his reaction. He would no doubt be horrified. He would never be interested in someone like her.

For that reason, she knew she needed to make the most of this moment while it lasted. She shifted her feet and pressed herself closer to him, to feel his heartbeat against her shoulder, to enjoy his warmth and smell.

Lucas took in a deep breath and groaned as his arms tightened around her.

"Oh no, you're in pain." Laura moved away quickly. "I'm sorry, I forgot about your shoulder. I must be hurting you."

Lucas paused. "My shoulder is fine, Laura. It's just..."

"I know. It's late, and you've had a difficult day. We need to drive home."

Laura reluctantly moved away from his hold and turned to face him. His eyes were filled with an emotion she couldn't place. She'd been as close to him as she would ever get, his heartbeat against hers. It would be the benchmark for every relationship she would ever encounter. Nothing, or no one, would ever surpass this. The thought of that almost stopped her own heart from beating.

"I'll drop you off at the surgery and walk home." Laura pulled her seat belt around her. "You'll need your car in the morning."

Lucas shook his head. "No need. Aiden is on call tonight, not me. Drop me off at the surgery and take this car to the B&B. You can drive it back when you come for surgery tomorrow afternoon, okay?"

As they pulled up outside the surgery, Lucas turned to her. "You've been quiet tonight, Laura. Have I upset you?"

Laura shook her head and smiled lightly. She needed to be careful about hiding her emotions. "I'm just tired. It's been a long week."

"Is this too much for you? The afternoon surgeries. You can stop coming anytime you wish, I'll understand."

"NO!" Laura said, with such ferocity that Lucas laughed. "I mean, it's not too much for me. I'm enjoying it."

"You mean you enjoy watching me humiliate myself, diving across floors for small furry animals, just so I can clip their nails?" He rolled his eyes in mock frustration.

It made Laura giggle, despite her melancholy.

"Drive home safely, Nurse Nightingale. I'll see you tomorrow."

CHAPTER 32

She slammed her alarm clock down and groaned. The chilly air made her shiver, reminding her to change the heating settings to come on earlier. She opened her curtains, peering outside into grey drizzle and cloud.

She longed for another fifteen minutes, but as her B&B was full this morning with another rambling group, she needed to be ahead of the game. At least they were all leaving today, which meant she could stay in bed tomorrow morning. She got up, showered and dressed, last night's events coming back to her with each movement.

The oven warmed the main kitchen as she prepared for breakfasts. The solitude of early mornings always calmed her soul, knowing she had a full hour to herself, uninterrupted.

What on earth? The massive crash came from her front room. With shaking legs, she ran through the hallway to find her front window smashed, a brick lying on the middle of the rug.

At first, she felt too stunned to move, then the adrenaline kicked in. She ran to the front window. Nothing. Her heart banged against her chest. Who would do this to her and why?

Glass splintered around her feet. She found a dustpan and brush and started to sweep up as much glass as she could.

"Oh my God, Laura. What's happened?" Amy stood at the front door, her mouth wide open. "Has someone just chucked that brick through your window?"

Laura nodded shakily. "They have, but I don't know who or why. I couldn't see anyone. It's too dark."

"You need to ring the police." Amy said angrily. "If for no other reason than claiming on your insurance. Do you think it's kids?"

"I honestly don't know. I feel so shook up."

"Where's Lucas?" Amy looked around, as if expecting to see him.

"I don't know. Probably at the surgery. Why?"

"His car's outside. I just presumed he was here. I thought maybe..."

"Well, you thought wrong," Laura snapped, walking back into the kitchen.

Amy followed, putting her hand on Laura's shoulder apologetically. "I'm so sorry. That was insensitive. Please forgive me."

Laura sighed and turned to hug her best friend. "I'm sorry too, Amy. This has really shaken me up. Lucas isn't here. I had to drive him out for an emergency yesterday evening. I kept the car after dropping him off. He didn't spend the night here."

Amy cringed. "I'm sorry, Laura. It's none of my business either way."

A few of her guests approached the kitchen after breakfast to offer their support at the mindless vandalism. Laura thanked them but encouraged them not to worry.

"When did that happen? I never heard a thing." John walked down the hallway, two newspapers under his arm.

"About forty minutes ago," Amy replied. "We know no more than you do right now. Laura has phoned the police. I'm trying to find someone who can replace the window-pane."

"I can do that," John offered quickly. "I'll have it done in a few hours. Is Bronte ill, by the way? Lucas' car is outside."

"Ssshh," Amy whispered. "Laura helped him with an emergency last night. She drove him home and kept hold of the car."

"I did wonder," John replied quietly. "They've been spending more time together recently."

John disappeared off down the garden to wake Olly. Within ten minutes both men were outside the front of the B&B, looking for evidence. They returned empty-handed.

After the police had left, Olly put his arm around Laura's shoulders. "Do you think this is Leon? Why didn't you mention him to the police?"

"It was the first thought on my mind. I can only think he's suddenly lost his temper over Sam's letter. But why now, why this morning, is beyond me. I just hope he doesn't do anything else. I've enough on my plate. I didn't mention him to the police because I want to speak with Sam first. It may harm my case against him if I accuse him of this."

"Well, John and I were talking earlier. I'm going to stay on in the hut for a while longer, keep my eye on things," Olly replied. "I don't like the thoughts of you alone here at night if Leon's playing silly buggers."

Olly saw Laura's frightened face, and he backtracked, trying to reassure her. "I don't think he'll do anything to hurt you, Laura, but you've got to admit, this has shaken you up."

Laura nodded her thanks. She felt more than shaken up. How much more could she cope with? Leon seemed intent on ruining her life. If he'd wanted to make her feel as miserable as sin, he'd succeeded.

CHAPTER 33

Laura drove down into the village in Lucas' estate car, parking outside the Harbour Café. The figure ahead stopped her in her tracks.

"Well, look who it is," Leon snarled. "Don't think those threats from your posh solicitor are going to frighten me, Laura. I've no intention of paying for any of that work or giving you any friggin' money. I've told you already, it's eighteen grand, or you pull that shed down. Got it?"

Laura shook from head to toe, but she had no intention of letting Leon know how much he'd frightened her. "Leon, I request that you deal directly with my solicitor."

Leon stood directly in front of her, so close she could count all the open pores in his skin. His breath smelled of beer and his eyes were bleary, his slight sway indicating he may be drunk, and it wasn't even midday. She tried to sidestep him, but he blocked her path. For the first time, she felt physically threatened by him.

"Where's your friend now, Laura? Your fat, loud-mouthed friend, who thought it would be funny to humiliate me in front of everyone. What about your gimp? What is he, ex-soldier? Recuperating, while you lick his wounds. I know what's going on with that vet of yours, too. I know he stayed the night. Tut, tut, he's using my castoffs already, I hope he enjoyed the ride. Does the village know you're shagging in that B&B? I bet you charge extra for those services, don't you? Keep them coming back for more."

Laura couldn't believe what she'd just heard. She knew he could sink low, but these words and insinuations were just horrible. A few weeks ago, they'd have brought tears to her eyes, but not now. This man and his foul mouth should be no match for her.

Leon stood back; his chest puffed out. His eyes shifting in and out of focus as he continued to sway in front of her. "Not denying any of it, are you? I always knew you were cheap."

Laura guessed his game. He wanted to provoke her. "Are you quite finished?" she asked calmly.

"No, I'm not," he spat back, spittle landing on his chin.

Laura noticed some of her rambler guests coming out of the newsagents. They waved to her, completely unaware of the altercation unfolding in front of them. Leon spotted them too. He retreated, like the coward he'd become.

"I'm watching you," he whispered. "Keep everything ticking over nicely for me. I'll own it all soon enough."

Leon banged shut his shop door, leaving Laura standing outside, shaking. She now had no doubt whatsoever that Leon had put that brick through her front window. He'd seen Lucas' car outside her B&B and jumped to the same conclusion as Amy.

*

Aiden took one look at her pale face and pulled her inside. "What's happened, Laura? Come on, let's sit you down in the kitchen."

Lucas stood up quickly, concern written all over his face. He put his arm around her shaking shoulders. "Talk to me. What's happened?"

She sat down, her chin wobbling, determined not to cry. Aiden made her a cup of tea and ordered her to drink it, while Lucas knelt at her side and held her shaking hand.

"It's my ex-boyfriend, Leon. He owns Rupert's sweet shop. I've had a few problems with him lately. I've just had an argument with him. It wasn't pleasant."

"Did he hurt you?" Lucas demanded.

Laura shook her head. "No, not physically."

"Did he threaten you in any way?" Aiden asked with concern.

Again, Laura shook her head, "Not in a violent way. He's just upset me with some of his vile insinuations."

"What has he said to upset you, Laura? Is there anything we can do to help?" asked Aiden.

"I really don't want to repeat what he said. Thank you for your offer of help, but it's complex. Sam Pickwick is dealing with a legal case between us. It's obviously turned nasty."

Lucas looked up at her, his face stern, his eyes dark. "He shouldn't be upsetting you, regardless of any legal case. Do you want me to go and have a word with him?"

"No, honestly, it won't help. It would only make it worse."

Laura took a deep breath. She knew Aiden and Lucas would hear via the village if not from her. "Someone put a brick through my living room window this morning. I think Leon did it."

Lucas jumped up and ran his hands through his hair. "You could have been hurt. I'm going around there now!"

Aiden put a hand on his shoulder. "Lucas let's try and support Laura in the way she feels is best. Are the police involved?"

Laura nodded. "They are now. I'll leave it to them and Sam to sort out."

Lucas sat down on one of the chairs, still running his hand through his hair. "We can't just do nothing."

"It's not our place, unfortunately," Aiden replied. "Laura, one thing I will say. When you are travelling to and from this surgery, you do it with someone, okay? I don't like the sounds of this Leon. Either Lucas or I will pick you up and drop you off. Is that understood?"

Laura nodded. "Thank you, but I'm sure I'll be fine."

"Regardless, that is my rule. Otherwise we will end your contract with us." Aiden looked for confirmation from Lucas, who nodded in agreement.

"Thank you, both of you. I really appreciate your support."

Aiden looked at his watch. "I do have to be on my rounds. Lucas, if you need me this afternoon, just ring and I'll come straight back."

What a morning, Laura thought as she changed into her uniform. She dreaded to think what else Leon would do if Sam continued with this legal battle. Laura washed her face to freshen herself up. The strong coffee Aiden had given her started to work. She felt less shaky.

Lucas jumped back when she opened the door.

"You look guilty, Lucas."

Lucas grinned and shook his head. "No, I was just walking past when you opened the door. It took me by surprise, that's all."

Laura watched his face turn colour. "Are you blushing? It makes a change for someone else blushing instead of me."

Laura watched his reaction as the blush crept slowly across his face. He laughed nervously. "I wasn't hanging around or trying to see inside."

"That's a shame. I've got matching undies on today."

This time Lucas turned a deep crimson. "Laura, you'll be the death of me. Stop trying to embarrass me."

"Come on, Lucas." She laughed. "You're very easy to wind up."

Despite her horrible morning, she had a good afternoon with Lucas in the surgery theatre. She learned so much watching him perform some of the procedures.

Lucas insisted that Laura help with some of the processes, like counting swabs and learning the instruments. She worried at first about the gruesome aspects, but instead found herself fascinated by the intricacies of his work. By late afternoon they were finished.

Lucas pulled off his gloves and stretched his back, grimacing slightly at his still sore shoulder. "I love Fridays. It's my favourite day of the week, but it takes it out of me. I'm shattered."

Laura filled the kettle to make them both a cup of strong tea. She suddenly realised she hadn't thought about Leon all afternoon.

She was reaching for another cup from the cupboard when Lucas coughed. She turned around to see him watching her. "What's wrong?"

He gave her his usual amused smile. "You said you were wearing matching undies. Your bra is white, and your knickers are black."

"What!" Laura pulled her uniform tight against her to see if she could see the colour of her knickers through it, but then she caught sight of him grinning.

"I'm sorry." He laughed. "I'm trying to get you back for embarrassing me about the bathroom door. I'm glad you've cheered up, Laura. I don't like seeing you sad."

"To be honest, I've not thought about Leon much today. The theatre operations have been a good distraction."

"Good, you seem a lot more relaxed than I've seen you in ages. I'm pleased this afternoon helped."

Laura sat at the kitchen table and placed her chin in her hands. "I've had fun today."

Lucas passed her a packet of opened biscuits. "I want you to have fun. You deserve to have fun."

She looked at him as he munched away on a chocolate biscuit, his eyes animated and his lips still smiling. She longed to kiss him, to see what his reaction would be. Would he kindly but politely turn her away, or would he not wish to offend her and return the kiss, only to tell her later that it was his fault and it must never be repeated?

Lucas caught her looking at him. He put his elbows on the table until their heads were at the same level. "Penny for them. Are you worrying about Leon?"

Laura shook her head. "Surprisingly, no. In fact, I was thinking about you."

"Me?" he asked, genuinely surprised. "Why me?"

"You're so different to the person I thought you were."

"And is that good or bad." He cringed. "Please don't hurt my feelings. My shoulder is painful enough."

"Good, actually. I like spending time with you."

He looked at her thoughtfully. "Laura, I need to ask you something. Please be honest with me. Lately I feel that we…"

Lucas' words were interrupted by a whining noise coming from the hospital bay.

"What was that? It sounded like howling." Laura turned to face the door, feeling scared.

"Nina." Lucas stood up suddenly. "That was definitely Nina. Come on, Nurse Nightingale. It sounds like we're going to have some kittens."

Laura followed him excitedly down the corridor and into the little hospital bay. She wondered what Lucas had been about to say. It puzzled her, and she made a note to ask him about it later.

They found Nina panting and lying on her side. Lucas gently stroked her contracting stomach. Nina meowed and turned herself around as a tiny kitten appeared. She started to lick her newborn straight away. Nina's stomach continued to contract, and she gave another meow of pain. Laura reached out to stroke her, but Lucas gently held her arm back.

"She'll be very protective of her surroundings now one of her kittens is born," he whispered. "I just want to ensure she doesn't reject them. She's been so sick, she may not have the strength to feed them."

Laura sat back on the floor with Lucas and watched as Nina turned her body and meowed as another kitten appeared. Lucas watched Nina's reaction intently as she reached behind her and gently licked both her newborns.

"One more kitten to come," he whispered. "It looks like she's bonding with these two. Can you see how she's washing them?"

Laura moved gently towards the cage. She felt honoured to be part of one of nature's wonders. The two tiny kittens wriggled around while Nina prepared for the birth of her final kitten. She stretched as another tiny form left her body. Nina reached round to clean all three little bodies.

Lucas leaned forward and frowned. "The third kitten isn't moving." He shifted position to be closer to the cage. "I'm going to try and put my hand inside the cage and see if it's alive."

Lucas gently placed his hand inside the cage and stroked Nina's head. She responded with a purr. Her eyes looked tired, but at the same time, Laura noticed her claws had come out.

"I'll try again in a few seconds. I can't risk stressing her out and making her ill again."

He waited a few more minutes, then repeated the action. This time Nina's claws retracted, and Lucas reached around for the still kitten. He placed it on a towel and brought over an oxygen tube. He asked Laura to hold the tube near the kitten's nose while he used his thumb to start chest compressions.

After a few minutes, the kitten's mouth started to move. Lucas stopped the compressions and rubbed the animal briskly with the towel, until it started to make a small cry.

"All done." Lucas placed the kitten back with the mother, then locked the cage on Nina and her three newborns. "I'll feed her in a bit, once she's settled."

He sat back on the floor next to Laura and peeled off his gloves, still watching Nina carefully with her new litter.

"Lucas, you are amazing. You knew exactly what to do."

"It's my job to know what to do. To be honest, you could have done that yourself. Quite often, common sense takes over."

"I couldn't have done that myself. You've just saved its life."

"You're very easily pleased, Laura." Lucas laughed at her astonished face. "That was just basic CPR for a kitten."

All three kittens wriggled around, making little wailing noises. Laura sat at the side of Lucas for a good while, fascinated by them. "I've never seen anything, or anyone, born before. It's a miracle, isn't it?"

"It's one of the good parts of this job, seeing new life. It goes wrong sometimes, though, and you're reminded that nature can be cruel, but most of the time things go well."

Laura sighed happily, and Lucas nudged her. "Don't go getting sentimental on me, Laura. Nina is a Bengal cat, which means these kittens will sell for a fortune. She's been bred intentionally."

"So, she'll not get to keep her kittens?"

"Probably not," he replied, standing up and wincing as his shoulder moved. "Come on. It's getting cold sitting on this floor. Let's go upstairs to my apartment and I'll turn the heating on. You can have a hot drink, then I'll run you home."

Laura followed him up the stairs to his apartment, feeling nervous as she remembered the abrupt ending from her last visit. Lucas threw her one of his fleeces to keep her warm.

Laura looked outside the window onto the village green, currently deserted due to the heavy rain. The sound of the constant downpour hitting the windows sounded cosy and comforting as she sat on the sofa and snuggled up in Lucas' giant fleece.

"You need to buy some thermals." He passed her a cup of hot tea. "Drink up, you'll soon get warm."

Laura sipped at her tea. She giggled as her stomach rumbled. "I'm sorry. I had no dinner because of the Leon fiasco. I've only just realised."

Lucas rolled his eyes. "You've not eaten all afternoon? That's madness. I'd never have let you help in theatre if I'd known. I feel awful now. What kind of boss does that make me?"

"A bossy one." Laura laughed. "It's my fault."

"Well, that's something I can rectify. Friday night means take away." He passed her a handful of menus. "You choose. Pizza, Indian, Chinese. I don't mind. I'll ask them to deliver. I can't let you leave without eating."

Lucas phoned their order through. He started to set the small dining table when his phone beeped. He checked his messages and shook his head, smiling. "My mates are in The Goose. It's quiz night and they're cheating, texting me for answers."

"Don't you go in The Goose on Fridays after surgery?"

"More often than not, I do, but I only drink if I'm not on the Rota. Otherwise I drive down and come home after."

"Are you on the Rota tonight?" Even though Laura had worked in the surgery all week, she still didn't understand how they managed their weekend working patterns.

"Nope, I'm done now until Monday." Lucas grinned. "I am officially off duty."

"So why aren't you in The Goose having a few beers with your friends?"

"Because I'm here looking after Nina and her kittens with you. I promised Nina's owner I would try to be at the birth to ensure a safe delivery, and that I'd keep my eye on her for a few hours after. I wouldn't have gone to The Goose tonight for that reason."

Laura nodded. "But you can have a drink, can't you? I can get a taxi home. I know Aiden wanted one of you to be with me, but a taxi is just as safe."

Lucas paused. "It does seem a shame not to celebrate Friday evening and Nina's kittens. I've got two bottles of champagne that someone bought me this week as a thank you. Fancy opening one and celebrating?"

"That's a pathetic excuse to open an expensive bottle of wine, but I won't argue with you." Laura thought she could have one glass and then ring for a taxi. The sooner she left, the better.

They ate at the small dining table. Laura felt herself relax as the champagne took effect.

Lucas topped up their wine glasses. "Well, here's to the new kittens."

Laura clinked her glass against his, thinking this would be her last. Champagne always went to her head.

She offered to wash and clear the plates while Lucas went back down to the hospital bay. Twenty minutes later, she filled up both their glasses and headed down the stairs to join him.

He apologised as she came through. "I've had to change their bedding. I can't risk infection while they are this young."

"How's Nina?" Laura asked, passing him a glass of champagne.

"Perfect. She's bonding well. I'm pleased with her."

Laura kneeled and watched how Nina curled around her baby kittens while they latched onto her.

"I bet you've had more interesting Fridays than this one?" Lucas sat by her side.

"I'd say it's quite memorable, for the right reasons," Laura replied.

"But you could be out and about, perhaps meeting a nice handsome man."

"I've had enough of men."

Well, enough of them all, with the exception of Lucas. Would he ever look at her the same way she looked at him? It seemed unlikely. His boundaries were clearly set. They worked together; they were friends. End of.

Laura suddenly remembered their conversation in the kitchen, "You wanted to ask me something earlier." She frowned as she tried to remember. "You wanted me to be honest with you. What were you going to ask me?"

"Nothing important. I'm just grateful for your friendship." He twiddled with the stem of his glass. "Don't give up on looking for love, Laura. You'll find the right person, eventually. There's someone out there for us all."

Laura felt like crying. If ever she needed confirmation that he felt no romantic tenderness towards her, that was it.

Lucas seemed to sense her sadness. "It's Friday night and you've had a difficult day. Let's open that other bottle of champagne and make an evening of it. Text Olly, let him know you're safe and I'll walk you home later."

The rain continued to beat against the windows while the streetlights from the village green cast warm shadows across the dimly lit apartment. Laura searched through Lucas' music selection to find something uplifting. "We need some happy music, Lucas. What do you have?"

He pointed to a selection of CD's. "Help yourself."

Laura put on one of her favourite albums, then searched through his book collection. "Hey, you have a draughts board."

"Yep, I'm pretty nifty. Fancy a game?"

"Why not. I'll set it up."

Lucas walked over with a bottle of champagne. "I'm warning you, I'm good at this."

"I heed your warning."

An hour in and Laura revelled in the frustrated look on his face. "Is there anything you can't do? No one has beaten me before."

"I've been brought up with board games, Lucas. However, one thing I can't do is dance. I'm your traditional Bambi on ice."

"Now that's something I can do." Lucas grinned. "It's one of the advantages of having a gay best mate."

"So, can you fox-trot?" Laura's face lit up with mischief. She didn't have him down as a ballroom dancer.

"Stop making fun of me. If you must know, I can salsa, jive and tango. Aiden had a crush on a dance teacher many years ago. He made me go for lessons with him."

Laura giggled. "I can just imagine you dancing to Saturday Night Fever in your theatre scrubs."

"Right." Lucas pulled her up off the floor and held her to him. "Watch and learn, Nurse Nightingale. We're going to Foxtrot."

Laura burst out laughing, "Lucas, I can't even walk in a straight line."

"I'm a good teacher, trust me. I put my arm around you like this and place it on your back. You need to put your arm around me and place it on my back. Right just remember this, slow, slow, quick, quick slow. Then forward with your left, forward with your right, forward with your left…"

Laura collapsed in a heap. "I can't do it. I can't stop laughing."

Lucas still held her tight. "You weren't joking. You're Bambi through and through."

The party hits stopped, replaced by the slower, softer beats. Lucas held her gently while they swayed along to the music. He rested his chin on her head, folding his arms around her more tightly.

Laura breathed in the scent of him. His body toned and taut beneath her hands. She placed her cheek against the bare skin exposed at the top of his shirt, allowing the effects of the champagne to wash over her.

Lucas pulled her in tighter, his hand on her hip towards the curve of her bottom. His other hand traced the line of her spine, stopping as it reached the fastening of her bra. Laura held her breath as his hand followed the strap around to her side, barely centimetres from her breast. She pushed herself closer to him and sighed.

Her sigh broke the magic spell. Lucas placed both his hands on her shoulders and held her slightly away from him. "We're drunk, and I'm behaving inappropriately. I'm sorry, Laura."

He rubbed his tired eyes and turned away from her. He looked absolutely shattered, so vulnerable and so beautiful. Laura wished they could have carried on dancing. If she hadn't pushed herself closer to him, then maybe he would have continued to hold her. It may have led to something they both wanted and needed.

Lucas put his head back against the sofa and closed his eyes. Laura covered him with a fleece blanket and then tried to ring a taxi. She had no luck, just a constant engaged tone.

She lay down on the rug, soon falling into a deep sleep.

CHAPTER 34

The sun filtering through the window shutters in Lucas' apartment woke her. She wriggled comfortably on his sofa. Lucas must have woken in the night and swapped places with her. The thought of him struggling to lift her with his bad shoulder made her smile. She hoped she hadn't been snoring.

A note at her side told her Lucas had gone for a run, but to help herself to breakfast. She wondered if he'd be feeling just as confused as her this morning. If only he hadn't pushed her away. Their bodies had fit so well together. She could still feel his touch along her spine. Damn his self-control. Did he have to behave like a gentleman all the time?

She quickly ran her fingers through her messy hair, hearing Lucas running up the stairs. "Morning, Laura. I've brought coffee."

Laura smiled. "I bet that will get the jungle drums beating. You buying two coffee's this early in the morning."

Lucas cringed. "Yeah, it did raise a few eyebrows."

She watched him run a hand through his wet hair. Laura felt herself blush, remembering how much she wanted him last night, and still did now. "I'll go in a few minutes. Let you get on with your morning."

Lucas bit his lip nervously. "Laura, I need to apologise. My behaviour last night was inappropriate. I'm sorry. I hope I haven't offended or upset you."

"It's fine, Lucas. You've not offended me." Laura knew his speech would have taken some guts for him to say. He was so proud, a man of few words most of the time. "We both had too much to drink. I should have stopped at one glass."

Lucas laughed lightly. "You sound like me now. I am truly sorry, though. Your friendship means a lot to me. I'd never risk losing it."

Laura nodded, fighting back her tears. That word again, friendship. God, this hurt so much.

"Are you okay, Laura?"

"Yeah, of course I am. I'm just tired. Thanks for swapping places with me last night. Did you sleep on the rug?"

Lucas smiled. "I did. You were curled up in a little ball on the floor. You looked so cute, but I couldn't leave you there."

Laura laughed, grateful no awkwardness existed between them. It would be awful if last night had damaged their relationship. At least she wouldn't be feeling uncomfortable about coming into work next week. "I had a really good night, Lucas, thank you. Remember, I'm not here on Monday. I'm in London, but I'll see you Tuesday."

"Have fun, Nurse Nightingale."

How would she cope for three days without seeing him?

CHAPTER 35

John paced the kitchen floor as they waited for the taxi to pick them up. Laura looked outside the window into the morning darkness, breathing a sigh of relief as car headlights came up the road.

"Have you got everything you need?"

John patted his coat pocket and nodded. "Aye, come on, lass. Let's get moving. London awaits."

"We may as well find our seats and sit in comfort," Laura said, as they navigated through the crowds at Whitby train station. "I booked us seats with a table. I thought it would offer us more space."

"Thanks for coming." John patted her hand as they sat down. "I'm not worried about the journey. I've travelled a lot in my career, but your company will help to take my mind off things."

"It's a pleasure, John. I have to admit I'm looking forward to a day in the city."

Laura had bought newspapers and treats to eat on the journey. She handed them out as they settled down, letting the train rock her gently as she thought about Lucas. He'd probably be setting up his surgery now and ensuring his medical bag was packed. She wondered if he would have spent the weekend with his friends, drinking in The Goose. A horrible thought suddenly passed through her mind. What if he'd met someone, a girl, and they'd gone back to his apartment and made love on the sofa? He had his needs, after all. He'd proven that on Friday, although he'd done a good job of controlling them, more's the pity. Laura shook her head. She didn't want to think about Lucas with another girl.

John put down his newspaper and looked out the window, his eyes glazed, no doubt thinking about the outcome of today's meeting with Alice. Laura felt for him. His thoughts must be all over the place.

"Did you never fall in love again, after Lizzie, I mean?" Laura asked, hoping to distract him.

John gave a rueful smile. "I did marry once." He laughed at her shocked expression. "Did I not tell you about that?"

"You didn't." Laura leaned forward across the small table. "Come on, spill the beans."

"I was in my thirties, based in San Francisco. Sally worked behind the bar near where I was stationed. She'd been married before, but it had broken down. She couldn't have children, you see, but that didn't matter to me. Lizzie and my daughter were never far from my mind even back then. I had no desire to make another baby with anyone else. Anyway, we dated for a short while, and then one night I proposed. Don't ask me why, perhaps it was the whiskey talking."

"How long were you married? Presuming you're not still married, of course."

"No, lass, I'm no longer married. Sally and I were together for six years. Bloody miserable affair, excuse my language. She was a gloomy sort of person, even back when I met her, but as the years went by, she got worse. She complained about everything. She moaned if I was at home. She moaned when I had to work away. She moaned if I tidied up, or didn't tidy up. I couldn't do anything right.

Eventually, we both admitted it wasn't working, and I filed for divorce. It was the best decision I ever made. I don't know what she's doing with herself these days. We stayed in touch for a short while, but the letters soon dwindled, and I didn't care enough to do anything about it. I've never bothered with marriage since. Don't get me wrong, I've had dates in my years, met some nice ladies, had short romances, but nothing to tempt me to put a ring back on my finger."

Laura's question burned on her tongue; she had to ask. "What would you do, John, if you found Lizzie? Would you marry her?"

John snapped his fingers. "In a flash, but a beautiful woman like my Lizzie, she wouldn't have stayed single for long. I've no doubt she has a large family by now, grandchildren even. I hope she's happy and content. That's all I ever wanted for her."

John picked up his newspaper, folding it and unfolding it nervously. "Love is precious, Laura. Sometimes it only comes around once, I should know. If ever you meet someone who makes your world explode, someone who you can't stop thinking about, someone who makes you smile just by picturing them, don't let them go. I lost mine, and given the chance, I'd never let her go again."

Laura turned towards the window to hide her quivering lip. John and Lizzie had loved each other equally. That made a whole lot of difference.

"We should arrive on time." John glanced at his watch. "I've already Googled the most direct route from Euston to the café. I've given myself plenty of time, just in case the area is not as I'd thought."

Laura linked John's arm, more for her own comfort than his, as they made their way up the escalators of Euston Train Station to the main entrance.

John looked at her and took a deep breath. "Well, this is where we part company. Wish me luck."

Laura gave him a kiss on his smooth cheek. "You've got a full three hours before we need to be back here. Take your time, and don't expect too much too soon. This is a big deal for her, too. Things are bound to be strange at first."

"I bet she'll have Lizzie's smile," John said, patting the photos in his jacket pocket. "How do I look? Am I smart enough?"

Laura took in his suit and tie. "John, you look just fine."

She stood and watched him walk away. Lizzie would have loved him dearly.

CHAPTER 36

Excited, Laura rushed through the crowds on Oxford Road. She had really missed shopping. The small towns near Lambsdale were well stocked, but they were nothing compared to three stories of the latest fashions. She wandered happily around all the goods on sale, picking up a few Christmas gifts as she went by. For Lucas, she bought a black leather wallet. Not too personal, but kept in his pocket, close to his heart.

Satisfied with her seasonal gifts, she bought herself a sandwich and made her way to Green Park.

When did the world get so busy? Had she become so familiar with country life already? Everyone rushed by, phones to their ears, faces frowning in concentration, all eager to get back to their small office spaces on the fifteenth floor, where windows didn't open, and the air-con buzzed all day.

Would she want to return to city life now? Most likely not, she considered. Lambsdale had worked its magic on her. Even in the rain and drizzle, she still appreciated the beauty of the scenery around her. The fresh tang of salty air, the wide expanse of ocean, green hills, fields, rivers and streams.

Three o'clock soon came around. Laura found John standing where she had left him. His face broke into a wide smile when he saw her.

"Well?" Laura asked, placing her shopping bags down on the floor. "How did it go?"

"Oh, Laura, so much better than I expected," John replied excitedly. He picked up her shopping bags. "Follow me. I know what platform we're on."

Laura waited patiently for more news until they were settled on their train. "Don't keep me in suspense. Tell me everything, from the minute you walked through the café door to the minute you parted company."

John laughed at her animated face. "Alice was already inside when I arrived. She recognised me instantly. We had a coffee first and just chatted about my journey down. I told her about you coming too. It was a bit awkward at first and I'll admit I struggled with what to say, but she broke the ice. Her exact words, 'there's no point ignoring the elephant in the room'."

"She strikes me as direct. Firm but fair." Laura replied.

"Aye, lass, she is, but nice with it too."

"So, have you learned anything?" Laura asked.

"A few things. She knows her birth mother gave her up straight after delivery, but she doesn't know why. Her adoptive mother didn't keep any of the documents."

"Was she curious about her past, John?"

"Not really. She didn't ask me about Lizzie, so I followed her lead. We talked about ourselves instead. She's a very successful editor in a magazine company, not married, no children of her own, but she has many good friends."

"Does she look like Lizzy?" Laura asked gently.

John paused as he pictured Alice's face again. "Do you know, she does a bit. She reminded me more of myself, though. The same green eyes, fair skin. Some of her mannerisms reminded me of Lizzie, the way she looked at me, as if she could see into my soul."

"Are you going to see her again, or at least speak to her over the phone?"

"Well, yes. She's agreed to a paternity test."

"Blimey, John." Laura turned to face him, shocked. "How did that come about?"

"She wants a definitive answer, for her own sake. She's happy to try and build a friendship with me once it's confirmed, but until then, she feels guilty for meeting me. She thinks she's being disloyal to the memory of her adoptive parents. I kind of understand what she was trying to say. She's not looking for a replacement, but if the original came along, she would respect that it needed to be acknowledged."

"So, what happens now, John? I don't know anything about paternity testing."

"I'm paying privately for both. It's a simple mouth swab these days. I've already researched the process. Once we've both had our sample taken, they go to a laboratory and I should get the results in around a week, all being well, of course."

"It's a brave thing to do, John, for you both, but sensible. Are you nervous about it?"

"Not really." He smiled. "She's got my eyes, and she's a stubborn bugger. She's my daughter alright."

CHAPTER 37

Their taxi drove through the cobbled streets of Lambsdale and up to the Harbour B&B. They shivered in the darkness, both tired, physically and emotionally.

"Thank you for your company, Laura. I've had a wonderful day."

"It's been my pleasure, John. I'm glad you've enjoyed it." Laura glanced at the light coming from the living room of the B&B and frowned. It wasn't like Amy to be so remiss as to leave a light on.

John caught her frown. "I'll leave you to it. Let you catch up. I'll see you tomorrow."

Laura hung her shopping bags off the handles of the bicycle, still propped up in the hallway. She jumped as Amy came out of the living room, followed by Olly, their faces solemn.

"We've had a problem, Laura." Amy looked at Olly, urging him to continue.

Olly took her shoulders and guided her into the living room. "Sit down, Laura. I want to show you something."

Olly took out his phone, selected his photo gallery, and handed the phone over to her.

A gasp of horror left Laura's mouth as she viewed the photo on the screen. "What? When did that happen? I didn't see it."

"I'm sorry, Laura." Olly replied. "It must have happened last night, Amy found it when she arrived here this morning. She woke me up."

Laura stared at the photo. The blood-red letters 'SLAG' painted all over her beautiful white picket fence.

Amy sat at the side of her. "We rang the police. They came out and took some paint samples. They are also going to ask around for any CCTV footage which may have caught who did it. We didn't mention Leon to the police. I tried to get hold of Sam for advice, but he's been in court all day. We didn't want to worry you, Laura. We both knew how excited you were about your shopping trip in London with John. I hope we did the right thing."

"I'm glad I didn't know, thank you," Laura replied quietly. "It would have completely ruined our lovely day."

She held her head in her hands and groaned. Where would all this end? Leon seemed determined to make her life a misery, and despite her best attempts to shield him off, he had succeeded. The words stung, 'SLAG'. It made her feel dirty and cheap. She'd been faithful to Leon the whole time they'd been together. She'd never given him a moment's worry on that score. Even now, though they'd split up, her chastity belt remained intact. What would he do next? Regardless of Sam's experience, Leon was holding firm, the eighteen grand, or the business closed.

"I'll have to buy some paint tomorrow and sort the fence out," Laura said wearily.

"We've already done it," Olly replied. "I went out this morning and bought the paint. It's taken three coats, mind you, and all day to do it, but there's no trace left of it."

Laura's eyes filled with tears of gratitude. "Thank you, Olly. You've gone to a lot of trouble for me today."

Amy knelt in front of her. "You've got some good friends, Laura. People in the village could see your fence this morning, causing tongues to wag, but only to source the culprit. No one thought you deserved this."

"Oh, God, I didn't think of that, everyone being able to see it. I bet I've lost potential trade because of this." Laura started to panic, desperately wanting to check her booking system to ensure no cancellations had come in over the day.

"Laura, no one cares about the paint," Amy said. "They just want to support you. Even Lucas rang me this morning to ask if he could do anything to help."

Laura groaned and rubbed her hands wearily across her face. Yet another humiliation in front of Lucas, and another reason for him to steer clear of a relationship with her. Could Leon see the damage and hurt his actions were causing? Opening up each one of her wounds slowly and painfully.

Amy poured her a glass of wine. "I'm going to stay the night with you. I'll sleep on the sofa and I won't take no for an answer," she said firmly, as Laura started to protest. "I've already got my things. I need to be back here in less than twelve hours anyway."

Laura nodded, too weary to argue. They spent the evening curled up in the annex, Bronte between them on the couch. Laura felt grateful for the company and the support, but it wasn't enough to prevent her from worrying about the future of her B&B.

CHAPTER 38

Laura pulled her towel from her beach bag and laid it out on the sand. The air felt chilly on the beach, but at least some warmth filtered through the clouds. Her hair flowed around her shoulders as she lay down on the towel next to Lucas. His body radiated warmth as she leaned towards him. Finally, the moment she had been waiting for. He leaned in towards her. His breath smelled awful. She really hadn't expected that. His tongue touched her cheek, rough and wet, and he licked her cheeks and nose whilst making little grunting sounds. Laura pushed him away, shocked at the amount of hair on his chest. Her eyes shot open to find Bronte sat at the side of her bed, tongue hanging out, tail wagging.

Can this day get any better? she thought as she helped Amy to prepare breakfasts. Her hands shook with tiredness and tension as she cleaned the B&B. Stepping into the hallway, she stumbled over the pedal of Jemima's bicycle, sending the contents of the wicker basket flying.

"Now look what you've done." Amy stood in the doorway of the kitchen, tea towel in her hand, giving her a sympathetic look. "Go and sit down and rest. I'll clean that up later."

Laura limped into the front room and slumped onto one of the sofas. She needed to get a grip. If Leon knew how this had affected her, he'd be dancing around in delight.

She sighed and picked up the mess from the wicker basket, boxes of chocolate-covered fudge and toffee. Their smell made her mouth water. How had she resisted them for so long? Giving in to her rumbling stomach, she took off the lid, expecting to find a selection of delicious sugary fudge. Instead, she found a sheaf of papers. She frowned as she read them, mostly bills from the shop when Mrs Henderson had owned it. Further papers proved to be accounts from years ago, some stretching back to the nineteen fifties. At the bottom of the pile lay an envelope with the words 'Rupert's agreement' written on it. Laura ripped it open, wondering what she'd find inside.

She read the contents, stood up with the letter in her hand and walked out of the B&B, straight into the village.

With her head in a whirl, she climbed the stairs to Sam's office and stood in bewilderment in his waiting room.

"Just the girl, I had plans to phone you this morning." Sam opened his office door and beckoned her inside. "Come and sit down."

"I've found this." Laura handed Sam the piece of paper she'd just read, her hands shaking. "Please tell me it is what I think it is?"

Sam looked up at her and smiled. "You're right, Charlie Bucket. It's the golden ticket."

"You've been spending far too much time with Amy." Laura laughed. "Are you sure?"

"Yes." Sam sat on the edge of his desk. "It's a legal planning permission for all the buildings, including your annex. Where on earth have you found this?"

"Remember that old bicycle from Rupert's? I found it in the wicker basket."

"So, it was under your nose the whole time," Sam replied. "Frustratingly, these things normally are. This is wonderful news, Laura, but I wanted to discuss something else with you. This may come as a shock. Leon has left the village. He won't be returning."

"Seriously? Where's he gone? Why's he gone?"

"First things first, Laura. How well did you know Leon, and what did you know about him when you got together?"

"Well, I'd like to say I knew him pretty well. We lived together as a couple for two years and dated for a year before that."

"What was his business?" Sam watched her face intently.

"Buying, renovating, and selling shop premises, mainly," Laura replied. "Leon waxed lyrical about how much work was involved and why he was often needed day or night."

Sam nodded. "I believe you, Laura, but that's not what he was doing. I've been carrying out a lot of research into our Mr Finch. Leon was indeed buying shop premises, but not to renovate and sell them on. He bought them for money laundering purposes."

Laura's jaw dropped with shock. "No! He can't have been. I'd have known."

"He owns three premises in Manchester," Sam explained. "One of them is a cleaning business, just like his plan for Rupert's. His crimes are mainly around knock-off jewellery, clothing, tobacco, the usual stuff. He would have continued under the radar if he hadn't pursued your land ownership claim."

Laura sat in shock as Sam placed evidence in front of her. Documents showing buildings that he owned or rented out and signed agreements from his employees stating their confidentially and waivers.

Sam raised his eyebrows. "While Leon was busy researching what land and property you owned, I've been engrossed in finding out why he owned a few small properties and yet earned quite a pretty penny from them."

"I had no idea, Sam."

"I didn't mention it to you deliberately. I needed to be absolutely certain."

"So, does Leon know you're aware of this, Sam?"

"Oh yes, he does now! I spoke to him yesterday, face to face in my office. I advised him that if he admitted his crimes and kept his nose clean, he may receive a lesser sentence. He will serve time for this, Laura. He's earned a lot of money and swindled a lot of people."

"Do you mean he's rich?" Laura asked, still incredulous at this news. She couldn't believe all this had been going on under her own nose for years and she hadn't seen it.

"Nope, not now he isn't. His business partner pulled out over the summer, leaving Leon to run this racket on his own. Leon, it seems, does not have much financial sense, and the money has been frittered away. He's completely broke."

"So that's why he came to find me? That's why he wanted me to pay him eighteen grand for my land." Laura clenched her fists in anger.

Sam nodded in sympathy. "It was his last attempt to save himself from bankruptcy. However, the letter you brought this morning proves that you inherited the land and the buildings. They were never Mrs Henderson's to sell. It's messy and complicated and no doubt someone will now lose out financially, Leon included. But not you, Laura."

Laura let out a massive sigh of relief that seemed to release all her tension and pent-up worries. Leon was out of her life for good, possibly serving time, and her B&B remained hers to keep for as long as she wished.

Sam glanced at his watch and apologised. "I need to leave for court. I would appreciate one favour, if you don't mind."

"Of course," Laura replied. "Sam, after everything you've done for me, of course I'll offer to help you."

"Tell Amy that Rupert's is back on the market."

CHAPTER 39

Laura skipped to Lucas' surgery that morning, via the Harbour Café, for the usual strong coffees they'd all come to enjoy.

She couldn't wait to give Amy the good news, Olly too. As for Leon and what he'd been getting up to, how could she have not seen what was going on under her nose? Money laundering? She'd never have imagined that. Her parents would need to know too. The news would break soon, no doubt. They deserved to know from her first, rather than via a local newspaper, or even worse, one of their church groupies.

Would her friends back in Manchester believe she hadn't known? That she hadn't been part of Leon's little schemes? She wondered if he'd swindled any of their friends, or if any of her gifts from him had been part of his illegal deals, like the Longines watch he had bought her last Christmas. Laura laughed at her own naivety. She'd sling it into the sea where it belonged. Leon was out of her life now, for good.

A beeping car horn caused her to jump. "Hey, I'm meant to be picking you up and dropping you off, remember? Or we'd sack you." Lucas wound his car window down and looked disapprovingly at her.

"Sack me then!" Laura said, climbing into the passenger seat. "I have news which means you don't need to ferry me anywhere."

Just the sight of Lucas made her heart melt. She looked at him out of the corner of her eye and visually traced his jawline, lips, and beautiful big brown eyes.

"So, are you going to fill me in?" Lucas gave her an amused look. "You look like you've just won the lottery."

"Sam has discovered Leon has been money laundering, for years, apparently. We think he'll serve time. Anyway, Leon has gone back to Manchester."

"So, you're free of him?"

"Yep, and the B&B won't get demolished."

"Demolished?" Lucas looked at her, confused. "Why would it be demolished?"

Laura cringed. She could have hit herself. She'd kept it a secret from him for this long. "I didn't tell you the full story, but Leon thought he owned the land my B&B is built on. He threatened to demolish the building if I didn't pay him a lot of money to buy the land back."

Lucas turned to look at her. "Laura, why didn't you tell me any of this?"

"For many reasons." She sighed. "Mainly because I didn't want you thinking I was a total idiot, getting involved in something like this."

"Laura, I would never have thought that. No wonder you've been so stressed lately. I wish you'd told me. I could have supported you more."

"It wasn't your problem, but I do appreciate your concern. Leon has been very full on these past few days."

"I know," he replied, his jaw tense. "I saw the fence painting."

"Yeah, well, small things for small minds." Laura paused, feeling herself blush. "Those words he used. They aren't true."

Lucas glanced her way and sighed. "I already know that."

"Good. Anyway, he's gone now, which means I can start thinking about my future and what it holds for me."

Lucas parked his car at the back of the surgery and turned off his engine. "What does your future hold for you?"

Laura put her head back and puffed out her cheeks. "I don't know," she replied. "I'm pretty sure I'll stay in Lambsdale with the B&B for a few more years. After that, well, who knows?"

Lucas simply smiled. "That will do. For now."

"A visitor for you." Aiden grinned as she walked into the surgery.

"I saw these and thought of you." Amy hugged Laura as she handed over a bouquet of flowers. "Which is kind of the truth. Also, there's the fact I need a reference to buy Rupert's and I couldn't think of anyone better than you."

"Amy, I'm so glad you're going to continue with buying the business. You'll smash it, I know you will."

"I couldn't believe it when you rang me earlier and told me the news. We can celebrate at The Goose later," Amy replied.

"Where are you going later?" Lucas asked.

Amy ignored Laura's warning look. "We're going to The Goose, meeting at seven. You're quite welcome to join us. Isn't that right, Laura?"

"Erm ... yes, of course."

Amy smiled mischievously. "That's Laura's way of saying she'd love you to come. We're meeting at seven. Are you joining us?"

Lucas looked at Laura for confirmation. "Would that be okay? I don't want to spoil your night."

Laura nodded, her face flushed. She'd kill Amy later.

"Great," Lucas replied, retreating to his room. "See you there."

"What was all that about?" Laura whispered to Amy. "That was embarrassing."

"Oh, Laura, don't dish it out if you can't take it. This is a bit of deja vu, I do believe!"

*

Laura could barely hear herself over the loud music competing with the sound of laughter and conversation. She smiled at the sight of Lucas carrying a tray of drinks, stopping every few steps while someone engaged him in conversation.

He sat at the side of her. "This is the problem with working and living in the same village. You never get away from the topic of worming tablets."

"So, Lucas," Amy interrupted, leaning across the table and twiddling one of her curls, "are you pleased Leon has left town?"

Lucas gave Amy a slight smile. "It's none of my business, but I can see it's made Laura happy."

"Hmm, it's made her happy and single." Amy smiled impishly.

Laura shook her head at Amy. "Stop it," she mouthed.

Lucas took a drink from his glass of lemonade and lowered his head, laughing. "Thanks for the update, Amy. I'll bear it in mind."

The pub quiz soon took over most of the conversation between their group, much to Laura's relief.

"Did you know," Amy whispered to Laura, as Sam, Lucas and Olly argued over a cricket question, "accidental physical contact is a real turn on for guys. Why don't you lean that way a bit towards Lucas, and—"

"Shhhhh!" Laura interrupted her. "Be quiet, Amy, he'll hear you."

"He's got a lovely bottom, hasn't he?" Amy giggled in her ear. "Buns of steel, I bet."

"Amy! Stop it now before I tip wine all over you."

"It'll cool me down if you do." Amy laughed, completely ignoring Laura's dagger stare. "What with Lucas' bum, Sam's lips, and Olly's thighs, I can't concentrate."

Laura started to laugh despite herself. "Stop it now, before he hears you."

"Before who hears what?" Olly asked, completely oblivious to their conversation.

"Nothing important," Laura replied, aware that her cheeks were colouring once again.

"Do you work out, Lucas?" Amy asked, coquettishly. "Laura and I were just admiring your toned legs."

Lucas raised his eyebrows at Laura.

"No, we weren't," Laura flustered, fanning her hot cheeks.

"It's the wine," Sam explained to Lucas. "She's always the same. Just ignore her."

"No one's admiring my thighs," Olly complained. "What am I doing wrong?"

"Not cycling enough, obviously," Amy replied mischievously. "So, Lucas, do you find you've more time for cycling now that you're single, like Laura?"

Lucas ruffled his hair and laughed. "I can see what's going on here. You're trying to pair me up with Olly, aren't you? I'm afraid he's not my type."

Even Laura had to laugh. He'd handled that well. As for Amy, she planned to give her a good talking to tomorrow!

The cold December air hit them as they left the pub. Laura huddled into her coat, feeling happy and relaxed.

Sam and Amy headed off home, giggling like a pair of teenagers, their arms wrapped around each other. Laura watched them enviously as they headed towards the harbour and Amy's house.

"I'll drive you two home," Lucas offered. "My car is on the car park."

"I'd rather walk, if you don't mind," Olly replied. "I quite fancy the fresh air."

Before Laura could protest, Olly had already made his way out of the pub grounds. She smiled to herself. His intentions were as concealed as Amy's matching-making earlier.

"Well, that leaves just you and me. Are you walking as well?" Lucas grinned.

"Absolutely not. I prefer warmth, heating, and blankets."

Lucas unlocked his car door. "I've got a car heater and two dog blankets, will that do? Unless, of course, Amy got here before us and planted a picnic for two and a duvet."

Laura cringed. "I'll kill her tomorrow. Amy doesn't like to see someone without a significant other. She feels the need to make a pair."

"I gathered." Lucas smiled. "Every sock needs a shoe."

"Something like that," Laura replied. "I bet Amy's Christmas list is full of requests for romcoms."

"Speaking of Christmas," Lucas said. "Are you staying in Lambsdale or heading back to Manchester?"

"Staying here. I'm not opening the B&B, though. I'm just resting. How about you? Are you returning to family?"

Laura cringed as soon as the words left her mouth. "I'm so sorry, Lucas, that was tactless of me. It was a stupid thing to say."

"Laura, don't be daft, I'm not offended. In answer to your question, I have absolutely no idea what I'm doing over Christmas, other than needing to be around for emergencies."

The words were out of Laura's mouth before she could stop herself, "Why don't you come here? I'll cook."

"Come here?" Lucas repeated. "To your B&B for Christmas dinner?"

Laura nodded, inwardly cursing herself. Why had she asked him? As if he would want to spend Christmas day with her.

"I'd love that. If you're absolutely sure?"

Laura almost choked. She had prepared herself to hear a million excuses. "I don't mind at all," she managed to say, after her state of shock had subsided. "It's daft us both cooking for one. I'll cook for us both."

"This will make Amy's day; you do know that. She'll have a wedding hat in reserve."

Laura smiled. She didn't know what else to say.

Lucas nudged her gently. "Don't worry, I'm not about to propose. Come on, Nurse Nightingale, you go inside and get warm. I'll see you tomorrow."

CHAPTER 40

The expected winter lull in bookings had finally kicked in. Laura only had two guests staying with her and they were both leaving that morning.

She'd given Amy the day off to concentrate on her application to buy Rupert's, which meant she could spend the morning pottering around the B&B, cleaning and refreshing the rooms. She washed down the woodwork and the bathrooms until they glistened, opening every window in the cottage to allow the crisp fresh air to filter through each room.

She stood in the window of one of the upstairs rooms and admired the view out to sea. The waves crashed lazily against the rocks just below, creating a comforting sound. With Leon out of the picture, nothing could stop her from enjoying this wonderful place and making a success of her business.

Lately, she'd been thinking of what to do with the hut once Olly had left. A recent trip to the farm shop had given her some inspiration. They'd advertised discounts for a nearby glamping site. She needed some advice from John, but surely not that much work would be involved in turning it into a shepherd hut? With the views it had to offer, and the cosiness of the log burner inside, it could hardly fail to be a success. She made a note to ask John about it later.

Laura showered after her morning cleaning, left Bronte with Olly, and headed down to the surgery. She found the waiting room empty for a change, both Aiden and Lucas busy going through medication cupboards, stock taking and filing old case notes.

She disappeared into the kitchen to prepare them all something for dinner, when bangs and shouts from the waiting room caused her to drop everything and run into the hallway.

The sight before her almost caused her to collapse. She leant against the wall to steady herself.

"Aiden, grab Laura before she falls," Lucas shouted, helping Olly into his surgery, both of them carrying a limp and unconscious Bronte.

Laura shrugged off Aiden's attempts to move her into the kitchen. "What's happened?" she cried as she ran to see Bronte. "Why's he not breathing?"

Aiden gently guided her away. "Leave Lucas to it, sweetheart. He knows what he's doing. Give him space to work."

Laura felt Aiden pass her over to Olly. He pulled her into his arms and sobbed. "I'm sorry, Laura. I'm so sorry. We went to the beach. Bronte was playing with his ball. He jumped to catch it and it stuck in his throat. I couldn't get it out. I ran all the way here."

"Is he alive?" Laura sobbed. "Please tell me he's alive. I can't live without him, I just can't."

"I don't know, Laura. I'm so sorry," Olly cried. "I just don't know." He clung to her tightly as they both sobbed into each other's shoulders.

Laura heard Lucas shout from his surgery. She watched on with dread as Aiden ran between the hospital bay and his room, carrying oxygen and other medical equipment.

The clock told her fifteen minutes had now passed. Laura fell silent and still. Instead of shedding tears, she prayed hard for Bronte to live. It would be her fault if he didn't. Her tears wouldn't help him now. Her beautiful, curly-haired, mischievous Bronte, who loved having his ears rubbed, who had protected her from Leon, who had lain on her feet and comforted her, now fighting for his life because of her stubbornness and refusal to listen to someone who only had his best interests at heart.

Olly still had his head in his hands, tears running freely down his cheeks. This big, brave man, who had so quickly become like a brother to her, felt so racked with guilt, that he broke his heart in front of her. Laura reached out to him. "Olly, it's not your fault. Please don't cry. This is all my fault. I should never have bought Bronte that ball."

Olly lifted his tear-stained face. "I'm so sorry, Laura. I tried to get it out, but I think all I did was push it further down. My fingers were too large to get a grip around the ball. I tried so hard; I really did."

Laura held this lovely man in her arms and let him cry.

She didn't hear Aiden approach them. "Come with me, Laura. Lucas is waiting for you."

Laura looked up at Aiden, her heart breaking. His face said it all. She felt like the world had just stopped. How could she go home now, knowing that Bronte would never run to greet her ever again?

She followed Aiden into Lucas' surgery, her chest refusing to rise and fall normally. Lucas took hold of her shaking hand as Aiden left the room and closed the door softly behind him.

Bronte lay completely still on the table, a large pipe coming out of his mouth, the horrible red ball in a dish at the side. Laura felt like her legs were about to buckle. What kind of life would she have without her little friend? He'd only ever wanted her love and attention. She had let him down so badly. Tears ran freely down her cheeks. She wanted to hold him for one last time, to bury her nose in his soft fur, to hear his little bark of excitement when she walked through the door. She thought about his bowl back at the annex which would never be refilled. His lead hung on the back of the door that would never attach to his collar. The end of her bed which would be forever cold. She couldn't speak, but she hoped he could hear her thoughts. *I loved you so much. You were so loved. You were so, so loved.*

Lucas stroked her hand softly. "I know it's not easy to see him like this, Laura, but all this is necessary. His throat will be sore for a few days, but we'll manage that with medicine. For now, he's sedated so his throat can relax without him panicking."

Laura gulped as she raised her hands to her face. "You mean, he's still alive?"

"He'll be fine now," Lucas replied. "He'll make a full recovery. Just give him time to come around."

Lucas held her hand as Aiden picked up Bronte and took him into the hospital bay. "Give me fifteen minutes to get him comfy, then I'll call you through, okay?"

Laura almost collapsed with relief as Aiden left the room with Bronte. Lucas held onto her tightly while she sobbed great big gulping tears that dripped down her face.

"I thought he was dead. I thought I'd killed him. My stupid, stupid stubbornness made me ignore you. You told me that red ball was too small for him, but my head was so mixed up, there was so much going on. I thought I hated you back then. You irritated me so much. You got under my skin and into my head like nothing I've ever known. I didn't know back then it was because I was falling in love with you.

I thought you were making fun of me and I retaliated at each point and..."

Lucas suddenly pulled her away from him with such force that it shocked her into silence. He bent his head to meet hers, his hands on her shoulders. "What did you just say, Laura? Did you just say you were falling in love with me?"

"Oh no," Laura whispered, as the enormity of her confession hit home. She turned away from him, her hands over her mouth. Now she'd gone and done it. She'd said those words to him. She'd just admitted it, out loud, to him. The incredulous look on his face said it all. She'd just ruined one of the most important friendships in her life. The clock couldn't be turned back. Now what would she do? She'd have to leave the surgery. Lucas wouldn't want to work with her now, knowing how she felt about him. He would be embarrassed and angry. He'd trusted her with his friendship. He'd opened up to her, and she'd mislead him into thinking she felt only friendship for him too.

Lucas shook her shoulders. "Laura, are you in love with me? Tell me the truth," he demanded.

She eventually turned to face him, knowing how much of a mess she must look with her swollen red eyes and snotty nose, but there seemed no point in denying this.

"I'm sorry, Lucas," she whispered. "I didn't mean for this to happen. I wanted … I still want your friendship, but I couldn't help falling in love with you. I know you don't feel the same, and please, don't say anything. I'll leave now, and if you don't want me to come back, I'll understand."

As she turned to walk towards the door, Lucas pulled her to him and held her so tightly she could barely breathe.

"Laura, I love you too," he whispered, his voice choked with emotion. "I've loved you for so long."

Laura looked up at him. Had she just heard right? Had he just said that he loved her too? Her heart banged against her chest and she shook her head in disbelief. "You love me?" she whispered.

"I love you," he repeated. "Laura, say something to me. You've gone so pale. Please say something to me."

"I love you, Lucas," she whispered, tears falling down her cheeks.

Lucas pulled her towards him and wiped the tears from her cheeks with his thumb. He tilted her head up with his hand and very gently kissed her cheek, tiny pecks that with each movement led slowly to her mouth. Laura held her breath as his lips gently touched hers, softly at first and then with more passion. He pulled her tightly towards him, kissing her deeply. She returned his kiss, folding her arms around his neck.

He pulled away from her, his eyes full of love and lust. "We need to stop," he said, his voice gruff with emotion.

"Why?" Laura asked, her body shaking against his.

"Do I need to explain?" he grinned, kissing her jaw and neck. "I've got a waiting room full of customers whose pets I need to be able to concentrate on. Right now, you are kind of making that impossible." He gently kissed the tip of her nose.

"I can't believe you love me," Laura muttered, still shocked at how her world had completely turned on its axis in the space of just one hour.

"I've wanted to kiss you for over five months," he murmured, stroking her hair back off her face.

"I never knew," Laura replied. "You were always so abrupt with me."

"Oh, Laura, I was abrupt with you because I didn't know how to speak with you. I've never wanted a woman so much in my life. Not just physically, although believe me, that's a main part of it, but emotionally too. The way you blush when I speak to you, your passion for your friends, the way you always wear your emotions all over your face, your caring nature, the way you cried when I told you about my parents. But Laura, I thought you only saw me as a friend, and you've needed a friend so much over the past few months. I didn't think it would be right to ask something of you. I persuaded myself that friendship with you would be enough. These past few weeks, having you here in my surgery, they've been some of the happiest, most infuriating times of my life. Your smiling face each afternoon when you walked in, the coffees you brought us each day, the way you teased me and made me laugh, those nights in my apartment. Laura, seriously, I had to fasten my hands to my sides to keep them away from you."

"I stayed away from you because of Keely," Laura whispered. "You weren't mine to love."

"I used Keely terribly. She had every right to be pissed off with me when I ended our relationship. I think she knew my heart was elsewhere, although I never admitted it to her. She came onto me so strong when I felt so vulnerable. I admit, I gave in and allowed it to happen. I was fond of her, don't get me wrong, but nothing like how I feel about you."

"You managed to hide your feelings so well," Laura replied, still confused.

"Aiden didn't think I hid it well." Lucas smiled. "He approached me within your first few days at the surgery, asking me did I have feelings for you. I already knew then that I loved you. That's why I swapped with Aiden for a day on the farm. I couldn't bear working alongside you and not being able to touch you. We considered swapping roles for a while until I could get my head around it all. But I was so miserable without you, even for one day, that we went back to the original plan of me just trying to put up with it."

Laura's eyes widened. "Is that what you were discussing at The Goose when I came over to say hello? You wouldn't even look at me properly. I thought I'd upset you."

"Oh, Laura, I desperately needed to get you out of my head. Just when I thought we had a plan, you appeared in front of me, all flushed cheeks and happy smiles. I just couldn't bear it. You wormed your way into my heart, and I couldn't do anything except let you."

Lucas pulled her to him again and kissed her gently on the top of her head. "We've so much to talk about. Let me sort Bronte out. He'll come around from his sedative shortly. I'll bring him back to you later and then we can talk? Does that sound okay?"

Laura nodded as he kissed her cheek softly. "Go home after you've seen Bronte. Reassure Olly that everything is fine, and I'll ring you in a few hours."

*

Laura walked back to her annex with Olly, both in a complete daze. She invited him inside, found a bottle of brandy and poured them both large measures. Olly wrapped his hands around his glass and almost downed the lot at once.

"Olly, please don't beat yourself up about this. You were amazing, getting him to the surgery so quickly. If you hadn't acted so swiftly, we would have lost him."

"I felt so helpless, Laura. I tried everything I could. I've never run as fast in my life. Thank God he's okay. Poor

Lucas, he's come to my rescue twice now. It's a good job he's a nice bloke, otherwise his head would be too big for this door frame."

Laura laughed softly as she thought about Lucas and their confession to each other less than one hour ago, but most of all she thought about that kiss. She smiled as she remembered his husky tones telling her to stop. He'd wanted her as much as she wanted him, that had been obvious. She felt like hugging herself and singing from the rooftops.

"God, Laura, you've got it bad," Olly said, rolling his eyes at her. "Are you ever going to 'fess up and tell the poor sod?"

Laura giggled. "Well, kind of ... well ... we ... you know ... well, basically ... he knows."

"He knows?" Olly repeated, raising his eyebrows. "He knows about the same thing I know about?"

Laura nodded, grinning at him like an idiot.

"And...?" Olly asked, holding his breath.

"And," Laura replied, "he feels the same way!"

Olly jumped up and hugged her tightly. "That is bloody amazing. I knew he had the hots for you, I just knew it. I'm so pleased for you. I'm so pleased for you both."

"He's coming here later with Bronte so we can talk."

"So you can ... talk?"

"Yes," Laura nodded. "To talk."

"To talk?" Olly repeated, looking doubtful. "I somehow don't think Lucas plans on coming around to just talk. You do know that, don't you?"

Laura hit him with a cushion. She knew that, but she had no intention of telling Olly.

*

Lucas finally arrived, carrying a now wide awake and tail-wagging Bronte. He passed Bronte to her as she buried her nose in his fur before kissing his soft head. He instantly started to lick her face, making her laugh. Placing him down on his rug near the fire, she turned to Lucas. "I know I've already said thank you, but I really do mean it."

"It's my job, Laura," he replied, his hands stuffed nervously in his pockets. "You don't need to thank me."

Laura thought he looked awkward. She walked over to him and took his coat. "I know we need to talk, Lucas, but I want you to know that I've no expectations. I don't even know where we go from here."

Laura thought how vulnerable, yet adorable, he looked with his hair all messed up. He'd obviously spent a lot of time running his hands through it today, something she'd come to realise he only did when he felt nervous.

He shrugged. "I don't know where we go from here either. All I know is I want to spend every minute with you. Knowing you feel the same way about me is just about the best thing I've ever heard. I tried so hard to break down the barriers with you, but I'm so awkward when I'm in a situation I'm not familiar with, and you brought so many emotions out of me that I really didn't understand."

"It's okay, Lucas. You don't need to explain," Laura replied gently, sitting by his side.

"Yes, I do. You need to know how I feel about you before we take this any further, and why I didn't tell you any sooner. That night at The Goose when you had too much to drink. I got the impression you were upset over a man. When you asked did I want to come into your annex and have a drink with you, believe me, I wanted nothing more, but I felt you needed time to move on from whatever, or whoever, had hurt you."

"I was upset over the land ownership case," Laura explained. "I've never been that drunk before, believe me!"

"You looked so sexy in that red dress. I couldn't stop staring at you. I fell in love with you even more after that night. You were so funny after drinking so much, yet so vulnerable. I wanted to wrap you in cotton wool."

"I was sick on your shoes." Laura cringed. "How could you have found that attractive?"

Lucas laughed. "It brought your defences down. You said a few other things to me too while I carried you. Believe me, if you'd have been sober, our relationship would have started that night."

"I don't remember saying anything to you." Laura blushed. "Although I do remember leaning against you on the bench."

Lucas grinned. "Funnily enough, I remember that too, most likely for different reasons. I spent most of that night trying to keep my thoughts innocent. You made that quite difficult!"

Laura smiled as she remembered the evening. She honestly had no idea those thoughts had been going through his head.

"The night I told you about my parents, when you got upset. I knew you wanted me to kiss you."

Laura groaned with embarrassment. "I thought I'd gotten away with that one," she mumbled into her jumper.

"I'm a bloke, Laura. I knew. I didn't kiss you because I'd promised to be a gentleman. If I'd have known how you felt, things would have been very different. Believe me, Laura, you tested my willpower a few times. That night Nina had her kittens, I could have made love to you there and then. How I stopped myself, God only knows."

Laura giggled. "I could have hit you when you stopped dancing with me."

Lucas reached for her and pulled her towards him. "I think we've spent long enough getting to know each other. If I have your permission, could I continue where we left off? I think my willpower has just run dry."

CHAPTER 41

Laura ran across the lawn to the B&B as quietly as she could. She'd run out of milk in the annex and desperately needed a coffee. Bronte followed her noisily, his bark still hoarse after his brush with the deadly red ball.

"Shhh!" Laura begged him to be quiet. "You'll wake Olly."

She padded back to her annex, her feet squelching in her flip-flops on the wet lawn, the only footwear she could find at this dark hour in the morning. A familiar cough stopped her in her tracks. She sighed with resignation and turned around to greet its owner.

"You're looking happy, Laura," Olly said, his face completely deadpan. He beckoned Bronte to him and held his collar while he checked him over. Trust Olly to be up and about this early in the morning.

"I see the good vet stayed late last night. You must have done a lot of, erm, talking."

"Olly, I'm warning you."

"I'm only saying, that's all. It's good to talk."

Laura threw him a black look as he retreated inside. So much for keeping secrets.

*

"I'll have a Christmas gingerbread latte and a chocolate muffin. I'm celebrating. My shop opens in a few days. I'm so happy!" Amy sat down at the table in the Harbour Café window.

"That's fantastic news," Laura replied. "I'm so pleased for you."

"Eeeekkkk!" Amy shrieked. "I can't believe this is finally happening."

"You deserve this, Amy. You've been a massive support to me over the last six months. I'm so glad it's all coming together for you."

Amy's shoulders suddenly slumped and she slapped her own forehead. "Laura, I'm a klutz. I'm so sorry. Here I am going on and on about how amazing my life is, while you've had a rotten time lately. I heard about Bronte, by the way. I rang you last night to ask how everything was, but you didn't answer. Is he okay?"

"Yeah, he's fine now, thankfully. Olly ran to the surgery with him, just in time by all accounts. Lucas managed to get him breathing again."

"Blimey, Laura, they always say bad luck comes in threes. You've just had all yours. Leon turning up, the land claim, and now Bronte. I think you're due some good luck."

Laura smiled, hugging her secret to herself.

"Lucas is going to expect repayment soon, all the lifesaving he's been doing. I wonder what you can think of." Amy winked.

"Actually, Amy, I've got a bone to pick with you. You promised me you wouldn't try any match-making skills on Lucas and myself."

"Ah, yes, the quiz night. I caught him looking at you quite a few times and he definitely didn't have cricket on his mind. He looked like he wanted to undress you. I think he likes you, Laura."

"Yep, he does. He kissed me."

It took a few seconds for her comment to register. "You what?" Amy asked. "What did you just say?"

"I said Lucas kissed me." Laura giggled, happy she now had her friend's full attention.

"Oh my God," Amy whispered. "Does he know how you feel? I can't believe it. When did this happen?"

"Yesterday," Laura replied quietly, keen to ensure the rest of the café didn't hear. "I thought we'd lost Bronte. It all came spilling out about how I felt about him, and guess what?"

"He feels the same way?" Amy asked, her eyebrows raised. "Oh, come on, Laura, don't look so shocked I'd figured that one out."

"I know." Laura sighed happily. "I just can't believe it."

"So, come on, tell me everything." Amy wriggled to get more comfortable in her seat.

"He brought Bronte back last night. We sat down and talked about our feelings for each other. I still can't believe he's in love with me. All those months, I never guessed."

Amy waved her hand, "I'm not interested in the talk. What happened next?"

"He went home."

Amy looked up in surprise. "Seriously? No hanky-panky? No seeing his stethoscope?"

"Nope." Laura smiled.

"And that doesn't bother you?"

Laura sighed with happiness. "We kissed. He kept his hands to himself. It was ... just perfect."

"But you wanted to?" Amy asked.

"Of course I did, but I took his lead. He didn't suggest it or make any move to make me think differently."

"Did he want to?"

Laura smiled. "Yes."

Amy frowned. "So why didn't you?"

"Because he's a gentleman," Laura replied. "And that makes me love him even more."

*

Laura walked back to her annex, feeling as if she floated on air. Her head swam with images from last night. She couldn't wait to see him again later.

A bottle of champagne sat on the doorstep to her annex. She laughed as Olly opened his hut door, waving a white handkerchief.

"I come in peace. I don't want any more black looks."

"This is so sweet of you, Olly, thank you."

"I'm sorry I embarrassed you this morning. I know how you prefer to keep that side of your life private. I've spent far too much time with fishermen, I'm afraid, but I'm a romantic at heart, you know." Olly put his arm around her and squeezed her gently. "You look good together. You're going to make beautiful babies."

"Olly, stop it! Now behave, because John is walking towards us. I've asked him to come across and look at your hut. Once you've moved into your home, I thought about renting it as a shepherd hut. What do you think?"

"I think that's a bloody fantastic idea," Olly replied. "John, what do you think about Laura's idea for a shepherd hut?"

"Well, I think it's a good investment." John passed Olly his morning newspaper. "In fact, while you're here, you can help me assess the work I've done, so the path runs smooth for her."

Laura smiled at the sight of John and Olly working together. "You're like two peas in a pod when you've both got your glasses on and pencils behind your ears."

"Except I've more padding." Olly grinned, patting his stomach.

"And I've more wrinkles." John laughed. "Olly told me about Bronte, how is he?"

"He's fine, thanks." Laura nervously fiddled with a ring on her finger. "John, if I was to tell you that Lucas and myself are dating, what would you say?"

John looked at her over the top of his glasses. "I'd say it's about time. That poor lad hasn't been able to think straight since you arrived in this village."

Laura laughed quietly. "It seems everyone could see it except us. I'm glad you approve."

"There's no approval needed for love, Laura," John replied. "My only advice to you is, don't let him go."

Laura nodded. She knew exactly what he meant.

CHAPTER 42

Bronte wagged his tail happily on the decking outside the annex, barking excitedly.

Laura opened the door to find Lucas on her doorstep. He gave her a shy smile. "How's Bronte?"

Laura's heart skipped a beat. Less than twenty-four hours had passed since she'd first kissed him. Her knees gave a slight wobble as she focused on his deep brown eyes and inhaled his familiar aftershave.

"Back to normal, as you can tell," Laura replied, aware of the electricity that zinged between them. "Have you been out on an emergency?"

"Yeah, helping Aiden." Lucas put his arm around her, kissing her longingly. "I've not been able to stop thinking about you. It's driving me mad."

Laura giggled. It still felt strange to be held by him so closely. She wound her arms around his neck and returned his kiss.

"I can't think straight," he said with his amused smile. "I only came over to check on my patient. I don't normally get this kind of treatment on home visits."

Laura blushed as he kissed her neck. Did he have to be so gorgeous? She gently pushed him away. "You're getting me all hot and bothered."

"Good," he replied, putting his arms back around her and nibbling her ear. "You put me through months of misery. This is payback time."

Laura jumped as a high-pitched ringing noise came from the B&B. Bronte started to bark frantically. They ran quickly across the lawn towards the boot room, finding that Olly had beaten them to it.

"The fire alarm," she said, panic in her eyes. Olly and Lucas pushed open the boot room door and ran inside. Her heart pounded in her chest while she waited in the garden, her hand protectively on Bronte's collar. Olly returned after five minutes, looking grim, holding a burned and foul-smelling package.

"This is the culprit," he said with sympathy. "It seems someone thought it would be funny to put a burning newspaper full of dog muck through your letterbox."

"Seems as if Leon is back," Olly said. "Your car has been scratched too."

"Oh no," Laura groaned. "Not again. Sam didn't say anything about him being back." Laura slumped on the step to the boot room. She felt like she'd come back to square one. "Where's Lucas?" she asked.

"Talking with John. He's thrown away the rug near your front door. It wasn't salvageable. That's all you've lost, though."

"And my car," Laura sighed. "I'll have to get that sorted."

"John and I can do that for you. You need to contact the police. This could have been much worse, and you'll have to mention Leon now. Each act is becoming more vicious."

Laura sighed. "We've no evidence. That's the problem. The police asked around for available CCTV footage, but they found nothing trained on my house. It's almost as if Leon knew that. I'm definitely going to have a camera installed at the front now, for my own peace of mind, if nothing else."

"Hold on a minute," John held a hand to his mouth, thinking. "I have a garden camera attached to my house. It captures wildlife. I've not looked at it in ages, mind you, so it might not be working anymore. Shall we have a look at it?"

Olly set up the laptop on John's dining table, rewinding the images from the garden camera. "It seems to be working. This footage is from around an hour ago."

As the screen came to life, they all bent forward, squinting at the images in front of them. A figure wearing a baseball bat and large coat walked past the camera. Laura shivered. This felt creepy, and she almost didn't want to watch. Lucas pulled her to him and kissed the top of her head, offering comfort.

"Can you zoom in on that picture?" Lucas frowned at the figure now paused in front of them.

"That doesn't look like Leon?" Olly stared at the screen, confused.

"Shit." Lucas turned away from the camera and ran his hands through his hair.

"It looks like a female, and much smaller than Leon." Laura squinted at the frozen frame. "Lucas, do you know who this is?"

"I'm afraid I do," he replied, sighing deeply. "It's Keely."

John rewound the video, "It's the same figure on each occasion. The brick through the window, the fence painting."

"It's the fringe and petite height that gives her away," Olly replied. "It's a shocker, I'll give you that. What on earth are we going to do?"

Lucas ruffled his hair. "Laura, I know you'll probably not like my suggestion, but can I have a chance to explain? I've hurt Keely badly, and this is her way of retaliating. I don't agree with anything she's done, especially not the fire this morning. That was stupid and irresponsible, but I think these are the actions of someone who needs a lot of support. Please, can we keep the police out of this for now? Let me talk to her. If I feel I'm not getting anywhere with her, I'll take this recording into the police station myself."

Laura rubbed her hands across her face. "I don't want any more trouble. If you think she'll listen to you, then give it a go, but she needs to know how serious this is."

Olly shook his head in pretend annoyance as Lucas left to confront Keely. "You two are disgustingly in love. I preferred it when you were pining after him. You didn't make me vomit then." He stuck his fingers down his throat and pretended to gag.

"Shut up, Olly." Laura stood up to leave. "You wet your pants the night you were unconscious on my bed, I bet you didn't know that, did you?"

"I didn't!" he squeaked in high pitch denial. "That's a lie!"

"Children, children." John laughed. "Honestly, you two are like school kids. You certainly fight like it."

Olly laughed as he put his arm around Laura. "But kick one and we'll both bark."

"Laura?" John asked. "Would you be able to pop round later this afternoon? If you have time, of course."

"Not a problem." Laura replied, wondering what he wanted to see her for. "I'll stop by when Lucas gets back."

Laura worked with Olly to cover as much of the damage to her car as they could.

"Are you shocked about Keely?" Olly asked, as they worked together on polishing the paintwork.

"I am. I honestly thought it was Leon. I've spoken with Sam and told him. I don't want Leon being accused of things he hasn't done."

"You've a very forgiving nature," Olly replied. "I'm not sure I could be that amenable, given all the aggro he's caused you since he arrived here."

"I'm just trying to be fair," Laura replied. "It's not a weakness. I just don't see the point in making other people's lives a misery."

Olly put down his cloth and looked at her. "Laura, weak is one thing you are most certainly not. Not many people could have coped with all the stress you've had. Plus, you've made this place an absolute gold mine. You should be upping your room charges next year. Believe me, people will pay it."

"I'll do it after Christmas. Speaking of Christmas, what are you doing, Olly?"

"Well, Katie and Danny will be here. I'm hoping to get the house sorted in the next few days, then we can all have Christmas there, my mum included. She's come on leaps and bounds since her operation. By the way, I'll need your help with my insurance forms when they come through. I need to fill them in to claim for my accident. I'm no use with a computer."

"Just let me know when they arrive, I'll help you. I'm going to be so sad to see you leave. I don't know what I'll do without seeing you every day."

"Ahh, but you've got lover boy now. You'll not notice I've gone. It's been great, though, hasn't it? Me, you and John all together. I'll miss him too. He's coming to our house for New Year's Eve. You and Lucas are welcome too, a bit of a housewarming for close friends only. Are you up for that?"

"Try and stop us." Laura smiled.

CHAPTER 43

Laura sniffed the air appreciatively. "John, is that a curry you're cooking?"

"Sure is," he replied, busy stirring and chopping. "My signature chicken curry."

Laura noticed a bottle of single malt whisky on the worktop. She smiled to herself. "What are you celebrating?"

He handed her a letter without comment.

"What do you want me to do with this?"

"I want you to open it," he replied. "It's the DNA test results."

Laura gasped. "John, they've arrived really quick, but it should be you opening them, not me. It's not my place. You've waited so long for this news."

"I will read it," he replied. "After you've read it, lass. I want to share this with you. Once it's confirmed, then I'll tell Olly."

"I don't know." Laura held the envelope gingerly. "I still think you should do it."

"Well, I'm insistent it's you, and if you don't do it soon, this curry will be ruined, my glass of whisky will be too warm, then my whole evening will be spoiled."

Laura took a deep breath and ripped open the envelope. "I don't even know what I'm looking for," she said, unfolding the letter with trembling fingers. She noticed

John's steady hand, stirring his curry. "Are you not even nervous?"

He shook his head in response. "There will be a box top left. It will say either 'Match' or 'No Match'. I just need to know the content of that box."

Laura's eyes went straight to the box. She looked at John, still stirring his curry.

"What does it say, lass?"

"No match," Laura whispered, as a tear trickled down her cheek.

John's shoulders moved slightly. "Thank you, Laura, that's all I needed. Have a good evening."

Laura watched him turn off the cooker, placing the spatula in his freshly prepared curry. He took off his apron and stood rock still, his back still to her. His hands gripped the edge of the worktop.

"John," she whispered. "It's okay to be upset. Sit down and talk to me."

John didn't reply. He scraped his curry into the bin and poured his glass of whiskey down the sink. He picked up her coat and handbag, handing them gently to her.

"Goodnight, Laura," he said firmly.

Laura didn't want to leave him like this, but John had his pride. He wouldn't let his guard down in front of her. She desperately wished he would. She wanted to share his hurt, pain and loss. She wanted to sit with him and talk about what his future held, to say that they would try again to find his daughter, that their search would continue, and they'd do it together. But that wasn't going to happen, John had made it clear he wanted to be alone.

CHAPTER 44

Instinct told Laura something looked different as she opened the boot room door. Bronte laid himself down on the mat, content with a bone to chew on. As she pulled back the drapes in the living room, it came to her. There had been no light in John's kitchen. Neither had his heating come on. Normally she found herself enveloped in the steam his boiler emitted as she opened the boot room door.

Her throat constricted in panic. Maybe he'd decided to have a lie in, but something in the pit of her stomach told her differently. A flash of white on the rug in the hallway alerted her to an envelope lying there. She picked it up with trembling fingers, recognising the handwriting.

Dear Laura,

I know you are aware yesterday's news affected me greatly. I need time to process it all. It's not something I can do while still living here. I had hoped for Christmas this year with my daughter and the hope of a link to Lizzie, but we both know that is now as far away as it ever was.

I booked a flight last night, with no return date planned. I hope to be able to clear my head while visiting friends back in America. I have deliberately left no contact number, but I promise to write to you regularly.

You and Olly have been such a support to me. I owe you both so much. I hope you will forgive me this cowardly way of dealing with my emotions, but it's the only way I know how.

Please feel free to tell Olly as much as you wish. He will no doubt wonder about my disappearance, but please let him know that his friendship has meant the world to me.

Yours,

John

Laura didn't know whether to feel relieved or sad. The fact being, she felt both, just as equally. She hoped that the friends he planned to visit would support him and that eventually, he would open up to them and share his troubled soul.

Olly sat with his head in his hands, Bronte at his feet. "Why didn't he tell me?" he asked Laura. "I would have supported him and helped him."

"He didn't want to mix the pleasure of your company with the anxiety of finding his family. He's loved being with you, setting up that hut, all those beers you shared, late night fishing, cricket matches, buying you a paper each morning. Those were his moments of release from this stress."

"So, he has a daughter?"

"Yes, he does. He doesn't even know her name, where she lives, or even if she's still alive. He thought he was so close when we went to London, but obviously not."

"I thought that London trip sounded dodgy." Olly sighed. "At least now I know he wasn't ill. That's what bothered me the most."

"I'm sorry." Laura squeezed his arm. "I couldn't talk to you about it. It wasn't my story to tell."

"Don't apologise for being a good friend to him. I would have done the same. God, I'm going to miss the old man. I grew so fond of him."

CHAPTER 45

Aiden opened the surgery door, raising his eyebrows in mock annoyance. "I hope you don't distract the good man today. I've never seen Lucas smile this much on a Monday morning. I'm pleased for you both, sweetheart. About bloody time."

Laura smiled shyly as she passed Aiden his coffee. His approval meant a lot to her.

Lucas looked up at her and grinned. "Don't expect favouritism in my surgery," he said, stacking up a pile of case notes. "I'll still crack the whip if I need to."

"Is it safe to leave you two alone?" Aiden laughed. "Should I not act as chaperone?"

"I'll behave myself," Lucas replied, holding up his hands. "She'll be safe."

Laura changed in the small bathroom, aware of Lucas standing outside in the reception area. Goosebumps ran all over her body. She buttoned up her uniform with shaking hands, half expecting him to open the door and undress her, but she knew Lucas wouldn't push her. He wanted her as much as she wanted him, but he'd never overstep the mark.

She shivered as she thought about his touch. They'd only been together a few days. They were still getting to know each other. Some things were worth waiting for.

She opened the door tentatively and his eyes immediately sought her out. "If you're trying to tempt me by wearing that uniform, you're succeeding."

Laura gave him a slight smile, enjoying the look of frustration on his face as he approached her and kissed her neck.

"I'm sure you've deliberately waited until five minutes before surgery starts. You smell gorgeous." He held her close as he stroked her hair. "Hey, I forgot to tell you. Keely rang me last night. Don't worry, she's not trying to cause trouble. She rang to apologise. I don't know if it's me that talked some sense into her or someone else. Nevertheless, I think we can safely say it's all water under the bridge. So, I thought we could celebrate. I can cook for us later if you wish. If you've nothing to rush back for?"

Laura looked into his eyes and nodded. "I'd like that."

Any inappropriate thoughts were pushed to the back of her mind as the surgery became busier.

"It's always like this just before Christmas," Aiden said, returning from his farm rounds early to cope with the number of unexpected emergencies. "I think everyone panics in case they can't get hold of us over the next few days."

Lucas looked through the long list of appointments and rubbed his eyes, "We'll still be here at midnight at this rate. I'm sure that phone hasn't stopped ringing all day."

Laura grimaced as another phone call came through. "Shall I answer it or let the machine take it?"

"I'll take it," Lucas replied. "Hopefully, I can put them off."

As four o'clock came around, they still had over half the appointments to see. Laura helped Aiden filter quite a few down as they triaged animals in the waiting room and offered reassurance or medication on the spot. This infuriated a few of the lipstick brigade, who flounced off in disappointment.

"The waiting room is a lot emptier." Laura's stomach rumbled as she helped Lucas in the surgery.

"Hungry?" he asked, stitching a cat's ear that had caught itself in barbed wire.

"A bit. I've normally eaten by now."

Lucas glanced at his watch. "I'll make us something to eat as soon as we're done. Has Aiden gone home?"

"Yeah, he's just left."

"Good. He's done a good job today clearing the waiting room. He's quick thinking like that."

"I don't think the lipstick brigade appreciated it, though."

"Who?" Lucas asked, looking confused.

"The women who turn up with their healthy dogs. I'm sure they only come here to see you."

Lucas groaned. "They drive me round the bend. I find their confidence quite scary."

"I thought you liked a strong, confident woman," Laura replied.

Lucas shook his head as he washed his hands. "Nope. I much prefer subtle."

Laura looked at him thoughtfully. "I've much to learn about you, haven't I?"

"And all the time in the world to do it."

Lucas cooked them something to eat while Laura locked up the surgery and fed the animals in the hospital bay.

Her heart fluttered against her chest as she made her way up the stairs to his apartment. Unlike last time, they now understood how they felt about each other, but it didn't make this evening any less difficult. It would be so easy to just give in and let the emotions take hold, but what would happen if he decided their relationship wasn't working? Trying to rebuild a friendship with him would be difficult enough without the added complication of any intimacy they might share.

Her body and heart argued with each other as she reached the door to his apartment. Why couldn't she be one of those girls who reacted on impulse? Lived as if they only had today. Why did she have to overthink everything?

She walked into his apartment and gulped as she took in the sofa bed, lit candles and soft music.

Lucas followed her line of sight and cringed. "Oh God, I've just seen that through your eyes. I didn't fold the bed up this morning. I have no expectations, I promise."

Laura let out a sigh of relief, causing Lucas to raise his eyebrows at her.

"I've had compliments in the past," he said wryly.

Laura fumbled with her watch strap. "I'm sure you have. I'm just not...."

"Hey, stop worrying." He took her into his arms and kissed her. "I've waited five months. I can wait longer."

Laura kissed him, grateful for his understanding. Her hands snaked around his neck as she pulled him closer.

"Be careful, Laura," he murmured, nibbling her ear. "I'm made of flesh, not steel. Go and sit down and pour yourself a glass of wine. The food is almost ready."

Laura sat at the table and watched him clear the plates. "I feel like I know you, but I don't know you."

Lucas turned to her. "That made no sense what-so-ever."

Laura glanced at him, feeling self-conscious. "Well, I know you're a good kisser."

"Naturally." He grinned. "Carry on."

Laura took in a deep breath, "And I know you went to university with Aiden, and you opened this surgery to keep your dad's memory alive. I know you don't like cows. I know you like cycling and non-scary women and low-fat mayonnaise on your sandwiches, but I don't know your birthday."

Lucas sighed and nodded. "I get where you're coming from. You've worn your heart on your sleeve from day one of working here. I know lots about you. What do you want to know?"

"Well, your birthday would be a good start."

"Twenty first of June. I'm a year older than you. My middle name is James. My best friend at school was called Peter. My first kiss was in year seven with a girl called Grace. I broke my left arm falling out of a tree when I was eleven, then three days later my right arm playing football. I fell asleep on a beach in France and got arrested for being naked at the time. Don't ask, it was my twenty-first birthday. I prefer to read rather than watch TV, although I did once cry watching Toy Story, and I lost my virginity in the back of a car aged eighteen to a girl called Phoebe. An awful experience. I lasted twenty seconds. I've got better at it. Will that do or do you need to know more?"

"Twenty seconds!"

"Seriously, all that information and that's the only thing you remember?"

"How many women have you slept with?"

Lucas smiled. "More than five, less than ten, including my twenty seconds of fame. Despite what Aiden may lead you to believe, I don't sleep around."

"Your first love?"

"You."

Laura gasped, "Seriously?"

"Yep, I'm entering uncharted territory with you, Nurse Nightingale."

Laura stared at him. Did he even know how absolutely gorgeous he was? Probably not. "I hope I don't disappoint."

"You haven't so far." Lucas pulled her into his arms and pressed tantalising kisses down her neck.

"Apart from the no sex theme."

Lucas tenderly kissed her forehead. "Best things are worth waiting for. All thirty seconds of them. Stay the night, Laura. No funny business, just you and me, curled up together, talking. What do you say?"

Laura looked up into his eyes, knowing she could trust him. She nodded.

CHAPTER 46

Amy looked in her element, her arms full of twinkly lights as she decorated the window of her sweet shop.

The shelves were once again stocked with tubs of brightly coloured sweets. Wreaths, candy canes and baubles hung from the ceiling, and swags of holly and ivy covered almost every surface.

"It's only a few days until Christmas, and I've sold absolutely loads today."

Laura looked around in amazement. "It's like a grotto, Amy. I can't believe how hard you've worked."

"I know, I checked the website this morning and I've received more orders in the past three hours than I did the whole of yesterday. I'll need to take on extra staff at this rate."

"Right, show me your website. I'll deal with a few now for you. I'm not due in the surgery until later this afternoon."

Amy logged Laura into the system. "You can't fool me, Laura Thompson. You're avoiding going back to the annex because Olly moves out today."

Laura sighed, caught out by the astute Amy again. "I can't believe he's leaving, although I'm pleased for him. He's missed Katie and Danny desperately."

"Their house looks amazing. He's worked hard on it. At least he's living in the village, so you'll see him around. Has his mum arrived yet?"

"Yes, she came yesterday. She's lovely, very friendly and unassuming, but she certainly keeps Olly in check. I can see where he gets his sense of humour from. They dote on each other."

"No news from John, I take it?"

"No," Laura replied sadly. "I've received a postcard from him and a few letters, but no news as to whether he plans to come home anytime soon. I miss him."

"Yeah, I know," Amy sympathised. "At least you've got Lucas to take your mind off things."

Laura smiled. "Aiden's offered to be on call over Christmas, so we get to spend some quality time together."

Amy grinned wickedly, "There's a few things of his I'd like to unwrap, I can tell you."

Laura giggled. She still couldn't believe they were together. Sometimes, she found herself just staring at him, taking in everything about him. He still looked at her with the same amused smile that used to drive her mad. "I've got to admit. I'm smitten with him."

"Yeah, and so is half the female population of the village. It will break a few hearts when they find out he's off the market."

Laura headed back to her annex, looking forward to settling in with a cup of tea in front of the log burner. She had treated herself to a real fir tree, which filled the small annex with its unmistakable sweet and fresh scent. Olly had found a large box in her attic filled with Christmas baubles, which she hung with mixed emotions. Each one was a memory of Jemima's past, her time abroad, making friends and memories, possibly finding love, and maybe also losing it. It made life seem so precious, so fragile, so perfect, and at other times so unbearable.

Her heart constricted to see the door to the hut closed and no sign of Olly. She knew they had agreed to do it this way. It would have upset her so much to watch him lock the door for the last time. Although permission to turn it into a shepherd hut was well underway, it would always be Olly's home in her eyes. She decided her Christmas present to Olly would be to name it after him. She wished John would be around to see it.

She walked into her annex and found Olly's key slid under her door along with a note. She opened it with shaking hands, her eyes already brimming with tears.

Laura, thank you ... for everything. Olly x

The note broke her. She sat on her decking with Bronte and shed some much-needed tears. With one hand, she had gained Lucas, but with the other, she had lost the daily companionship of Olly and John. She wiped her eyes as her phone started to ring, Olly's name flashing up on the screen.

"Bastard pipe,!" Olly shouted down the phone. "Bloody bastard cheap shite from that friggin' warehouse."

"What on earth is the matter, Olly?" Laura asked with amusement as he continued with his choice language down the phone.

"The soddin' pipes have burst upstairs in the house. All the ceiling has fallen in. It's a right fucking mess."

Laura heard his mum shouting at his choice of language. Despite the drama, Laura had to smile. Bea certainly had him in hand when she needed to.

"I've got my mum, Katie and Danny, and no bloody house to live in." Olly groaned. "This is going to be a completely shite Christmas."

Laura thought quickly. This went against her plans for a relaxing Christmas, but given the situation, she felt she had no choice. She took a deep breath, hoping Lucas would forgive her.

"Come and stay with me," Laura replied. "I've got five empty bedrooms here all ready and prepared. You'll all have to help out though, cooking, breakfasts, cleaning, but as long as you all pull your weight, there'll be no charge."

"Laura, I can't ask that of you. It's your business!"

"The rooms are doing nothing. It doesn't matter to me whether someone is in them or not. As I said, I don't intend to get up and cook breakfasts, change beds, or clean your bathrooms."

"Laura, have I told you how much I love you?" Olly sighed with relief down the phone. "You've just saved my life."

"I did that over summer, Olly. Right now, I'm just offering you a room."

CHAPTER 47

From her position near the cliffs, Laura thought the whole harbour glistened like a grotto. Even in the early morning, trees and pergolas were filled with sparkly white illuminations, and the windows of shops and restaurants glowed with tiny twinkly lights. Laura wrapped her scarf tightly around her as she made her way down to the surgery.

"Last day of madness." Aiden greeted her wearing flashing Rudolf ears. "I'm praying for a quiet day, then we can all head home early. What's your plan for Christmas day, Laura?"

"I've got a house full." She grimaced. "No doubt you know Olly and his family are staying with me. I'm cooking for them, plus Amy and Sam, and Lucas, of course."

Aiden nodded. "Yes, he did say. So, you're looking forward to your first Christmas as a couple?"

Laura smiled. "If we ever get any time on our own, but yes, I can't wait."

"Good, his last Christmas wasn't too great. He refused to join Martin and me. He thought himself a gooseberry, which is ridiculous. Nevertheless, he took himself off to Thailand for the fortnight."

"On his own?"

"Yep. Although given his looks, that wouldn't have lasted long."

Laura giggled as Aiden rolled his eyes. She didn't feel any jealousy for what relationships Lucas might have had in the past, but she did feel sorrow that he'd spent last Christmas in the arms of someone for only a brief amount of time.

The visitors to the surgery arrived wrapped in wool coats, hats and scarves, all exclaiming about the sudden drop in temperature.

Aiden looked through the window, frowning. "I may need to leave earlier if this freeze continues or I'll never get home. Would you and Lucas be okay if I left within the next hour?"

Laura had a quick glance at the appointments. "Yeah, it's all routine. Just head off when you feel it's best."

The temperature dipped even further as the surgery started to empty and a few flakes of snow fell past the large windows.

"Any bets on a white Christmas?" Lucas grinned, walking out of his surgery.

"I love snow." Laura sighed, opening the front door to watch the village green turn into a winter wonderland. "I really don't understand my aunt. She closes her hotel every winter and heads to Gran Canaria. She'll be there now, warming her toes in the sand. I'd rather be warming my toes against a log burner."

"Well, if I don't get moving, I'll be warming my toes against a car heater." Aiden picked up his coat and medical bag and gave Laura a kiss on her cheek. "Have a fabulous Christmas, you two."

Lucas clapped Aiden on his back, before hugging him tightly. Laura watched on with fondness. They were so close.

No matter what happened to them in their lives, they would always stay by each other's side.

"What now?" Lucas asked, after waving Aiden off. "We could head to The Goose for a drink if you like. The world is your oyster."

"I'll take Bronte for a walk first, then meet you in The Goose. Does that sound okay?"

Lucas looked at her doubtfully. "Walking in this weather on your own. Will you be okay?"

"The snow's not too bad. I'll just let him have a quick run. Shall we meet in an hour? Give me a chance to get changed."

Lucas kissed her nose, "Just don't keep me waiting."

*

Laura couldn't see anyone on the beach for miles. Bronte ran ahead, enjoying the freedom and space. The tide came in slowly, the blueness of the sea contrasting with the pale sand, slowly turning white under the thin blanket of snow.

She walked briskly, enjoying the eerie quietness you only experienced during a snowfall. As the sun started to set, leaving a faint orange glow over the sea and white sands, she turned around and walked back to the cliffs, taking in the view of her beautiful B&B.

"Arghh," Laura cried as she tripped over a piece of driftwood, badly twisting her ankle. She limped to a nearby rock, sitting down to nurse her throbbing foot. Taking off her boot caused more agony and then panic as the swelling started almost immediately.

"Damn," she muttered, attempting to stand up and put weight on the injured foot. Bronte whined, sensing her discomfort and concern.

The incoming tide seemed to be approaching faster. Laura's heart banged against her chest as she realised her predicament, her anxiety heightening as no signal appeared on her phone. Taking hold of Bronte's lead and her boot, she limped slowly along the shoreline.

The sun had almost set by the time she reached the steps that led up to the garden of her B&B. Given her pain, climbing up those ledges seemed impossible. Laura sat down for a few minutes and took a few deep breaths. She didn't have far to go now. Hopefully her phone would gain a signal soon.

"Laura!"

She turned to see two figures approaching across the sands. Recognising them both, she sighed with relief.

"I've been worried sick about you. You were supposed to meet me over an hour ago."

Lucas knelt by her side and looked at her swollen foot.

"I'm so sorry. I fell and hurt myself. There's no phone signal on this section of beach. I had no way of contacting you."

"Why on earth would you walk on the beach in this weather?" Olly asked her. "We've been walking around the village looking for you. It didn't enter our heads you would be daft enough to come down here."

Laura looked into their concerned faces and grimaced. The truth being, she just hadn't thought. The beach had looked so peaceful and calm under its winter blanket. She hadn't planned on falling.

Olly shook his head at her lack of response. "You need to keep a better eye on her, mate. She's trouble, this one."

"I'm beginning to see what you mean," Lucas replied, half smiling. "Come on, hop along. Let's see if we can get you home."

Olly and Lucas supported her as she hobbled between them, biting her lip with pain. She could sense Lucas' frustration with her. His face looked pale, even against the whiteness of the snow.

"How much pain are you in?" Lucas asked her. "Be honest."

Laura sighed, admitting defeat. "About twelve out of ten."

"Right, hang on tight." Lucas picked her up and carried her in his arms until they reached her B&B.

"I'm storing this one up, Laura." Olly grinned as he left them to walk down the garden to her annex. "I'll live off this tale all next year."

Lucas kicked the annex door shut and placed Laura on the sofa. "You had me out of my mind with worry when you didn't turn up at The Goose. I rang you, no reply. Came here, no reply. I did wonder if Leon had come back and hurt you in some way."

Laura looked into his face, etched with concern. "I'm sorry. I didn't mean to worry you."

"If anything had happened to you, Laura, I don't know what I'd do. Do you have any idea how much I love you? This is no passing phase for me. It's not a lust-filled attraction. I love you completely and utterly with every ounce of my body. Do you know what I went through, not being able to find you?"

The look of fear in Lucas' eyes reached into her soul. All the time she'd felt hesitant, wondering if he loved her as much as she loved him, she'd missed his own lack of confidence. If ever she needed confirmation that this was forever, the moment had arrived.

Laura held his freezing body in her arms. "I'm so sorry," she whispered.

Lucas wrapped his arms around her and held her tight for a few moments. "You're shivering," he eventually said, rubbing her arms. "Go and get changed into something warm, I'll look at your ankle too."

Laura wriggled in discomfort. "Even my knickers are wet after sitting in the snow."

Lucas shook his head, smiling. "I'm fast losing patience with you, Laura Thompson. Go and get changed."

"How about you?" Laura asked. "Are you okay?"

"I'll be fine. I just need to get warm. Have you got anything I can change into if I have a shower? My clothes are wet. I didn't have my waterproofs with me."

"I've got some of Olly's old clothes. He asked me to take them to a charity shop. They should fit you."

Lucas' words echoed in her ears as she heard him turn on the shower. Their relationship had just turned a corner. They'd admitted their love for each other so many times over the past few days, but his words tonight, they were from a depth she never knew existed in him, a depth that mirrored her own love for him. Suddenly, her throbbing foot didn't matter anymore.

Laura opened the bathroom door. She took off her damp clothes in the warm steamy room, until she stood completely naked. Gently, she pushed back the shower curtain.

Lucas turned to look at her, water dripping down his face and body. He slowly took in her naked form, his eyes eventually meeting hers.

"You are stunning," he whispered.

Those words were the only encouragement she needed. She stepped into the shower and joined him under the warm water.

"Are you sure?" he asked, his voice filled with longing.

"Yes," she replied. "I've never been more sure of anything in my life."

CHAPTER 48

Laura found Olly and his mum in the B&B, arguing over dinner. True to their word, everything looked beautifully clean.

"How's your ankle?" Olly asked her, grinning like a Cheshire cat. "It must have been bad for Lucas to stay the night."

"It's fine, thank you," Laura replied, giving him the evil eye. "Don't think you can start embarrassing me in front of your mum."

"I've had words with him already," Bea said. "I hope he's not been a nuisance while he's been staying with you. He needs keeping in check."

"I've been as good as gold, haven't I, Laura? I've not made any remarks about you and Lucas sharing that small bed, both of you cramped together, naked, holding onto each other tightly."

Laura shook her head. "Just remember, Olly. I remember the night you spent on my little bed, crying because we had to cut your trousers off."

"At least I was wearing trousers, unlike you with just a nightie on."

Laura gasped. "How do you know about that nightie? Did Lucas tell you?"

"He mentioned it briefly." Olly laughed. "He said I'd ruined your mattress, bedding and nightie. Why? Is there a story behind this item of clothing?"

Laura blushed. "No, nothing important."

"Oh, I get it. All these months you've been teasing me about what I did that night and you've had a little secret yourself."

"No," Laura replied. "There's nothing to tell."

"Were you naked under that nightie?"

Laura blushed furiously.

"Ha, no wonder Lucas quizzed me about you after my accident. I've got to admit, I'm jealous."

"Shall I hit him for you, love?" Bea asked. "Just say the word. I'll enjoy doing it."

"My mum is the only woman that scares me." Olly laughed. "Sorry, Laura, you know I take great delight in embarrassing you. Anyway, I should be trying to sweeten you up. Those insurance forms have come through. Can you help me when you get a chance?"

"Not a problem." Laura rolled her eyes in mock frustration. "Just give me an hour to wrap a few Christmas presents, then come over to the annex. Lucas should be home by then. He can help with the medical sections."

*

"Thanks for this." Olly sat down, spreading his paperwork on her small coffee table.

"Where's Katie and Danny?" Lucas asked.

"Katie's putting the little one to bed. He's shattered after running on the beach all day. We'll not be long. Hopefully, these will be straight forward."

Laura noticed Bea had brought a bag of white wool and knitting needles with her. "What are you making, Bea? I didn't know you knitted."

Bea held up a small woollen item and frowned. "I've offered to knit hats for the babies in my local maternity ward. I don't think knitting is my forte though."

Olly laughed. "Looks more like a handkerchief to me."

"Right, Olly, behave yourself." Laura placed the laptop on her knees. "I need your forename and surname."

"Patrick John Dearden," Olly replied, sorting through his paperwork.

Laura and Lucas looked at each other, surprised.

"I thought your name was Olly, short for Oliver? Is it not?" Laura asked, confused.

"Nah, it's a nickname," he replied, still searching through his papers and frowning. "I've lost my driving license. I know I had it earlier."

"Why the nickname?" Laura asked.

Olly found his driving license and grinned, "I'll let my mum tell you. She loves this story."

Bea looked up as she placed the knitting on her knee. "Well, complete chaos reigned the night Olly was born. There had been a fire in the maternity ward. We all had to evacuate. I was in the final stages of labour when my midwife bustled me into a wheelchair and took me over to the village hall opposite. Well, our Olly has never been early for anything in his life, apart from his birthday. There was no way he was going to wait until I got into that hall. I gave birth in the middle of the street." Bea laughed.

Laura gasped. "Oh no! What did you do?"

"Thankfully, my midwife was quick on her feet. She caught him and wrapped him up in her coat until we could get inside the hall. I couldn't see much of my baby at all, other than a mass of black hair and a big bawling pink mouth. Anyway, they wheeled me inside and took Olly away while they checked him over."

"I bet you were scared," Laura replied. "Giving birth sounds stressful enough without it happening in the middle of the street with no support."

"I felt terrified, I'll admit, but I knew I could trust Jean, my midwife. We'd got to know each other quite well over the months I was pregnant. I had every faith in her. Anyway, they brought my baby back after they'd checked him over. I looked down and thought to myself, *what a beautiful baby girl.* I'd always loved the name Holly, and given the time of year, I felt it fitting. It was only a few hours later when I came to change his nappy that I noticed my Holly was actually male."

Laura burst out laughing. "Olly, I can't believe you had a girl's name for the first few hours of your life."

Olly had the grace to blush. "Yeah, have a good laugh at me, white nightie girl."

Bea chuckled. "It tickled me and Jean for years after. It still does. That's how he ended up with the nickname Olly, a take on Holly. We didn't mean for it to stick, but whenever he had a tantrum as a baby, or even as a teenager, then the name Olly would pop back up."

"I can just imagine you as a stroppy fourteen-year-old." Laura giggled as Olly stuck his tongue out at her.

"As Olly grew up, he preferred being thought of as an Oliver rather than a Patrick. He unofficially adopted the name himself. I didn't mind, I understood he wanted a more modern name. My grandfather was called Patrick. I was very close to him as a child. I didn't have a good relationship with my own parents."

Bea looked wistful. She smiled at Olly, who held her hand and winked affectionately at her.

"So, we ended up with an Olly. That makes sense now," Laura replied, "but tell me, why did you think Olly was a girl when you first saw him? I know he's got a feminine side to him, but I didn't think that would be so obvious at birth."

Olly gave her the finger, wincing as his mum slapped his head. Laura snorted with laughter.

"The chaos from the fire, I presume. They'd wrapped Olly in a pink blanket, I never thought to query it. I just assumed pink meant a little girl. We laughed about it after. It was Christmas day, after all, the staff were so busy."

Something zoomed through Laura's mind so quickly that she struggled to hold on to it. She frowned as she tried to recall key words from the story Bea had just recounted. Something had just set her mind whirring. Almost like when somebody says something, and you're reminded of a dream you had the night before. It comes into your head for split seconds, then leaves just as suddenly. This felt like one of those occasions. Laura shook her head. Maybe it would come to her later. She continued with the insurance form.

"Olly, what's your date of birth?"

"Twenty fifth of December, nineteen seventy-four. I'm a Christmas baby."

Laura gulped. She'd suddenly remembered. The date of birth brought it back to her. The pink blanket, that's what had triggered her mind. John's photograph of his daughter. Laura encouraged her mind to think of the wording on the back of the photo. Did it say baby girl? She screwed up her face, trying to remember. No, she didn't think the gender was given, just 'Baby Flanagan - 25/12/1974'.

A crazy thought ran through her head. "Where were you born, Olly?" she asked, her heart beating a tattoo against her chest.

"I don't know," he replied. "Mum should know."

"Well, it should have been Queen Victoria, Surrey, but I'm not sure if your birth was registered there, because of the fire. Why, love, do you need to know a place of birth for this insurance form?"

Laura nodded, her heartbeat getting faster. *Surely not. It can't be.*

She swallowed a nervous lump in her throat, her clammy hands shaking. "I need to know your full name, Bea. For the insurance records."

"Of course, love," she replied, picking up her knitting. "Elizabeth Anne Flanagan."

Laura put her laptop down on the floor, her breathing unsteady. She stood up, feeling light-headed.

"Laura, what's the matter?" Olly took hold of her arm.

"I need some fresh air," she replied, taking deep breaths. "I'm sorry. I just need some space."

Lucas guided her to the nearest garden bench. He knelt in front of her. "Laura, tell me what's wrong. Are you not well?"

Laura shook her head and took another few deep breaths. "He's been right under our noses all this time," she whispered.

"I don't understand. Who's been under your nose, Laura? Talk to me, I'm worried about you."

Laura steadied herself before continuing. "Remember I told you about John and his daughter? The reason he left for America."

"Yes," Lucas replied, frowning. "He went to London. It wasn't his daughter. What's this got to do with now, this form and Olly?"

"John thought he was looking for a baby girl. The picture he had showed a baby wrapped up in a pink blanket."

"I'm still not with you." Lucas sat at her side on the bench.

"On the back of John's picture, it didn't say a baby girl. Just 'Baby Flanagan 25th December 1974'. The mother of the baby was called Lizzie Flanagan. Do you see what I'm getting at, Lucas? Olly is John's son."

Lucas stood up and rubbed his hands through his hair. "I don't know what to say. Are you sure?"

"Well, you've got to admit it's a bit of a coincidence," Laura whispered. "I've no contact details for John, though. I can't tell him. What do we do?"

"Hey, guys, are you okay?" Olly walked over to meet them at the bench. "I know this is a busy time of year. I shouldn't have asked you to help with this form. You've done enough for us."

"It's fine, Olly. I'm sorry," Laura replied, hoping to reassure him. "I just felt light-headed. It must be the heat from the log burner or pain killers for my ankle. I hope you don't mind, but could we do this another time?"

"Yeah, of course," Olly said with concern. "I'm sorry, Laura, I didn't know you were feeling so much pain from your ankle. I would never have asked."

"Don't worry about me. I'll be fine," Laura reassured him. "I'm probably just hungry and tired. I'm sure I'll feel much better in the morning."

Olly looked at her strangely. "Did you feel ill this morning, too?"

"Erm, I don't know."

"Okay," Olly replied, raising his eyebrows at her. "Well, look after yourself and don't over-do it. Your secret is safe with me."

"What secret?" Laura asked, confused as Olly walked away.

"He's thinking you're pregnant." Lucas grinned. "Talk about a comedy of errors."

CHAPTER 49

Laura curled up on the sofa with Lucas and Bronte. "I just can't get my head around it all. Should we tell Olly?"

Lucas shook his head. "It's not our place. There may be a reason why Bea didn't get back in touch with John. We've no idea how she will react."

"I understand that," Laura replied. "I just wish John was back home, then the decision would be taken out of our hands. I look back now, and in some ways, it seems so obvious. I often commented on how much they looked alike. Even their mannerisms were so similar. Two peas in a pod, I often called them."

"You'd never have guessed this, though," Lucas replied, stroking her hair. "It's just too extreme."

"I know, but these things do happen. I'm not a great believer in fate, but there's something about this that seems destined. Olly being hurt on this harbour, ending up recovering in the hut, alongside John for company. Bea coming here this Christmas."

Lucas nodded, "It's a funny one, I'll give you that."

"Except John isn't here to seal the fate." Laura sighed. "He's on the other side of the world. I just hope he comes home soon."

"Yeah, he's going to have one hell of a shock when he comes home. If he does come home, Laura. You may need to prepare yourself for him wanting to stay in America."

"But he'd have to contact me, then I could tell him," Laura replied.

"Not the best way to tell him he's a dad to a strapping great fisherman, and grandfather to a little four-year-old, though, is it?" Lucas said.

"Oh my God! Danny is his grandson." Laura sat up quickly. "Oh Lucas, this is so unfair. If only he knew. They dote on each other. I really need John to come home." Laura groaned.

"Not going to happen anytime soon, is it? He's spending Christmas and New Year in San Francisco. We'll just have to wait and see what happens."

CHAPTER 50

Laura rushed around in the Christmas Eve madness. Bea offered to come to the farm shop with her to buy all the fresh food for Christmas day. Laura bit her tongue to stop herself from mentioning John. All those missed years, and even now, on his own doorstep, John was still missing out.

Into her car boot went the massive turkey she had ordered a few days before, alongside a hamper full of condiments, desserts and wine, compliments of the farm shop. Laura felt grateful of the large oven in the main kitchen. At this rate, she would be up at six o'clock Christmas day just to cook the giant turkey.

"Where's Lucas?" Bea asked as they pushed all the small dining tables together.

"He's been called out on an emergency," Laura replied. "The second one today. He'll be shattered. He had to get up at one o'clock this morning to help Aiden with an emergency at the surgery."

"Ah, the life of being in love with a vet." Bea smiled.

"I love it," Laura replied. "It makes me adore him all the more."

"So, what do you think?" Bea smoothed a red tablecloth over the makeshift long dining table.

Laura looked around at her transformed dining room. A mini Christmas tree twinkled in the corner and a garland dressed the old Victorian fireplace, now filled with candles, ready to light on the special day. She closed her eyes and thought of Jemima. She would have loved this, her B&B filled with happiness, love, and laughter. Life was too short to waste.

"I think it looks amazing. We've done ourselves proud." Laura replied, her voice shaking with the effort of trying not to cry.

Bea placed her arms around Laura's shoulders. "Olly told me about your godmother. I bet you miss her."

Laura nodded. "It's taught me we only have one chance to do something with our lives."

Bea smiled with understanding. "I know what you mean. Look forward, never backwards. You can't trip over what's behind you, after all. Look, it's gone midday. I think we can celebrate with a glass of sherry, don't you?"

Bea opened a bottle of sherry and pulled two mugs out of the kitchen cupboards. "To us!" she said to Laura as they clinked mugs together.

"Are you drinking already?" Lucas laughed, taking off his muddy wellies in the boot room, stepping to one side to allow Olly to join him. "I've been delivering puppies while you're getting intoxicated!"

Laura giggled. "This is why I love him."

"Oh God. Is she getting sloppy again?" Olly groaned. "I agree with Lucas. I've just come home after trying to dry our house out, and I find my mother getting plastered on sherry."

"Less of the plastered," Bea warned him. "Where's my grandson, by the way?"

"Katie's took him to a pantomime with a group of school friends," Olly replied.

"So, it's grown-ups only this Christmas Eve." Laura grinned. "I think we all deserve a trip to The Goose!"

*

No tables were free, but that didn't bother Laura. Christmas music blasted from the jukebox and everyone sang along in high spirits.

"Fancy a dance?" Lucas pulled her onto the dance floor, and they joined Sam and Amy.

"I remember our last dance." Laura smiled. "You pushed me away."

"I won't be pushing you away tonight, Nurse Nightingale. Believe me, I intend to make the most of dancing with you in the future, inappropriate as it may be."

"There's nothing inappropriate about your dancing tonight." Laura giggled.

Lucas picked her up and kissed her passionately as the pub cheered and clapped him enthusiastically.

"Was that inappropriate enough for you, Nurse Nightingale?"

As they strolled back to her annex, Laura couldn't think of a time when she'd been happier. Her little dog waited for her at home, no doubt warming his paws in front of the pre-lit log burner, and the most handsome, eligible bachelor of the village had just given her the most amazing kiss. What more could she want?

CHAPTER 51

Laura looked out on her snow-capped garden and hugged herself. It had been so long since she'd experienced a white Christmas. Not that it mattered greatly. How could she be disappointed, waking up next to this gorgeous man in her own annex, with the sea stretched calm and endless at the bottom of her winter wonderland garden?

She screwed up her toes and whispered excitedly to Lucas, "Come on, let's see if Father Christmas has been here."

She dragged a sleepy Lucas out of bed and into the front room. Bronte jumped on their knees the minute they sat down to open their gifts, wagging his tail in their faces as they ripped off the wrapping paper.

"I've got another gift for you." Lucas presented her with a long thin box. Laura took off the top to find shrouds of delicate tissue paper and underneath a beautiful white silk nightie.

"It reminded me of a certain evening over summer, when I desperately wanted to know what might be underneath it." Lucas gave her his amused smile.

Laura shyly held up the almost transparent material. "There's no stripy red and white socks, Lucas. I can't wear half an outfit."

Lucas reached under the sofa and pulled out a pair of knee high red and white socks. He put them around her shoulders and pulled her in for a kiss. "Life is never boring with you, Laura Thompson. I never thought my first Christmas present to my girlfriend would be red and white socks."

"I never promised you boredom." Laura smiled as she returned his kiss. "I have another present for you, too. A weekend in Paris, just us. Aiden has already agreed to cover your Rota."

"I think you're very sneaky, Nurse Nightingale, but I kind of like the idea of you having a side I don't know about. It keeps life interesting."

The lights were on in the B&B as Laura and Lucas walked over a few hours later.

"He had us all up at five-thirty this morning to open presents," Olly complained, pointing to the living room where Danny could be heard shrieking and playing with toys. "I'm too old for this lifestyle."

"You wanted kids!" Katie laughed, as Danny shouted for Olly to come and play.

"I played with Olly all the time when he was a baby." Bea smiled. "He constantly wanted attention. I'll admit I made a rod for my own back and always gave in. Not that I regret it, mind you. It made us closer."

"Olly and Danny are like that." Katie sighed. "Two peas in a pod."

"As father and son should be," Bea smiled wistfully.

The smell of roast turkey soon filled the B&B. Amy ran around with Laura, setting the table and preparing the vegetables.

"We've no champagne flutes, but I think we'll cope with drinking from cups." Amy giggled. "Come on Lucas, are you going to open that bottle of champagne or not?"

From the corner of her eye, Laura noticed Sam nod at Lucas as he turned off the music. Everyone stopped talking and turned to look in their direction.

Sam coughed nervously. "Amy, you walked into my life almost six months ago, bringing happiness, colour and joy. You've turned my world upside down. You're my light, my fire, my reason for waking and breathing. My reason for living. When you realise you want to spend the rest of your life with somebody, you want the rest of your life to start as soon as possible. Amy, will you do me the great honour of becoming my wife?"

Everyone held their breath as they waited for Amy's response.

"Yes!" she finally managed to squeak in between her sobs.

Sam picked her up and kissed her as everyone clapped and congratulated them.

Laura wiped her eyes as she watched Sam slip a beautiful solitaire ring on her finger. "Did you know about this?" She whispered to Lucas.

"Only since last night. They look kind of cute, don't they?"

"I think they are wonderful," Laura replied tearfully. Lucas laughed as he kissed her nose. "Come on, Nurse Nightingale, don't get emotional on me. We've got a giant turkey to carve."

Amy's eyes shone as she showed off her ring. "I hope you'll be my maid of honour," she whispered to Laura.

Laura kissed her cheek. "Thank you. Of course I will. I'll make sure you have a fabulous day and an amazing hen night. Just don't put me in a big meringue, okay?"

"Talking of big dresses," Amy whispered. "Do you know Olly thinks you're pregnant? You aren't, are you?"

Laura laughed, shaking her head. "It's just Olly overhearing something and making assumptions. Don't worry, I'm not pregnant."

Amy breathed a sigh of relief. "Thank God. That would have totally ruined my hen night."

"Hey, Laura. Have you invited Santa to our party? He's knocking at your front door." Sam stood at the dining-room window, looking out.

Laura frowned. She wasn't expecting anyone else today, and she certainly wasn't expecting a Santa Claus. She opened the front door, wondering who it could be. Her breath stuck in her throat as she recognised the face partially hidden behind a fake white beard and a large Santa hat.

"Happy Christmas, Laura," came the familiar American drawl. "Can you forgive me, lass? I had to get away. It all got too much for me. I'm sorry if I caused you hurt or concern, but it was something I had to do for myself. Look, I can hear you're having a party. I'll come back later if that's okay?"

Laura didn't know what to say. She grabbed hold of John and hugged him tightly. She had missed him desperately. Her hands shook as she pulled him inside. *Are they prepared for this?* she asked herself. This moment had been playing around in her head for the past few days.

Her legs shook as she guided him inside the dining room where everyone sat waiting for Lucas and Bea to bring in the turkey. Danny jumped straight onto John's knee and began to tell Santa all about the presents he had received that morning.

Olly clapped John on his back, "It's so good to have you back, mate. I can't tell you how much I've missed our fishing trips. I hope you're okay. We'll have a catch up later over a few beers?"

"We will, lad," John replied, trying to keep a wriggling Danny on his knee. "I'm looking forward to a beer or two later."

Olly looked at Laura and grinned. "All your chicks in one nest, Laura. Does that make you happy? I'm over the bloody moon."

Laura sat down on the nearest chair, still stunned at John's sudden appearance. She had no idea what would happen next, but try as she might, her legs would not work, and neither would her voice.

She watched as John kissed the top of Danny's head and cooed with him in amazement over his new toys. They looked so perfect together. They always had, and Laura now knew why.

"I hope you're all hungry," Lucas said, interrupting her thoughts. "We need room for this giant turkey!" As he placed the dish on the table, his eyes moved straight to John in the window seat.

"When did he arrive?" he whispered.

"Just." Laura gulped.

Lucas raised his eyebrows as Bea joined him in the dining room, placing vegetables on the table.

Bea fussed with the plates and the table layout, before spotting the man in the Santa suit holding Danny. "Well, I can see Santa has come to see my little grandson."

Laura watched with fascination at John's reaction when he heard Bea's soft Lancashire tones. A mix of emotions washed over his face as he lifted his head. He looked confused, hopeful, bewildered, shocked. His head shook slightly from side to side as if he couldn't believe what his eyes were seeing. Lucas turned off the music and watched with concern from the doorway, while everyone else fell silent.

"Lizzie?" John's voice finally croaked.

Bea looked at him more closely, her eyes squinting as she tried to focus on the face framed by the white beard and large red hat. She angled her head to the side as if questioning what she saw.

Slowly, John removed his disguise.

Bea gasped, her hand straight to her mouth. "John?" she whispered. "My John? Is it really you?"

Olly looked on, confused. "Do you two know each other?" he asked, his eyes darting from one to the other.

Laura held her breath as Bea stood up and walked over to John. She stroked his smooth cheek. "They told me you were dead," she whispered. "They told me you'd died on your motorbike."

John stood up and took her hand. His eyes closed briefly, as if he couldn't cope with the emotion of finally doing something he'd wished for so long. He held her hand as if it were as delicate as a flower and placed it on his trembling lips.

"No, Lizzie. Stan, my brother died on my motorbike. I went to America."

Lizzie suddenly sank on the window seat and started to sob quietly as John held her tightly.

"I'll take Danny outside," Amy whispered to Laura. "I think you all need some space. We'll be in the annex."

Laura nodded. "I just need to make sure John is okay. I'll join you in a few minutes."

"Will someone please tell me what's going on!" Olly banged his fists on the table, his face angry and confused. Katie placed her hand on his arm to calm him.

"Lizzie, why are you here? Did you come to find me?" John asked as tears slipped freely down his cheeks.

Bea shook her head. "I'm here with my son. That's all."

"Lizzie," John whispered. "Please tell me you've brought our daughter."

Olly placed his hands on his head and shouted again, "Will someone please explain to me what's going on!"

"We need some answers," Katie said quietly, trying to calm her fraught husband.

Lizzie stood up and took hold of Olly's hand. "I never had a daughter, John. I had a son. We have a son. Olly."

"Olly?" John whispered. "Olly is my son? You had a son?"

"What?" Olly looked incredulous. "Mum, are you telling me John's my dad? I thought my dad died before I was born?"

Olly paced the room, his hands clamped around the sides of his head. "Did you know?" He turned to John. "Did you know all this?"

John shook his head. "I never knew until right this minute, lad. I swear, this is a shock to me too. I thought I had a daughter out there somewhere. I was never looking for a son."

"Am I the kid you were looking for?" Olly's voice cracked; his eyes full of tears.

"For years," John whispered, his own lips trembling. He pulled out the photo from his wallet, "I thought you were a little girl."

"Oh God!" Olly cried. "All this time and we didn't know."

"I'm sorry, sweetheart." Bea hugged the giant frame of her weeping son. "I truly thought John had died. I would never have lied to you about something as important as this."

Bea looked at John as she continued to comfort Olly. "I came back for you, John, after my parents died. They threatened to make me penniless if I went back to you. They died when Olly was just nine months old. I came back to Heppleworth, but your neighbours said the boy with the motorbike had died, and his brother had gone to America. I knew your Stan had always wanted to go to America. I assumed it was you who had died."

"No, lass," John replied. "I moved away because I couldn't stand to stay there with the memories. I've spent years since trying to find you both."

"You're a grandad, John." Olly wiped his eyes. "There's Danny, too."

"Danny," John whispered. The moment suddenly became too much for him. He sat and sobbed as Olly placed his arms around him.

Lucas ushered Laura out of the room. "They'll be fine," he said quietly as they walked to the annex. "Let's leave them be for now."

*

"What on earth?" Amy pounced on them as they walked into the annex. "Is John really Olly's dad?"

"Yes." Laura smiled. "It certainly seems that way."

"Wow!" Amy's eyes were wide with amazement. "And they didn't know?"

Laura shook her head. "They had no idea."

"Oh my God! That's like something out of a movie."

"I'm sure you'll find a quote for it, Amy." Sam laughed as he gave her a hug.

Laura watched Olly and John walk across the lawn together, smiling and laughing as she had so often seen them do. The resemblance now seemed unmistakable. Two peas in a pod. They both had a beer in their hands, their heads close together as they talked.

"We've come to say dinner is ruined, but the turkey still tastes good." Olly smiled sympathetically at the group all huddled in the annex. "Mum wants to know if you'd like turkey sandwiches. She's making some now in the kitchen. Come and join us. We've a lot to catch up on. We'd like you to be part of it."

Olly put his arm around Laura as her lips started to tremble. "Come on, Laura, don't get upset. This is an amazing opportunity for us. To get to spend the rest of our years getting to know each other. It's the best Christmas present I could have ever asked for."

"What, finding out I'm your dad?" John grinned as he accepted kisses and handshakes from the little group.

"Nah, having my name above that hut door." Olly nodded towards the converted shepherd hut.

"That was meant to be a surprise." Laura laughed as she punched him.

"Normal service resumed." Olly rubbed his arm. "She's hitting me already."

"You're a big lad, son. You can sort this one out yourself."

Lucas cupped Laura's elbow gently and held her back. "We'll just be a minute," he said to the group as they all headed back to the B&B.

Lucas guided Laura towards the end of the garden, looking out over the sea. From his pocket he took out a fine silver necklace with a single filigree feather attached.

"I'm giving this to you. I thought it would remind you of Jemima." Lucas kissed her neck as he fastened the necklace and placed the delicate feather on her chest. "It was my mum's."

"Oh Lucas, it's so beautiful." Laura held the feather gently in her hands.

"I'm glad you like it," Lucas whispered.

"Hey, it's okay." Laura held him as his eyes filled with tears. "Don't hide your sadness from me, and never cry alone. I know how much you must miss them."

"They're always with me," he said, desperately trying to hold back his tears. "And I'm sure they're watching us now."

Lucas held her tightly as they both stood at the bottom of the garden, looking out over the calm sea. "I love you, Nurse Nightingale. You take my breath away."

Laura and Lucas joined the group in the dining room of the B&B.

John stood up and asked them all to raise their glasses. "To absent friends and to the moments that take our breath away. Merry Christmas."

Thank you for choosing this book. If you enjoyed it, please consider telling your friends or leaving a review on Goodreads or the site where you bought it. Word of mouth is an author's best friend and much appreciated.

ABOUT THE AUTHOR

L ouise is a data analyst for the NHS which she has been for twenty-five years. An only child, she spent her childhood reading famous five and secret seven books in a makeshift tent in her garden. She adores rabbits which earned her the nickname of Rabbit Lou amongst her good friends. She loves gardening and being cosy in front of a fire with a glass of wine or a cup of tea, depending on the hour of the day! She's happiest when with her husband David and son Thomas. They are her world. While in her early thirties, she lost both parents very suddenly to terminal illness. The aching loss and feeling of being cheated worked to shape her book. She hopes they will be proud of her.

Printed in Great Britain
by Amazon